MW00532921

DEATHLESS

VENGEFUL GODS MC
BOOK 3

CRYSTAL ASH

Copyright © 2024 by Crystal Ash

Cover Art by MoorBooks Designs

Published by Voluspa Press

This is a work of fiction. Names, characters, places, and incidents either are the products of the author's imagination or are used fictitiously. Any resemblance to actual persons, living or dead, businesses, companies, events, or locales is entirely coincidental.

All rights reserved. No part of this publication may be reproduced, distributed, or transmitted in any form or by any means, including photocopying, recording, or other electronic or mechanical methods, without the prior written permission of the publisher, except in the case of brief quotations embodied in critical reviews and certain other noncommercial uses permitted by copyright law.

RECAP OF HARMLESS
VENGEFUL GODS MC BOOK 2

Rori has been released from Mystic Canyon resort while Torr and Santos remain imprisoned inside. She finds refuge with her cousins and begins to formulate a plan to save her men and liberate the gladiators from the resort. During this time, she deals with self-doubt and seeks advice from her cousins and Astarte, her companion goddess in the form of a white dove.

Back in Mystic Canyon, Santos and Torr are kept in the same cell and get to know each other. Devin, the Ghost, is left with Santos' jaguar, Tezcatlipoca, who nudges him toward trusting Rori, Torr, and another gladiator, the Hunter, who approaches him about a revolt.

After several days in a pitch-dark cell, Torr and Santos are released to fight in the gladiator pit. Being weak and disoriented, they struggle to stay alive. Rori, her cousins, and their riders arrive just in time and cut power to the resort.

Rori encourages the gladiators to fight united against the resort staff and shut it down for good. They agree, and a battle ensues. Rori demands Nella, the guest services manager and the one in charge of pimping out the gladiators, be captured alive.

Canyon staff call for backup, and Rori's side is pinned down by gunfire in the canyon. Eventually, Rori's backup arrives--her undercover friend, Gwen, and her friends in Chasing Death MC. The liberation is successful, but Nella has not yet been found.

Unbeknownst to everyone else, Devin is hellbent on killing Nella himself. He finds Nella in a parking garage, but Santos and Rori convince him not to kill her because they need information from her first.

With Nella captured, the bikers and gladiators head to two safe houses that Rori arranged with her aunt, Kyrie. There they meet Valorie (Val), another cousin of Rori's and Kyrie's daughter. Val has brought a truckload of supplies like food, clothes, and other necessities for the refugees.

While everyone adjusts and recuperates, Rori's cousin, Carter, keeps calling her, "Prez" and insinuating that she should bring these men into an official MC, with her as the leader. She keeps brushing him off while spending quality time with Torr and Santos.

Nella is questioned after a few days and reveals that the resort was run by a group of women called the Sisters of Bathory. Their core ideology is to seek revenge on all men for the subjugation of women through the centuries. They carry this out with enslavement and murder as sacrifices to their goddess.

Rori manipulates Nella into revealing the location of the Sisters' compound, then keeps her word to Devin and allows him to kill Nella once she has the information she needs.

Later, Rori gathers the ex-gladiators for a meeting and informs them what their options are in terms of jobs and starting new lives. She's surprised when they all want to fight with her to take down the Bathory cult. Carter again makes the suggestion of forming an MC with her as president. Rori's forced to accept it when everyone votes unanimously for her. She names Torr her VP and calls her father Shadow to design the Vengeful Gods MC patches.

After a few days, Rori's newly formed club heads out on their first official ride. Their plans are to scout the cult's main settlement and learn more about what they're up against. Astarte pulls Rori from her physical body so that she can fly over the village and see it from the dove's eyes. Rori witnesses a man being sacrificed, as well as several women who are pregnant and have young children. When she relays this to her men, Santos remembers Hudson, a friend he and Devin were imprisoned with.

Santos believes Hudson is being held in the village and being used as a stud to breed the next generation of cult members. With this information, the MC reforms their plan and decides to make this a rescue mission.

A small team sneaks into the village after nightfall, and Hudson is successfully rescued. However, he believes Rori to be aligned with the cult and shoots her in the leg, intending to kill her. Santos subdues him before he can do any more damage, and Devin carries Rori to safety.

They make a clean getaway with Hudson, but he is extremely hostile toward women due to his imprisonment. Devin advocates for him to stay with the club, saying that he will be responsible for Hudson's care and won't let anyone else get hurt. Rori allows it after some consideration.

That night, she's visited in a dream by the companion gods. They warn her about the fight she's in for next.

HERE IS WHERE DEATHLESS BEGINS...

CONTENT WARNINGS

This book contains the following:

Mentions of infanticide
Suicidal ideation
Human sacrifice
Bodily possession/loss of autonomy
Bondage/rope play
Group sex (including DP)

1

RORI

"Come here, sweetheart." My mother lowered into a squat, holding her arms straight out in front of her. Her face was lit up with love and adoration. "Come to grandma."

I looked down and noticed the child in my lap for the first time. A girl, going by the sparkly butterfly clip holding back waves of dark brown hair. She, my daughter, held onto the forefingers of each of my hands for balance. Tiny, chubby hands released me slowly as she started taking wobbly steps toward my mother.

Her grandmother.

"Yes!" my mom praised with a huge smile. "You're doing so good! Come here and give me a hug."

The little girl ventured forward, growing more confident with each unsupported step. She giggled, reaching for her grandma, her other favorite person besides me. My daughter was so happy and loved with the two of us to take care of her.

"Yes! That's my girl!" My mom swept her up on her last step, holding her granddaughter tightly, protectively, as she smothered her in kisses.

I watched, feeling as if it were recording being played. Or like I was a sheet of glass.

"What is this?" I asked, unnerved by the odd detachment from the two people before me, the two people I was supposed to love most. "I'm dreaming, aren't I?"

"It's real if you allow it to be." My mom stood up with a groan, lifting my daughter to settle her on her hip. "Isn't it, my love?" She tapped the child on the nose.

Or at least, it looked like she did. I had yet to see the little girl's face.

"What do you mean?" I looked around, finding small homes, cottages and trailers entering my vision. And women bustling about, some with small children as well. "This is wrong," I heard myself say.

"How so?" My mom grinned at the little girl on her hip, bouncing her up and down as she made funny faces.

"Where are her fathers?" I demanded. "Where are *my* fathers? Your husbands."

"Oh, we don't need them." My mom pretended to bite the little girl's nose. "We're a much better, happier family like this."

"No, we're not. This is wrong." Panic settled in; and I wanted to move, to run. But I felt stuck, as if swimming through thick mud. "What about my brothers?" I demanded. "Where's Daren and Nolan?"

"Where they belong."

"They're your fucking *sons*. What do you mean by that?"

The woman, entity, or whatever was wearing my mother's face, finally made eye contact with me. "I have no sons. Only daughters."

"Give her to me." I approached her with my arms out, even though it felt like I wasn't crossing any distance at all. "Give me my daughter."

The thing holding the little girl seemed to float backwards

in space, her arms tightening around the child. "You're not ready, Aurora." It gave me a twisted smile, distorting my mother's face. "But don't worry. You will be soon."

"Ready for what?" I demanded. "Give me back my daughter!"

"All daughters are mine, Aurora. The sooner you accept that, the sooner we can begin."

The little girl then turned to look at me, but in place of her face was just...a moving hunk of flesh.

It was smooth and grayish-brown, expanding and contracting on itself rhythmically as if controlled by a breath or heartbeat.

The faceless child reached its hand toward me and I careened backward, trying to get away. It was wrong. It was evil. It had taken everyone I loved and now it was trying to consume me...

It caught me, gripping my shoulder with a rough hand and shaking me.

"Rori, snap the fuck out of it!"

There was a falling sensation that made me kick, and then I was somewhere else.

In bed, sandwiched between two hard, masculine bodies.

Torr's face appeared in my vision, his hair mussed from sleep and a frown pinching his mouth. "Fucking hell. Again?"

I rubbed my face, my eyes, just to feel something real, solid and tangible. On my other side, Santos seemed to read my mind and placed a warm, lingering kiss on my shoulder. His calloused hand massaged my hip and thigh. The weight and heat of his touch shepherded me back to reality, this place of safety with my men.

"Yeah, again," I sighed in answer to Torr's hovering frown. "I'm sorry."

"You have nothing to apologize for." Santos kissed my

temple, his fingers running across my belly. "We're just worried about you."

"I'm fine—"

"Don't say that," Torr bit out. "Not to us. Not when you've been thrashing and screaming in your sleep for two weeks straight."

"It's just bad dreams." I couldn't convince myself of that any more than I could the guys. My hand shook as I rubbed my forehead.

Torr flopped down next to me with a huge sigh. "That therapist guy is coming today, right?"

"He's expected to, yeah." I pushed a lock of hair off of his forehead, then looked the other way at Santos. "You're both talking to him."

"Yeah, about that." Santos turned onto his side, bicep flexing as he propped up onto his elbow. "We think you should talk to him too, paloma."

My gaze bounced back and forth between them. "You two have discussed this?"

"It's like he said." Torr brought one hand behind his head. "We're worried about you. I've never seen you have dreams like this."

"Goddamnit." I covered my face with my hands and groaned.

"Don't tell me you're mad about this," Torr chided. "You can't be a hypocrite and tell us to talk to someone but make yourself exempt."

"I'm not mad. I'm annoyed because I want to be mad. But *noooo*." I sat up and stretched. "You two have to be all sensible and caring and talk to each other because you're concerned about me. I never get an opportunity to be mad at you guys, and that's really fucking unfair."

Santos laughed, deep and rumbling like the purr of his

jaguar, as he sat up next to me. "Sorry we're so perfect for you." He dropped another kiss to my shoulder, the slow brush of lips and smolder in his dark eyes making me want to shove his head between my legs.

"You're not sorry." I tried to use my best accusatory tone, but shit, it was hard to *pretend* to be mad too.

"No, ma'am." Santos kissed the crook of my neck and I felt his smile against the curve in my skin.

Still reclined, Torr's hand drifted over my hip and lower back. "You want breakfast?" His touch skimmed up my spine. "Or should we have a lie-in?"

Normally, not even breakfast could get me to skip extended time in bed with my men. It was the best feeling, waking up to the two of them. My head on Torr's chest, with Santos snuggled up to my back.

They were everything I wanted and never thought I'd have, devoted to me and secure enough in themselves to share me. It didn't hurt that they were two of the most gorgeous male specimens I'd ever set eyes on.

But if I was being honest, the dreams were unnerving me, and I probably did need to talk to someone. They were unsettling me to the point of not wanting to spend extra time in bed for fear of falling asleep and experiencing them again.

"Yeah, breakfast sounds good." I leaned over and kissed Torr, then came back up and did the same to Santos on my other side.

As the three of us got out of bed and dressed, someone else started to rouse. Tezcatlipoca yawned, showing off all his teeth before stretching long, the dark spots in his coat shimmering with his graceful movement.

"Good morning, beautiful boy." I scratched the jaguar's neck and kissed the top of his head, earning a chuff and a firm headbutt against my thigh.

Tezca led the way downstairs, where we found Devin already laying strips of bacon in a pan. The lean-muscled fighter was shirtless and his long hair was loose, spilling down his back nearly to his waist in glossy, untangled strands.

Really, it was unfair how some men had such beautiful features. Santos' eyelashes would make mascara companies cry with envy. Devin's hair had the body and shine so many women dreamed of.

"Morning," Santos greeted his ex-gladiator friend with a fist bump to the shoulder. Tezca walked right up to Devin and headbutted him square in the ass.

"Jesus! Trying to kill me here, cat?" Devin swatted at Tezca behind him, but I didn't miss that quick scratch behind the ear.

"That for Hudson?" Santos nodded at the bacon starting to sizzle.

"Yeah." Devin grabbed the handle of another pan and tossed some diced potatoes all casually like he was a professional chef. Though he was likely the best knife thrower in the world, so maybe there was some shared skill there. "Dude needs to put on some calories."

"Invite him to come eat with us." Torr got the coffee started. Our tools were pretty rudimentary at the safe house, so he was putting some muscle into a manual grinder as a pot of water boiled.

"I did." There was a note of annoyance in Devin's tone. "I do, for every meal. Every day."

Silence fell over the kitchen as no one wanted to say what was on their mind. We'd rescued Hudson from the same cult of women who had enslaved Devin and Santos and forced them to become gladiators. Hudson had been so delighted at being rescued that he'd taken Santos' gun and shot me in the leg.

After staying for two weeks at the safe houses of my newly formed motorcycle club, the Vengeful Gods MC, Hudson didn't seem to be improving when it came to being around women. And with me as president, that was an issue.

"Should we revisit the idea that maybe this isn't the best place for him?" I ventured. I truly wanted to be sympathetic to Hudson. I couldn't imagine the amount of trauma he'd been through, being used as a captive breeding stud for this cult for years. But my priority was to my club and the safety of the women within it.

Hudson had shot me in the leg only because Santos had tackled him as the gun went off. While I could understand violence being his first reaction toward me, I did not want my or any other woman's life in danger because of this man's trauma.

Devin flinched at my question as if I had thrown something at him. "And where *would* be the best place for him?"

"I don't know. But it might be worth bringing up to Dr. Corwin when he arrives."

Devin's eyes remained steadfast on the stove in front of him. "He's not dangerous."

Santos snorted at that. "Come on, dude."

"We've kept all the weapons out of his reach," Devin argued. "He doesn't leave his room because he doesn't *want* to hurt anybody. Is that such a bad thing?"

"It's concerning if just seeing a woman will trigger him into a violent outburst." Torr set up the pour-over cone onto the coffee carafe and dumped the freshly-ground beans.

"He used to *want* to hurt people. Now he doesn't. That's an improvement," Devin argued.

"A very impressive amount of progress in two weeks," I deadpanned.

Devin whipped around to glare at me, every long, slender muscle on his body bunched with tension. As much as I loathed to admit it, he was still beautiful even when pissed off.

"You don't get to decide how long it takes for someone to

heal," he spat. "Not everything can happen the moment you snap your fingers and command it, *President*."

"You're right. You can explain that to my aunt and uncles if their daughter ends up dead," I replied. "Or to the Hunter if something happens to Paige. He's been through this shit with you guys. I'm sure he will be most understanding. Oh no, wait." I held up an index finger, pretending to think about it. "As president, *I'm* responsible for everyone in my club. So that means any bad shit that happens falls on me."

"So what would you do?" Devin asked coldly. "Stick him in a padded room? Put him on a cocktail of meds? Throw him out into the world to be retraumatized over and over?"

"Like I said, I'm willing to let the doctor give his professional opinion."

"Right. The therapist that a woman recommended."

Oh hell no. This man was not going to insinuate any misogynistic shit about my mother. "Fuck off with that. There's no ulterior motives here," I said. "We all want Hudson to heal. I don't want to punish him or make him struggle any more than he already has. But I'm not going to put my people at risk for his benefit."

Devin faced the stove again, effectively done with the conversation. He turned off the burners with more force than necessary, plated up the food, and stormed out of the kitchen.

"Another highly productive conversation," I sighed at his departure.

2

DEVIN

"**B**reakfast," I called, rapping my knuckles on Hudson's door. When no answer came, I knocked again. "Hud, you up?"

After more silence, I turned the knob and stuck my head inside. "Hudson, you okay?"

Like every morning, his bed was neatly made. Actually, the entire room was neat as a pin, which was a nice change of pace from the rest of the house occupied by ex-gladiators.

Books were stacked neatly on a bedside table. Laundry was either hanging or folded in the open closet. The attached bathroom door was closed, which alleviated my worry at the silence in the room.

"Hey, you taking a shit?" I went inside to put the food down on the table with a single chair next to the window. "I'll get you some coffee if you want."

"Not a good time, Dev!" came the tense reply through the bathroom door.

I paused. "You okay in there?"

"Fine!"

I couldn't place what it was, either just instinct or something in his voice, but I had a feeling he wasn't working his way through his usual morning ritual. Keeping light on my feet, I moved closer to the door. "Hudson?"

"Go away, Devin!"

"If you're really taking a shit, I will. Believe me, I have no desire to interrupt."

He could have just said, *Yes, fuck off.* But he didn't. Instead, a moan floated through the wood. The sound could have been pain or...the complete opposite of pain.

My pulse quickened and I held my breath, not wanting to miss another sound that came through that door. I wanted to make sure he was okay, and if he was, maybe, for stupid, selfish reasons, I wanted to hear that sound again.

"Hudson," I said again, my throat feeling tighter. "What are you doing?"

"Nothing!"

"Are you hurting yourself?"

The silence from the other side of the door spurred me into action. "I'm coming in."

"No, don't—"

I swung the door open wide to find Hudson leaning against the sink's counter, scrambling to tuck his erection back into his sweatpants. He was shirtless and breathing hard, skin flushed under all his tattoos.

"What the fuck, man?" he demanded, blue eyes seething with embarrassment.

I laughed, rubbing my face both with relief and as an excuse to not stare too blatantly. "You could have just said you wanted some privacy to jerk off."

"I wasn't!" The flush raced up his neck to his face.

I stopped laughing, taking in his body language like I was sizing up a target. "Dude, it's okay. Nobody cares."

16

"No, I was trying to make it go away! I don't want to be waking up with this shit, feeling like..." He trailed off, shaking his head. "I don't *want* that. I mean, I don't want to want it."

It dawned on me what he was saying, and I had to fold my arms to resist giving the poor guy a hug. "Hudson." I gentled my voice as if talking to a child. "It's okay to feel, uh, aroused," I said in an effort to not be crass. "That's totally normal. And if you touch yourself because it feels good, that's fine too. It's your body, you get to have control of it now. No one is going to take that away from you again."

"You don't get it," he hissed. "It reacts like clockwork every day. Like when I used to take cigarette breaks at work, the cravings always hit me at the same time."

"Shit." That was an aspect I hadn't considered, the involuntary conditioning and habits instilled into him after all these years. "I'm sorry."

"I'm losing my shit, Dev. Going through withdrawals for something I don't even want."

"We have a therapist coming out soon. A man," I added. "He'll be able to help you with this, I bet."

Hudson tilted his head back and laughed mirthlessly. "A fucking head shrink. Whose idea was that?"

"Rori's."

His gaze returned to mine, expression going cold at the mention of her name. "And you trust...*her*?"

"With this, yeah." It was a truth I could say confidently. In spite of the friction between Rori and me, I believed she was doing her best for all in this situation. If it were me who'd been shot by the guy we were trying to rescue, I might not be so forgiving. But she was actually compromising a lot, letting Hudson stay here and bringing out a professional to help him. Even I could admit that.

Hudson shook his head. "I don't know how, man. I know I

sound like broken record, but how can you believe a fucking word she says?"

"Because that's not the kind of person she is." Obviously I wasn't Rori's biggest fan, but I was astounded at how much defending of her I had to do with him. "She's not the same people who put us, put *you,* through all that shit. She led the charge to get you out. She changed up her original plans to make *your* rescue the number one priority. And..." I hesitated but decided to go through with that thought. "Santos loves her. Like, deeply loves her."

Hudson gave that a dismissive scoff. "He loves any woman who looks his way."

"Have you lived with him for the past four years? I didn't think so." I crossed my arms. "Maybe in the early days he was a sucker for some female attention, but this life has sucked the soul out of him too. The only difference between him and us is that he still had enough soul left to find happiness when he got out."

I used to be just as dismissive as Hudson when Santos and I were gladiators. His eternal optimism had been so annoyingly naive. Every day, we saw people slaughtered, and Santos refused to believe that would ever be him. He'd escape one day, find a way to make a living, find a woman who loved him, raise a family, grow old together, blah blah blah. I'd made myself blue in the face telling him to snap out of it and face reality—we were gonna die on the sands just like the rest of the faceless, nameless gladiators.

But that didn't happen. And I got up this morning to see him coming down the stairs with an easy smile on his face, hands around the waist of the woman he'd woken up next to. He'd really fucking done it.

Back at Mystic Canyon, I'd joked about being envious of

Santos' head-in-the-clouds pipe dreams. Now, I was dumb-founded that he'd actually made it happen.

"Well, good for him." Hudson's tone dripped with sarcasm. "At least one of us still remembers what happiness feels like."

"I dunno, man." I ran a hand back through my hair and noticed Hudson following the movement. "There may be hope for us yet. We're out of that hellscape. The world is our lobster or however the fuck that saying goes."

"Oyster."

"Yeah, that's the one."

Hudson laughed, and this time, there was a touch more humor to the sound. The slightest pull of a smile at his lips. "I feel like getting past this shit would be so much easier if I wasn't attracted to women, you know?"

My throat tightened again while I attempted to keep my focus on Hudson's face, not the tattooed, lean body that had started to fill out ever since he'd started getting balanced meals every day. But shit, he had a heartbreaker's face too. Baby blue eyes. Brown hair with a tint of red.

Don't say it, I told myself. *Don't even think about asking the question.*

But what if you could help him...in another way? asked another voice.

In the end, the weaker side of me won.

"Well, have you ever considered...guys?"

Hudson didn't bat an eye, didn't even seem to notice my internal debate. "Sure, why not? I mean, if I could get this issue," he gestured at his crotch, "resolved without ever having to touch a woman again? Sign me the fuck up." He touched his mouth, eyes focusing some-where else as gave it some more thought. "If I could ever, you know, learn to enjoy the act again, that would just be a bonus." His gaze fell on me again, eyes narrowing skeptically. "Why, you know anyone?"

Oh, fuck me. Why did I crack open Pandora's box if I thought even for a moment it would lead to this?

Because you want it, that weak, treacherous side of me said. *Because your dirty little secret is twofold: your savior complex and your jealousy over Santos having someone when you don't.*

All terrible, selfish reasons that I was fully aware of. But if I really, genuinely, could help Hudson in this way, wouldn't the good outweigh the bad?

"I know, uh." I cleared my throat and tried again. "I mean, well, there's me."

The guy's chin lowered, his eyebrows going up. "You?"

"Yeah. I mean, I'm the only bi dude I know of around here. But if it's awkward or I'm not your type or whatever, it's cool." And that was how I learned Pandora's box was actually a hole, and I just kept digging myself deeper.

"No, Dev. It's not that. I'm just surprised." Hudson rubbed his lower lip with his thumb, his gaze intense. "Although, I guess I shouldn't be."

"Why do you say that?"

"No reason. It's just..." He stroked his chin. He'd been letting his facial hair grow and it was coming in dense and full. "Whenever I thought back to that time, when it was the three of us, I always thought of you more than Santos."

I swallowed. "You did?"

"Yeah. I just clicked with you more, I guess."

"Look, man." I brought my palms up, eager to backtrack. "Something like this can get messy, so—"

"How do you mean?" he challenged. "Other people in this house are fucking, aren't they?"

"Sure, but—"

"You don't have to treat me like I'm made of tissue paper, Dev." His expression hardened. "In fact, I'd really prefer it if you didn't."

"Okay." I lowered my hands. "How do you want me to treat you then?"

One shoulder went up in a lazy shrug. "I dunno. Like anyone else you'd hook up with."

"Alright. Well it turns out everyone is different. You have to tell me what you expect, what your limits are."

He started to roll his eyes. "Come on—"

"No, this is how it's gonna be." I straightened my spine, firming up my stance. "You have to use your words and tell me what you want and don't want, or this doesn't happen."

"Way to make it fucking awkward," he groaned.

"This is how people make it enjoyable for each other. You discuss this shit."

"Doesn't make it any less weird."

I shoved my hair back and sighed. "Okay, I want you to ask yourself a question. Repeat this in your head: 'Do I trust Devin?' If the answer is no, that's fine, but if that's the case, I'm definitely *not* fucking you."

"I do trust you." Hudson's throat bobbed, and he said more quietly, "You're the one I trust here the most."

"Okay. Then be a little awkward and communicate with me. It's hard to be vulnerable dude, I know. But I'll never ridicule you for what you've been through. And anything you share with me stays between us."

For some reason, an image of Rori popped into my head, shrewd green eyes missing nothing. I shoved her away just as quickly as she came.

Hudson remained silent for a long time until he said, "I don't want you on top of me."

"Okay, that's good. What else?"

"I don't...I..." The poor guy clammed up, harsh breaths rushing in and out of his nose.

"Hey, it's okay." I took a chance moving in closer, standing next to him at the counter. "We can start there, or even ten steps before that. You're in control here."

"That's all I really want," he admitted. "To be in control of what happens to me. And not just there for someone else to..."

"Good. I'm glad you told me that." I knew, even when I thought this would be a far-off fantasy, that I would have to tread carefully with Hudson. To not only show him what pleasure was again, but to make him feel confident and safe. My goddamn savior complex was riding high, and I was too much of a sucker to do the hard thing and think about long-term consequences.

"Can I take your hand?" I asked.

Hudson looked surprised, like he thought I'd want to touch something a lot more X-rated, but then nodded.

I went for his closest palm, then took several steps back to gently pull him out of the bathroom. Hudson followed, cautious but curious. His eyes flicked to his bed when he realized I was heading that way. Just like throughout our entire conversation in the bathroom, I made every effort to focus on his face and not what was happening in his pants.

Taking a seat on the edge of the bed, I released his hand so I could scoot all the way up the mattress until I was reclined in the middle. Once there, I freed my trapped hair and relaxed with my palms behind my head.

"What are you doing?" Hudson asked in a rough voice.

"Nothing." I tilted my head to meet his eye. "But you can do whatever you like."

"What?"

"Get on top. Use your hands, mouth, whatever you want. Or just sit back and look at me." Only then did I allow myself to drink him in. The handsome face, the tattoos subtly moving with every breath, the slender hips that the oversized sweatpants could barely hang onto.

"Take control, Hudson," I told him. "Do what will make *you* feel good."

3

RORI

"You got a cigarette?" I asked Torr.

He patted the inner pockets of his leather jacket. "No, I'm all out."

"Goddamnit," I groaned into my coffee cup.

"Sorry, Reaper." He laughed. "When did you become such a smoker, anyway?"

"Being a leader is stressful, okay? Now I get why Reaper was such a dick when he didn't have his cloves and whiskey." I tapped my fingernails against the ceramic mug, watching the driveway from the front porch. "They should have been back by now."

Torr propped his boots on the porch railing. "Did you try calling LJ?"

"Yeah, straight to voicemail."

"There's a lot of dead zones out there. I'm sure they're fine."

"And if they're not?"

"We can't make decisions based on what we don't know. Only what we do know."

"Thanks, Carter," I grumbled.

Torr just chuckled, all Mr. Calm and Collected while I

watched the road like a hawk. Last week, I'd sent LJ, the Saint, and another ex-gladiator, the Bull, to watch the Sisterhood's village. After making sure they didn't follow us, I wanted to know how they'd react to us taking Hudson, their prized breeding stud. Would they increase patrols? Sacrifice or kidnap more men? Those women were nothing if not tightly controlled and organized. I needed to know the ins and out of everything they did.

Scratching my head, I thought back to the dreams I'd been having ever since we'd gotten Hudson out of there. They always started the same way, some idyllic scene playing out like I was watching a film about my future. There was love, laughter, family. Sometimes even children that didn't exist yet. Then it would slowly morph into something horrifying. My men with chains around their necks and limbs, if they were present at all. Me, sometimes with other women, standing on the bodies of men I knew.

And there was always that gross fleshy thing that looked like a cross between someone's liver and a giant slug. That seemed to be the source of everything. It felt immensely powerful and dangerous. Like if I wasn't careful, it was going to slide its way into my ear canal and control me like an alien parasite.

The gods, Astarte, Lupa, and Tezcatlipoca, had given me a warning. And I couldn't shake that it had something to do with these dreams.

A distant roaring pulled my attention back to the road, and I stood at attention, squinting at the horizon. "Do I see riders?"

"Yep. Our boys are back."

I was already off the porch and heading down the gravel driveway before Torr brought his feet down to follow. We passed by Santos, the Hunter, and some of the other guys working out on our way out to the road.

26

"That them?" Santos sheathed his machetes and wiped the sweat from his face with his shirt hanging around his neck.

"Yeah. Coming?"

He shook his head, grinning as he pointed to Torr. "This fucker owes me deadlifts. I'm waiting here until he gets back."

"I got you, Santos, but it has to wait until I'm done with VP business." Torr gestured to me like it was obvious.

"Sounds like stalling to me," the Hunter chimed in, gulping water down as he leaned against one of the supports of a pull-up bar. "Who knows if he's got it in him to do five-hundred?"

"I'll do the five-hundred and then your ass on top of it," Torr hollered back.

"You guys are all very cute together," I chuckled once we were a good distance away.

"They're good dudes." He rubbed the back of my neck, rough fingers gently pinching and massaging the way I liked it. "I wasn't sure at first, but you've got a good club here, President."

"I hope the same can be said for these two." I shielded my eyes from the sun, squinting to make out the approaching riders. My cousin LJ was the only one I trusted implicitly among them, and I was eager to get a full private report from him later on.

"Who's giving you doubts?" Torr asked.

"The Saint," I admitted. "I can't decide if he's just an eccentric guy or if he's trying too hard to throw suspicion off him."

"I've felt the same," Torr admitted. "Can't get a good read on him. Santos and Devin aren't sure either, and they would probably know him best."

"It's frustrating when you're not sure if you can trust someone. I hope LJ's able to tell us something from this mission."

"It was a good idea to put him in charge of this. That's what a wise president does."

"Don't kiss my ass, Torr."

27

"Fine." He leaned in close, lips trailing the shell of my ear. "Can I eat it instead?"

I couldn't hold back the grin, even as the riders were coming close enough to make out their faces. "If you're a good boy."

Torr groaned as he leaned away. "Damn, I can see why Santos loves being owned by you."

"Stop." I laughed. "I can't have both of you collared and leashed."

"Why not? You have two hands."

"Too much power going unchecked is a dangerous thing." I bumped into him with my hip. "I need someone to keep me in line, and that can only be you."

"Fair enough." Torr planted his feet wide like the guard he was, eyes on the approaching riders. "But I wouldn't mind a 'good boy' now and again."

"You gotta earn it."

He groaned again. "Trying to give me a hard-on in front of these guys?"

"Stop trying to make me laugh."

We continued bickering playfully until the three motorcycles pulled up in front of us. LJ, leading the trio, yanked down the bandanna tied over his mouth and nose. "Hey, Pres! VP."

"Welcome home," I greeted. All I wanted to do was give my cousin a big hug, but that would have to wait until we were in private. Right now, I was his president and he was my sergeant-at-arms. "What are our friends up to?"

LJ glanced over his shoulder as the two ex-gladiators pulled up to flank him.

"You are a sight for the sorest of eyes, President," said the Saint, leaning over his handlebars with a grin.

"If it's bad news, get it out," I snapped. "You won't soften me with flattery."

"We came up to the settlement as they were in the process of splitting up," LJ said.

"Splitting up?" Torr echoed. "The fuck does that mean?"

"They packed up and they're moving," elaborated the Bull on LJ's other side. "They split up into three groups, all heading in different directions."

Torr and I looked at each other, then back at the riders. "Why would they do that?"

"We were just as baffled as you are." LJ, rarely without a smile, sat higher in his seat, his face stoic. "It makes no sense from a strategic standpoint to divide up their forces."

"What directions did they go in?" I asked.

"Two of 'em headed north, then they split. One heading northeast, the other northwest."

"And the third?" I prompted at LJ's silence.

He chewed his lip, hesitating a moment longer. "South."

"Toward us."

"Yes, but." My cousin dragged a hand through his russet brown hair. "It was the smallest party. Just four older women and a baby. They all fit into one van with a few belongings."

"A baby?"

"Yes, we thought it was unusual," the Saint chimed in. "All the other children seemed to be going with another group, the one heading northwest."

"You're sure it was a baby?" My instincts were stuck on this one detail for some reason, something niggling at me to probe further. "You saw an actual child with them?"

"Well, it was one of those old car seat carrier things. With an arm handle, you know?" The Bull tried to gesture helpfully. "It had a blanket over it, and one of the women kept peeking in there, tucking it in, you know."

"But you never actually saw its face?"

"I didn't." The Bull looked at the other two riders, who also shook their heads.

"Is there a reason why you wouldn't believe it to be a baby?" The Saint narrowed his eyes, compressing the tattoos on the outside corners.

"I dunno," I sighed. "It's just a weird detail. Anything else? Did you see any men with any of the groups?"

LJ shook his head. "None that we saw." My cousin's eyes bore intensely into mine. He walked to talk away from these fighters.

"Alright. Well, good work. We'll hold church tonight, so go ahead and rest until then."

"Ah, the church of Aurora." The Saint made the sign of the cross on himself. "I can't wait to worship."

The Bull snorted as the two fighters rode off together, then there were cheers and greetings as they came upon the second of our two safe houses, the one most of the fighters had taken up residence in. Torr affectionately called it the frat house.

Once there were three of us, LJ dismounted his motorcycle and chose to walk it alongside me and Torr. "Please tell me you have a cigarette," my cousin grumbled.

"No, Torr's out." I patted his back in an apology.

"Son of a bitch." LJ sighed.

"We'll have Val get a whole pallet of 'em on her next supply run."

The three of us walked up to the first house, which was where I, my men, and my cousins stayed. Paige and the Hunter had their own room too, since they were a couple and the frat house consisted of a bunch of single guys.

Rather than go inside, I led our trio around to the back of the house, where a wooded area gave us more privacy. Later in the day, more people would come here to practice shooting, but for now, it was blissfully quiet.

"So how'd it really go?" I lowered onto a tree stump while the two guys remained standing.

LJ shrugged. "Alright, I guess. I had to herd 'em like a couple of cats when the cult groups started splitting up, but that was the biggest friction point."

"How do you mean?" I asked.

"They wanted us to split up as well. So each of us could follow one of the cult groups to watch them more closely, then rendezvous after a few more days. I said no way in hell. The president's orders were clear; we stay together and watch each other's backs."

I beamed at him. "Knew I could count on you." I had said no such thing but told LJ he could order those two around if he suspected something fishy and to say the orders came from me.

"Who's idea was it to split up?" Torr asked him, arms crossed.

"The Saint said it first, but the two of them were pretty gung-ho about it. I had to argue with them about it for a good minute."

"What was your gut feeling?" I asked. "Do you think they were trying to pull something, or were they genuine about this plan?"

LJ let out a long breath, crossed his arms, looked up at the sky and then down at the ground before meeting my eye again. "I honestly couldn't tell you," he admitted. "If it was someone I trusted, like Val or my brother, who'd brought that idea forward, I'd be all for it. But these gladiators, cuz. I just don't know 'em well enough."

"Would you trust Santos out there?" I pressed. "Or the Hunter?"

"Yeah, but," LJ scratched the five o'clock shadow on his cheek, "neither of them would've gone against an order coming

31

from you. These guys were adamant until they realized I wasn't gonna budge."

"We can't let that fly." Torr slid a glance over to me. "They're testing boundaries. Seeing how much they can get away with when you're not around to crack the whip."

"Or they're trying to take initiative and impress me," I countered. "We could learn a lot by watching all three parts of the Sisterhood."

"I wouldn't advise that," Torr said. "That's probably what the cult is hoping we do, and we don't need to be more divided."

"That's what I'm thinking too," LJ said.

"So, this stays between the three of us." I stood from the tree stump. "I want you both to keep close eyes on those two fighters. Especially the Saint." When the two of them nodded, I added, "Let everyone know there's going to be church tonight. We're going to handle the Sisterhood as a club, nothing changes that."

"You got it, Prez." Torr headed for the back door to the house and reached to hold it open just as Devin came out.

"Hey, Dev," I greeted.

"Hi."

Torr and I watched him go by before exchanging curious looks. Devin was fully dressed with his hair up in his normal topknot, but we both noticed something different about him.

The tall fighter's cheeks were flushed. His lips were redder and more swollen than I'd noticed before. His hair, normally without a strand out of place, was a bit mussed like he'd just tied it up carelessly. His eyes even looked brighter, warmer than his usual cold detachment. And was that a *smile*?

I stared. Straight-up gawked as Devin laid out his throwing knives on the stump I'd just been sitting on. His lips were definitely pulling at the corners, a secret hidden smile as he checked his blades' sharpness before getting started on target practice.

"Did you get a blowjob or something since we last saw you,"

Torr looked at his wrist as if checking a watch, "like an hour ago?"

The hidden cheer in Devin's expression faded away. His dark eyebrows slashed down, mouth pressing into a frown. "How's that any of your business, Torr?"

"It's not, I'm just being nosy. I mean, the only thing that sets my mood on a total one-eighty is a good ol'—"

"Come on." I cut him off with a punch to the shoulder, surprising myself. "Not everyone's sex life is a casual conversation. Leave him alone."

I ignored both men's surprised expressions as I headed into the house.

4

HUDSON

T his was the best day I'd had in a long, long time. I couldn't stop grinning at the ceiling, couldn't stop thinking back to what had happened on this bed a few hours earlier. And thinking ahead to when it would happen again.

Sure, things were better in the last two weeks since I'd been freed, but they hadn't been *good*. Not until Devin came in this morning and offered something I didn't know I'd needed. I'd gone from feeling like my body was still under *their* control, an automated machine dialed in to perform on the schedule *they* subjected me to. Then Devin put the control firmly back in my hands, and I felt like something I hadn't been in years.

A person who could make choices.

Someone with the freedom and permission to explore a partner's body. Devin had encouraged me to touch him anywhere, do anything to him. I was so confounded by the freedom and the trust that I had barely known where to start.

All the while, he never made a move to touch me. His hands, with those long slender fingers, stayed under the back of his head the whole time. Except when his fists curled to grip the sheets at his sides, that was.

I wasn't ready for him to touch me, not yet. But I was starting to think it might feel nice when he did. Kissing him sure felt really, really nice.

"What is happening to me?" I laughed to myself, covering my eyes as if to hide myself from the empty room. I was a teenager with a crush again, but this bright, bubbly sensation in my chest felt so weird despite how good it was. Like I'd been injected with a drug and it was some foreign substance making me feel this way.

Three hard raps came to my door, knocking me out of my daydreaming.

"Devin?" I called hopefully.

"No, this is Dr. Corwin. I just wanted to come up and introduce myself."

My good mood deflated into sour disappointment along with a healthy dose of anxiety. I didn't trust this man, least of all because he was a stranger. Most of all because he came at the behest of that woman, Rori.

"Hudson?" the man called through the wood. "Would you mind opening up for just a moment? I'd like to put a face to your name."

I rolled out of bed, then dragged my feet across the room, hoping he'd get impatient enough to leave once I reached the door. No such luck.

Turning the knob, I pulled the barrier open an inch, just enough to look through. A middle-aged man with medium brown skin, a shaved head, glasses, and a salt and pepper five-o-clock shadow smiled at me.

"Hi there, Hudson." Dr. Corwin gave me a friendly wave. "It's nice to meet you. Would it be okay if I shook your hand?"

He held his palm out toward me, but didn't attempt to wedge the door open wider.

He asked the question. Left it up to me to open the door wider if I wanted to. Already, Devin had taught me something important so quickly. If someone gave me a choice, the opportunity to refuse or accept, they just may be worth trusting.

I let the door swing wider and reached forward to clasp the doctor's hand, which he took in a solid grip before releasing me quickly. "It's a pleasure. You can call me Malik if you'd like."

"Um, okay." I stood there awkwardly, not knowing what else to say. Having conversations with other people would be another thing I'd have to re-learn. Talking to Devin felt so natural. I forgot other people would be different.

The doctor, Malik, didn't seem to mind though. "Do you go by Hudson or anything else? I met some of the ex-gladiators, a lot of them seem to prefer their fighting names, which is interesting."

He sounded genuinely interested, without a drop of condescension, and I found myself feeling a little more at ease. "Uh, Hudson is fine. I wasn't a gladiator."

"I know that," Malik said gently. "I just wanted to make sure you didn't prefer anything else." He stepped away from the door, giving me plenty of space. "Well, I'm going to make more introductions and get settled in. Perhaps I'll see you later, at dinner maybe?"

"Oh, I dunno. I don't really eat with everyone else. Usually, I just stay up here."

"I see. I understand Rori is holding a meeting in the other house this evening, so most of the fighters will be there." Malik kept his tone even and light, but I could feel him watching my reactions to every single word. "Maybe if it's quieter here, with less people around, you'd give coming downstairs a shot? If you're feeling up for it."

"I don't know, maybe."

"Sure, give it some thought." He shot me another friendly smile as he turned to leave. "See you later, Hudson. It was nice to meet you."

* * *

A FEW HOURS LATER, as the sun was going down, I found myself pacing back and forth in front of my bedroom door. For the first time since arriving here, I felt restless. Antsy. Like this bedroom I'd hidden away in was suddenly way too small. Instead of feeling safe here, away from everyone else, I felt...trapped.

"He might be fucking with your head," I muttered to myself, thinking of Malik. I played our earlier interaction over and over in my head, trying to figure out what ulterior motive he might have, and kept coming up with nothing.

He'd been polite. Didn't invade my space. Waited for me to shake his hand. And then left. Our whole conversation probably happened in less than a minute.

Devin made it clear that he'd wished I'd leave my room more often, but that he wouldn't force the issue. I'd never been tempted to leave the safety of these four walls until now, after Malik mentioned there would be fewer people downstairs.

Too many people was overwhelming. I'd get panic attacks. But if there were only a few, in a bigger space than this room, maybe I could handle it.

I stopped the repetition of my pacing to look out the window. Fighters were walking to the other house, talking amongst each other in pairs or small groups. On the porch of the other house, watching everyone enter through the front door, was her.

The woman in charge. Rori, she was called.

Next to her stood the tall, dark-haired man who was always at her side. He was speaking to her, mouth moving with a cocky smirk pulling at his lips, but his eyes were focused on the men walking in. Every fighter got a thorough inspection, whether they realized it or not.

Santos was on the woman's other side, and his focus was entirely on her. The Butcher was clearly smitten, one hand resting on the machete's handle sheathed at his hip, the other hidden somewhere behind her back, probably touching her.

"What's so special about her?" I asked the windowpane. "How is she so different that she doesn't remind you of everything they did to us?"

As if she heard me, the woman's gaze flicked up. Her amused smile fell away, leaving behind a hard mask of disapproval as our eyes met.

I backed away from the window, walking clear across to the other side of the room, as far away from her as possible. My chest burned, pulse and breath tight with adrenaline. I had to force myself to calm down, remind myself that she was roughly a hundred feet away. She couldn't get up here. She didn't even *want* to come up here; she was about to hold a meeting, for fuck's sake.

"She doesn't want me. She doesn't want me," I repeated under my breath to reassure myself. "She wants nothing to do with me."

That phrase, more than anything else, broke me through the panic. Santos could keep staring at her like the sun shone out of her ass. Devin could tell me again and again that she wasn't a bad person. None of it sank in. Nothing could convince me that she was worth trusting.

But as long as she had Santos and that other man, plus all the other fighters wrapped around her finger, she had no need for me. She had all the attention and power she wanted. Why would she bother with me? I was nothing to her.

I would rather be nothing than anything to a woman. Especially this one. Women who had power over men were the worst of all. Better to be forgotten in this case. And for the next hour or so, her attention would be well-occupied by her devoted followers.

Once my heart rate slowed to a normal pace, I returned to facing the door and pulled it open. I moved slowly through the hall of bedrooms, then took note of all the windows and doors on the lower floor once I reached the stairs' top landing.

There was noise coming from below, and I leaned over the railing to take a cautious glance. Malik was the only one in the kitchen, his sleeves pushed up to his elbows as he dried dishes with a towel. He sang something under his breath, whistling on occasion. The guy just seemed...content. Happy, even. I wondered if that would change once the fighters and I began unloading our traumatic stories onto him, or if the good doctor stayed cheerful because listening to horror stories just rolled off his back like water off a duck.

I didn't know which would be worse.

Something must have alerted him to my presence, because he stopped whistling and turned around to look up at me. "Hudson! Good to see you again." Malik smiled like we were long-time friends who hadn't seen each other in weeks, rather than strangers who'd met only a few hours ago. "Are you hungry?"

He made no mention of me coming out of my room, which was a relief. I didn't want to be praised for every little thing like a child.

"Um, I could eat, I guess."

"Good! The rice just finished cooking." He pointed to a pot on the stove with a lid that was too big. "There's vegetables and chicken in the fridge that need to be cooked before they go bad. I figured we could do a simple stir-fry. How does that sound?"

I shrugged. "Works for me."

"Great! Have a seat. Would you like anything to drink?"

"I'll just get water from the tap, thanks." Despite Devin's constant reassurances that nothing was tampered with, I couldn't bring myself to accept drinks from just anybody yet. It was just a few days ago that I'd started to feel okay about the food that was made.

Malik was all over the kitchen in a way that was very energetic but also controlled. He wasn't chaotic in the slightest but actually calming. Whether he was chopping, tossing things in the pan, or stirring up a sauce for the stir-fry, he kept that warm friendliness he exuded when he first came to my door.

It made me feel like I was at my dad's house years ago. He'd make pancakes for breakfast while I sat at the table, my feet swinging because I was too short to reach the floor. And he'd talk to me about anything and everything while he cooked, just as Malik was now.

"My son is a chef, and he taught me this little trick." Malik tapped a white powder from a box into his sauce mixing bowl. "A little bit of cornstarch to thicken your sauce and make it richer. Might sound silly if you know what you're doing in the kitchen, but it was like magic to me! I never learned this."

"I think my grandma told me something about that. Or it might've had to do with baking. I don't remember."

Malik smiled broadly at my reply. "Cooking and baking really are art forms in the right hands, aren't they?"

I dropped into a seat at the table. "Never thought about it that way, but I guess it's true."

"Well, I'm no artist, but I can promise a meal that's edible. Maybe even flavorful." The doctor returned his attention to the stove. "So, what do you like to do, Hudson? What's your art form?"

My fingertips tapped together as I thought about how to answer. An honest response would be, S*it in my room, hide from the world and half the population in it. Hate everything and almost everyone.* But that was melodramatic, and probably not what the good doctor was looking to hear.

While ruminating on polite responses, it dawned on me how far removed I felt from all that churning, bitter hatred already. It wasn't even like my imprisonment was long ago, I'd only been freed for two weeks. But today, it felt like I'd shed a layer of that anger, discarded it like a shirt that no longer fit. Something transformative had happened today, and it started when Devin helped me take control of my body back.

Fuck, my mind was wandering back to him again, the sight of him stretched out and panting on my bed. And Malik was still waiting for me to answer his question.

"Um, I don't know," I finally said. "I haven't really pursued any hobbies or anything since they got me out." I stared at his back facing me. "You *do* know where I've been the last six years, right?"

"I do," he said lightly. "And I understand it's been an adjustment since you've been rescued. Hopefully I'll be able to help with that process."

"So how's that gonna work?" I placed my elbows on the table and crossed my forearms. "You gonna have me talk about how it felt to raped on a daily schedule, and tell me how it's important to trust women again?"

"No, Hudson. I'm not going to do that." Malik brought down a couple of bowls from a cabinet and began scooping rice into them. "You relive your trauma often enough as it is, don't you think? When you're about to fall asleep at night. When you're alone and your thoughts wander. When you're minding your own business, and then you're suddenly back there with seemingly no trigger. Am I right?"

For a long while, the only sound was the gentle clink and scraping of the pan as Malik poured the stir fry over the rice.

"How'd you know that?" I whispered.

"That's post-traumatic stress disorder, my friend." He turned to face me, holding a bowl in each hand. "Your trauma becomes a monkey riding on your back. A body of water that always feels like it's about to drown you." Malik set one bowl in front of me and the other across the table. As he turned again to find silverware, he said, "What I'd like to work on with you is making that monkey smaller so it's not so heavy on you all the time. After a while, maybe we can turn that drowning sensation into a puddle you step in. Inconvenient, but not constantly triggering your fight or flight response." He sat down across from me and placed a fork next to my bowl. "How do you feel about that, Hudson?"

"That...sounds amazing," I admitted, and then swallowed. "But honestly, a little far-fetched. I don't know how this...being on edge all time, I don't see it diminishing."

Malik smiled kindly at me as he started to dig into his food. "I'm going to ask you to trust the process. It will take time and parts of it may be uncomfortable, but if you work with me, I promise you will have the tools to put yourself in a better head space than you are now."

"Okay. I'll give it a shot." I picked up my fork, twirling it through my fingers before stabbing some well-sauced veggies. "I just want a normal life again."

"First thing I want you to think about." Malik set his fork aside and looked at me squarely. "You already are a complete, whole human being. You always have been. You are *more* than what was done to you."

I froze mid-chew. When I resumed, my jaw worked in slow, methodical movements. "Thank you," I said when I swallowed.

"No need," Malik said. "I'm only saying what's true."

I liked this man already. The perpetual constriction in my chest released a little as we continued our meal together.

All because he'd told me something I never knew I'd needed to hear.

5

RORI

Everyone watched as LJ marked three places on a map we'd haphazardly pinned to the wall. "These are the directions we saw the Sisterhood go after they split up." He capped his marker and stepped aside so everyone could see. "The group heading south, obviously, is coming toward us and would be the easiest to engage, if we decide to do that."

"Uh, *yeah*, we wanna do that," Val declared from her armchair. "Shit, let's take out each group one by one. Might as well start with the closest."

"Easy, road captain." To LJ, I said, "Could you tell if these groups were split up in any particular way?"

"Yes. The southern group looked to be four older women with a single baby in a carrier."

"Pffft, piece of cake. Let me handle the grannies by myself," Val said. "I'll be back before lunch tomorrow."

I bit back my laugh. Only a few minutes left of playing president before I could let my hair down. "And the other two, LJ?"

"The northwestern group consisted mostly of children, plus a few armed adults."

"How many?" Torr asked.

"We counted twelve children and three adults." LJ pointed at the other X on the map. "Heading northeast appeared to be the bulk of the adult women, most of them unarmed. We counted twenty unarmed, three armed."

I looked to the Saint and the Bull, the two of them sprawled on one of the couches and having stayed mostly silent during the meeting. "Do you two agree with these numbers?"

"Yes, President." The Saint bobbed his head emphatically while his cohort only gave a slight nod.

"So altogether, this cult is thirty adults strong." I crossed my arms and chewed idly on a fingernail. "Seems like a small operation for all the resources they had to build the resort."

"There may be other settlements," Santos pointed out. "That may be the reason for the 3-way split. They could be reinforcing at other locations."

"I'll bet you the four on their own are the leaders, the ones in power," Torr said. "The armed ones are the muscle, the rest is the flock. The devoted followers breeding the new generation."

"Sure fucking hope they don't have any more Hudsons," Devin muttered. He stood next to Santos, who nodded his agreement. Devin had also been oddly well-behaved for this meeting, which threw me off more than I expected. I'd come prepared for barbs at every turn, having every decision questioned. But he'd seemed content to stand and listen.

"If they do, we'll find them. Well, actually, *you* guys will find them," I said.

"Not too keen on getting shot by the person you're trying to save?" the Hunter cracked, which earned some snickering from the peanut gallery. Apparently, the guys found it hilarious that my first time meeting Hudson resulted in a bullet taking a chunk out of my calf muscle.

Men. Gladiators. Bunch of Neanderthals.

Good thing I knew exactly how to deal with them. I picked

up a throw pillow and flung at the Hunter's head. "Exactly! You see what I do for you fuckers?"

Fighters erupted in cackles and crude jokes, shoving playfully at the Hunter as he brought his arms up to block the pillow assault.

"So yeah. It can be one of you assholes getting shot next time instead of your president."

"I will take a bullet for you any time." The Saint placed a hand over his heart. "Send me out, Aurora."

"Alright, let's focus and I can let you animals loose for the night," I said, pointedly ignoring him. "I do think we should scout the closest group. It'll be me with a small team." I scanned the room, weighing my options. "Me, Val, LJ, the Butcher, and the Saint. We ride out tomorrow." I looked at Torr. "You're in charge while I'm gone."

"Yes, President."

He said it with a reverent dip of his head, which sent heat pooling through me. I couldn't help but mouth, *good boy* at him. The look he sent back to me was just as heated, just as promising.

Forcing my attention back to my main responsibility, my club, I said, "Is there anything else that needs to be discussed?" When no one spoke, I said, "Oh, most of you have met Malik already. Don't fucking haze him, he's a family friend. And seriously, talk to him if you're struggling in any way or just need to get something off your chest. Anything you tell him is confidential, even from me. He's here to support you all, and he's great at his job."

"What does confidential mean?" one of the fighters piped up.

"It means he'll talk to you confidently," the Hunter said.

I couldn't hold back the squawk laughter before tearing into him. "I'm going to have your woman put a muzzle on you, *Levi!*"

"She already does that." He elbowed Paige, who was sitting right next to him, while wiggling his eyebrows.

As said woman groaned and rolled her eyes, I answered the other fighter's question without bullshit. "It means Malik will keep anything you've told him to himself. And you can trust him to do that."

The man who asked, and a few other fighters, nodded.

"Anything else?" The room remained respectfully silent. I let a few more seconds pass before clapping my hands once. "Great. Church is now dismissed."

Devin gave a quick, "See ya," to Santos, nodded goodnight to Torr and I, then made a big show of trying to look like he wasn't in any hurry to leave. He slid through the crowd of bodies heading out like a fish through water, agile and sleek. One thing the Ghost was good at? Moving without being detected. I blinked and he was gone.

"How would you say Hudson's recovery is going?" I asked Santos as the last of my club filtered out of the house and to their various rooms.

"No idea." He shrugged. "Haven't exactly been asking for status updates."

"You haven't talked to him yourself?" Torr asked him over my head.

Santos shook his head, his face grim. "Nah. Shooting my woman doesn't exactly put him on speaking terms with me."

"You're so sweet to hold a grudge in my honor." I went up on my tiptoes to kiss his cheek.

Even though it was a joke, the praise made him blush, and a smile teased at his lips. Santos just melted like chocolate in the sun whenever I praised or complimented him, and I loved to make him do it.

"What are we still doing downstairs?" The heat of Torr's breath tickled my ear while he gave a not-so-subtle squeeze to my ass.

I turned to face him, linking my hand in Santos' on my other side. "Lead the way, cowboy."

He didn't hesitate. With a grab of my free hand, he bolted toward the stairs, dragging me and Santos along. The long-legged bastard took the steps three at a time, which was quite a feat for me.

"Hold on, Torr." I laughed, resisting his pull. "You're not gonna get laid if I'm injured doing the splits out here."

"Why not?" he shot back, but paused and waited for us to catch up anyway. "Splitting you in half is exactly what I intend to do."

"Romantic," I drawled sarcastically, even though a shiver of anticipation ran up my spine. Sometimes his ego needed to be checked, but he was so damn good at being rough.

"You got him for being romantic." Torr nodded at Santos as he opened our bedroom door.

I twirled in Santos' arms as we stepped into the bedroom, wrapping my arms around his shoulders and kissing him deeply as we made our way to the bed.

"Anything you're craving tonight?" I asked my achingly sweet, brutal fighter. He would stay on his knees and worship me all night if I wanted him to, but I always checked in with him. Always made sure his needs were met as well.

"Hmm." Santos cocked his head, eyes lighting up as he looked at me. Damn, every woman deserved a partner who looked at her like that. Like she was a meal about to be devoured and a goddess to be worshiped all rolled into one.

"No ropes tonight," he said after some consideration. "I want to soothe you while Torr punishes you."

I grinned, delighted at that prospect. "Want me to boss you?"

"Yes, please," he groaned.

"Then get on that bed and make a nice seat for me."

Santos knew exactly what I meant and hurried out of his clothes. Once he was naked and finding the perfect spot on the wide mattress, I turned to Torr.

"Undress me," he said quietly.

The command was unquestionable despite the low volume of his voice. I stepped closer to him and pushed his jacket off of his broad shoulders, the creak of worn leather the loudest sound in the room. He lifted his arms and I gripped his T-shirt at his waist, my breath hitching at the slow reveal of muscle as the fabric rose higher, like a stage curtain drawing up at the start of a production.

This would be one hell of a show, alright.

I took a moment to drink Torr in, letting my eyes feast on all the swells and dips of his torso. The shadows in the low light made every muscle more pronounced.

"Do you want to sit down?" I asked demurely. "So I can get those boots off for you."

Torr ambled over to an armchair, dropping into the seat like it was his birthright, a king on his throne. His forearms came to the armrests, long legs splayed out carelessly. He asked for nothing, but I dropped to my knees at his boots. If he told me to crawl over to him, I would have.

My submissive instincts weren't as strong as Santos', but in this context, I loved to serve Torr.

I'd gotten both boots off when he reached down to stroke my cheek. "Good girl," he purred. I barely had time to melt under his praise when he added, "Now take care of this belt for me."

Scooting closer, I found myself between his heavily muscled thighs as I pulled apart his belt buckle. The clink of metal was followed by the soft hiss of leather as I pulled it through the belt loops. After dropping it to the floor, my hands rested on his thighs, fighting the urge to cup the thick bulge already pressing at his fly. But Torr was in a mood to give commands, so I waited.

"Santos," he said over my head. "Scoot a little further down, will you? Thanks, that's good."

Before I could react, Torr gripped the short hair at the nape of my neck in his fist, hauling me upward as he stood from the chair. I hissed at the sting, but relished in the sharp sensation all the same.

"Go on over and sit on your other man's face for a bit. With your eyes closed." Torr released me and with the same hand, flicked open the button on his jeans.

"I'm still dressed," I pointed out.

"Then fix that," Torr growled, yanking down his zipper.

"You don't want me to touch you?" I pouted a little, watching his hand dip into his jeans.

"You will," he promised. "But not yet."

Fine. If he wanted to tease, two could play at that game. I would take all my clothes off as slowly as humanly possible. We didn't have music on, so I closed my eyes and swayed to the beat of a song in my head as I peeled off each piece.

I never considered myself an exhibitionist, but the temperature of that room and the buzzing anticipation in my body skyrocketed as I stripped for my two men. I kept my eyes closed, not wanting to ruin the illusion and become self-conscious. Even as I hummed softly to myself, I heard their ragged breaths and the rhythmic whisper of skin-on-skin as they stroked themselves.

"Fuck, you're so beautiful." Santos' voice floated over from my right the moment I stepped out of my panties. "Please sit on my face, paloma. I need to taste you."

Just for the hell of it, I kept my eyes closed and navigated my way to him by sound and touch. He gently directed me to the right place, and when he kissed the lips between my legs, my body rocked with sweet relief and aching need.

I couldn't feel anything in front of me, no headboard or wall, so I planted my hands on the bed above Santos' head, but that was short-lived.

"Stay upright," Torr barked from somewhere else in the room.

My groan was both out of frustration and pleasure with Santos lapping at me, but I straightened as instructed, using my legs to hold myself up. Ever the sweetheart, Santos helped, supporting my ass with his hands while his tongue dragged long, slow licks over my pussy.

Moments later, I felt pressure on one side of the bed like Torr was climbing on. Then I felt a strip of fabric press against my eyes and wrap around my head.

"Since you're so committed to the part," Torr mused as he tied the fabric at the back of my head. The blindfold smelled like him, so it had to be one of his T-shirts.

"Well I *am* a good girl," I said in the direction of his voice.

Santos moaned like he was agreeing with me, the sound creating vibrations against my sensitive flesh. I reached behind me, pressing my palms down on his chest so I could grind against his mouth. He was doing that thing where he avoided my clit, and I was *not* having that.

Still, he sucked on my lips again, teased my entrance with his tongue, but he avoided any direct contact with my clit.

"You know how to make me come, so do it." I injected hardness into my voice, taking on the dominating persona that he loved. "You live to please me, so fucking please me."

A sharp pain suddenly lit up my nipple, the pinching of the sensitive peak making my breath stutter and a whimper squeak out of my throat. The moment it was released, Santos' tongue lashed over my clit.

"Oh, you fuckers planned this," I groaned, hips bucking against his face.

"The specifics only a minute ago," Torr admitted with a chuckle. "With lots of hand signals and mouthing to each other while you stripped so pretty for us."

My retort was cut off by rough treatment to my other nipple, this time by Torr's mouth. There was no softness as his teeth scraped and pulled. The sensation pulsed its way down to my clit, which was desperate for more attention from Santos' tongue. My sweet fighter didn't give it to me until after a short scream left my mouth, and Torr pulled away.

"Too much?" He took my chin in a hard grip, and even though I couldn't see, I could sense him watching me carefully.

"No," I panted.

Fuck, I was so close to coming already. The whiplash of having control and then losing it had me teetering on the edge. This place between them, the balance between my dominant partner and my submissive one, was exactly where I belonged. Exactly where I thrived. I needed to be Santos' domme just as much as I craved being submissive to Torr. And the fact that the three of us found a way to satisfy each other, all at the same time, felt nothing short of incredible.

"Is that all you got?" I taunted Torr. "Blindfold and some nipple play? I thought you were going to punish me."

Just because I let him dominate me in the bedroom didn't mean I wasn't also a brat.

There was a flurry of movement I couldn't track, like Torr was arranging himself on the bed somehow. The next thing I knew, a hand cupped my nape and brought my head down, forcing me to pitch forward. My hands landed on muscular thighs and the blunt head of a cock brushed over my mouth.

"Good girls don't talk back," Torr said. "Open your mouth."

I did as told, and hot, velvety skin pushed past my lips. Torr moaned as I formed a seal around him, making him wet with my tongue. I brought a hand up to grip his base, but to my dismay, he grabbed both of my wrists and pinned them against the small of my back.

"No hands. No eyes," Torr commanded. When I moaned in complaint, he brought a hand down in a hard slap on one side of my ass. "You can do it. Suck me, good girl."

Fortunately, I still had Santos' mouth between my legs. That tongue laved over my pussy, sucking and licking me like it was his full-time job. After Torr's no-hand command and the sting of his palm on my ass lingered, Santos rubbed over that same cheek, his hand soothing the heated, tender skin. Then he brought his fingers to join his mouth, stroking them in and out of me as he finally concentrated attention on my clit.

He was soothing my pains, pleasing me in equal measure to Torr's punishment. God, what more could a girl want? I had sweetness and pain wrapped up in one incredible package deal.

Torr continued roughly playing with my nipples and spanking the hell out of my ass while I took more of his cock down my throat. Every muffled scream, whimper, moan, and slap earned me more of Santos' treatment. Loving passes over my bruising skin, another finger to fill me, and the most perfect suction and pressure on my clit.

My hips ground down hard over his face, my orgasm moments away. At the same time, I felt Torr swell and stiffen between my lips.

"That's a good girl, take me deeper," he urged. "Let me shoot down your pretty throat."

He had loosened his grip on my hands and I took the opportunity to massage his balls. He was too far gone to punish me anymore, his release on the precipice. His curses and groans filled my ears, and Santos' moans vibrated all the way up my body.

It was both of my men combined that did me in, sending me over the cliff in a rush of sensation. Hot spray filled my mouth, and I swallowed Torr's release on the second wave of pleasure.

I removed the blindfold as I lifted away from Santos' face and just had to pause, soaking in the sight of my men. They were both panting, muscled bodies glossy with sweat. Torr's back was against the headboard, with Santos further down the bed and flat on his back.

To my surprise, there were stripes of cum on Santos' stomach and chest. His cock lay against his lower abdomen, softening as the tip dribbled. "Someone wanna get me a towel?" he asked sheepishly.

"Did you...is that from without any touching?" I asked.

"Just barely, at the end," he admitted. "If you and Torr would have taken a little longer, I might have been able to go completely hands-free."

"Now that's talent." Torr tossed him a towel from the bathroom. "I haven't been able to go hands-free since I was like thirteen."

Santos smiled up at me as he wiped himself down. "What can I say? It's pleasing our girl that does it for me."

"Our *very* good girl." Torr dropped onto the bed behind me, bringing an arm around my waist and a kiss to my neck. "You're so fucking incredible, you know that?"

He kissed my shoulder, my upper back, and caressed me with such adoration and care. I knew this was him saying he loved me without using those words.

"I love you both," I said on a contented sigh, kissing Torr over my shoulder first and then leaning down to kiss Santos.

"Love you, paloma," my sweet fighter whispered reverently with a returned kiss and stroke of my cheek.

The three of us shifted into our sleeping positions, scooting and wriggling up the mattress as a single unit. Once I settled into the middle spot, flanked by my lovers and protectors, I closed my eyes and willed my brain to settle down as much as my body had.

No dreams, I pleaded. *No nightmares, just for tonight. Just let me rest before I have to leave.*

I should have known it was pointless to ask.

6

RORI

T he dream started off normal enough, like all the others. This time, I was in the wooded area behind the safe house. A white dove sat on the mangled stump of a tree, one that had been used for target practice so much that it was little more than an abused fence post.

I came toward the dove, Astarte, my movement not fully perceptible. I may as well have been floating.

"What's happening to me?" I heard myself ask.

The bird said nothing, only stared at me as she moved her head around.

"I can feel something happening to me, but I don't know what it is. I need your help."

Astarte fluffed up her feathers before smoothing them down again. *Do you know the difference between a true god and a false god?*

Her voice in my head warbled, like there was some kind of distortion with the sound.

"I don't know." Some instinct prickled over me, and I got hit with the urge to run. Not just to move at the pace faster than walking but to run for my fucking life.

But where I was practically floating earlier, my feet felt cemented into the ground now.

"Astarte, help me!" Panic edged into my voice. "I don't know what to do."

Yes, you do.

The dove's form broke apart like she'd been made out of sand or pale dust, a delicate sculpture disintegrated by the wind. Now as tiny particles floating in the air, what had once been in the form of a dove came toward me.

I turned to run, putting all my energy into my legs to get the hell away. Whatever the hell that was, I didn't want it touching me.

No matter how hard I pumped my arms and legs, it didn't look or feel like I was crossing any distance at all. I was stuck, running in place from a swarming...something.

You only need to know one thing about false and true gods, Aurora.

My head pounded with the reverberation of the voice, like a bass speaker turned up way too loud inside my skull.

"Who are you?" I shouted at the top of my lungs, though I heard no sound except a constant, heavy buzz inside my head, pressing against my skin, all around me.

When I tried to scream again, it felt like sand was being poured down my throat, shoved up my nose, and rubbed into my squeezed shut eyelids.

This swarm thing was trying to get inside me.

All gods are false except for me.

"Rori. Rori! Fuck, come back to us."

I was falling, kicking, grabbing for purchase on anything I could. Something hard and flat smacked against my skull, and I wanted to sob with relief. Finally, something solid! Pain pounded at my temple the moment I finally woke up.

"Shit, she hit her head. I'm gonna get the doctor."

My eyes snapped open to the beautiful sight of the hardwood floor in my bedroom. Relief was short-lived though as I coughed like I never had before in my life.

"Easy, paloma. Take a deep breath."

Santos' voice was the most comforting sound I could have asked for. His broad hand making passes up and down my back were so gentle and grounding. Through gritty eyes, I made out the glass of water he set down next to me.

I was dying for a sip, but I couldn't breathe past the sensations of sand in my throat and nose. Coughing into my hand, I only caught saliva. I swiped a finger into my mouth and only felt the usual suspects—my teeth, tongue, the insides of my cheek.

And yet it felt like I had mouthfuls, fucking lungfuls, of sand that I needed to get out. It was dry, gritty, and everywhere. Fuck, it hurt so much.

Finally, after my throat was completely raw and I had exhausted myself, I could take a shaky controlled breath and a sip of water.

Santos remained at my side the whole time, watching me with a worried expression.

"I'm sorry," I choked out in a weak whisper. "That was a bad one."

He scooted closer to me on the floor, enveloping me protectively with his arms and legs and providing the solid wall of his chest to lean against.

"I don't think we should go on this ride." Santos brought his chin to my shoulder. "Not while this is happening to you."

I pulled in another shaky breath, relying on his strong, solid body to stay mostly upright. "These dreams aren't getting any better. We need to act."

Footsteps thundered up the stairs at that moment, and then Torr appeared in the door. "Malik is on his way," he announced.

"I don't need—"

"Shut it." Torr held up an index finger, his face so grave that I knew he was dead serious. "You were screaming in terror, moving your arms and legs like you were running in your sleep. We couldn't even keep you on the bed. You fell off and hit your fucking head, so you are seeing the fucking doctor."

"I was just telling her that I think we should postpone the ride," Santos said.

"Excellent idea. I agree."

"No! We're doing the ride." I pushed away from Santos and climbed shakily to my feet. "We need to find what these crazy cultists are planning."

"Have you seen yourself?" Torr asked, gesturing at me. "You look haunted. You're in no shape to ride, much less lead."

"Torr, we need to do this. I—"

"Like hell we do. We can scout them again later, but I'm calling it off."

"Will you fucking listen?!"

My frustrated demand came out sounding more like a raspy whine, but Torr's change in expression told me he heard me. As long as I was president, he would hear me out. He went to the bedroom door and closed it.

"Okay, I'm listening."

I took a few more panting, ragged breaths, trying to form my racing thoughts into coherent sentences.

"This has something to do with gods," I finally whispered.

Torr's eyes flicked to Santos and then back to me. "How so?"

"I don't know exactly but..." I went to sit on the edge of the bed, struggling to put it all together in a way that made sense. "That night we rescued Hudson, I heard a voice. It was in my head like when Astarte and Tezca talk to us." I swallowed. "And I had...visions, kind of."

The guys said nothing, just waited for me to keep talking.

"The Sisterhood has their own god. Goddess, I guess." Fuck, if that wasn't terrifying to say out loud. "They...willed her into existence." I felt sick using that deity's words out loud.

"How?" Torr demanded. "We don't just *make* gods, right? Astarte found you."

"It—she— told me she was the pain of all women who have been hurt by men. Like *all* women who have ever lived. We know how far off the deep end the Sisterhood is, they live and breathe hating men. And they've been doing it for decades."

"And making sacrifices," Santos pointed out. "Both the ritualistic ones like in the village and forcing the gladiators to kill each other."

"So it's made from years and years of extreme, single-minded devotion on steroids," Torr mused. "How the fuck is this possible?"

"How are talking doves and jaguars possible?" I snorted.

His head snapped up. "Did you see the animal it was in? What if we just killed the animal body?"

"I don't think it has a body yet," I said. "And even if it did, that feels too easy. What's to stop it from just going into another animal?"

Santos crossed his arms, his face pinched with worry. "How are we supposed to fight a god, then?"

"I don't know, but I'm glad we have two."

Torr pinned me with a hard stare. "So what else did this goddess say to you?"

I blew out an exhausted breath. "She says I'm on the wrong side and I should be a leader for the Sisterhood."

"Fuck." Torr turned away, rubbing his jaw.

"I think the dreams are a tactic to wear me down? Punish me for telling it to fuck off? I'm not sure exactly."

Santos chuckled softly. "You told a god to fuck off, huh?"

"Oh, I told that rotten bitch a lot of things. Like I would kill her and every one of her followers so she'd never fucking exist again." My gaze returned to Torr, who'd begun pacing back and forth. "That's why today's ride is still happening."

"No." He stopped abruptly with an emphatic shake of his head. "No, it's not."

"I'm not arguing about this, Torr." I stood from the bed, already feeling stronger than when I first woke up. "I'm going to shower and get ready for this ride."

Torr made like he was following me into the bathroom to keep arguing, but I closed the door in his face. Moments later, I heard his and Santos' quiet voices floating from the bedroom.

I smiled to myself as I turned the shower on. Santos might have been submissive to me but he was no pushover. He would make sure Torr came around.

By the time I finished showering and re-entered the bedroom, both men were standing with glum faces and Tezca the jaguar between them.

"The cat says the ride still happens," Torr grumbled. "Can't exactly argue with a god now, can we?"

"And this is why Tezca is my favorite boy." I grinned, holding my palm out to the jaguar.

The ancient voice stroked like a physical presence over my brain. *The Ghost is joining us as well.*

My smile and hand dropped, the latter hitting my leg just below the towel I had wrapped around my torso. "Devin? Why does he need to come?"

Tezca ambled over to me then, his forehead bumping into the hand I'd held out moments ago. He opened his jaws just as I went to scratch his chin, taking my hand between those massive teeth.

The pressure was gentle, but it did make my heart rate speed up. Santos told me how many gladiators Tezca had killed. Easily.

I got the message from that soft, warning bite, along with a feeling that seemed projected onto me. I felt like I'd been gently scolded, a child chastised by a parent. *Don't question me, mortal,* was the general gist.

He dropped my hand with a huff and turned toward the door. So polite of him to avert his eyes so I could get dressed.

"Neither of you want me to go, huh?" I dropped the towel and started rummaging around for clean clothes.

"After what you just told us? Hell no." Santos still looked worried, so much so that he wasn't even watching me prance naked around the bedroom. "At least I'll have eyes on you while we're out. Too bad this poor bastard won't."

He nodded at Torr, who was staring distractedly at Tezca.

"Devin, huh?" Torr mused under his breath, a muscle feathering in his jaw.

The jaguar nudged Torr's hand, as if warning he would get some teeth too if he didn't watch it.

I eyed the sun outside the window as I stuck my feet into my boots and hurriedly laced them up. "Let's go. We should've left by now."

Tezca went down the stairs first, followed by me and my two men. Malik waited for me in the kitchen, eyes shifting from the jaguar to me with a small smile and shake of his head. "You Wilders and their animals," he chuckled.

"What?" I took a bite out of a piece of toast on the counter and washed it down with some black coffee. Malik was a long-time family friend and colleague of my mother's. Naturally, he was a regular at our house parties. "Our biggest animal was a

Doberman, this guy belongs to him." I patted Tezca's flank and nodded at Santos.

"I seem to recall a rooster that was definitely larger than expected." Malik shuddered as if the memory traumatized him.

My laugh nearly had me choking on my food. "Foghorn was just intimidated by you. He thought you were going to steal all his ladies."

Malik chuckled, setting down his own coffee cup. "You doing alright, Rori? Torr was pretty concerned."

I nodded, trying to look as earnest as possible while my mens' eyes bore into me like lasers. "I'm good, I swear. Just had a bad dream and a dry throat. Had a little coughing fit when I woke up is all."

Malik was too damn smart and observant. I knew he could tell I was still rattled, but I wasn't about to explain the gods business to him. He might physically prevent me from leaving.

"You're sure? I understand you're going out for a few days?"

"Yeah. I promise you, I'll be fine, doc. I wouldn't put my people at risk."

He spent another good, long minute observing me before nodding. "Alright. Be safe out there, young lady."

"I'll be back before you know it." I gave him a quick hug before scarfing down more toast. "I know these guys can be a handful."

"Oh, they're no trouble. This group is surprisingly open to talking about their experiences. I'm seeing lots of support and camaraderie between the fighters. I'm thinking of hosting a group session soon."

"Really? That's great." A physical weight seemed to lift from my chest. I was really hoping the fighters wouldn't be extremely closed off or worse, hostile to Malik.

As if bubbling up out of nowhere, I got an urge to ask about Hudson's progress but ultimately chose not to voice it. With a final squeeze of Malik's arm, I headed for the door. "See you when I get back."

Torr, Santos, and Tezca followed me out to where my hand-picked team was waiting.

"Took you long enough," Val griped. "I could've slept in another half hour if I knew you were gonna drag ass."

"The president arrives when she is ready," quipped the Saint, sitting astride one of the borrowed motorcycles.

"No shit," Val grumbled.

LJ sat quietly on his ride, arms crossed in front of him while he stared daggers at the Saint.

I turned to Torr first, lifting on tiptoes and throwing my arms around his neck in an embrace. "Keep an eye on the Bull," I whispered in his ear. "We need to know if they're shady together or if one of them is instigating something."

"Okay." That was the only thing he said before crashing his mouth to mine, stealing all my air and apparently the bones in my legs as I wobbled. His forehead pressed to mine when he broke away. "For fuck's sake, be careful out there. Call me if you can."

He knew the likelihood of having a signal was slim, and he was worried enough to want a call anyway.

"I'll try." I cupped his face, running my thumbs over those sharp cheekbones. "I love you, Torr."

His lips tensed. Relaxed. Tensed again. He was trying to say it back.

Eventually, he gave up.

"You better fucking come back to me," he growled. "If I hear nothing for one week, I'm riding after you."

"You won't have to," I assured him, pushing his hair off of his forehead.

"I can't fucking lose you. To them, their god, or whatever—"

"You won't." I gave him another kiss, rising on my tiptoes to make it forceful, harder. Pulling away slowly, I was already smiling when we separated. "It's gonna take a lot more than some angry cunt of a god to keep me away from you."

We unwrapped from each other, and Torr turned to Santos. "Keep our girl safe, man."

"You know I will." Santos held out his hand with a smirk. "I'm still the Butcher."

Rather than take his hand, Torr grabbed him in a rough, back-slapping embrace. Santos returned the affection just as Devin came out of the frat house.

The fighter was annoyingly breathtaking as usual, his hair up with a few small braids running through it. Some of his knife collection was holstered over his shirt, but I knew there were plenty more that weren't visible. And why was that knowledge so hot?

"Hey, we match!" Val grinned, pointing at Devin and then her own hair, which was done up in more of a Viking braid style.

He gave a small nod and uneasy smile to her before looking at me. "I assume Tezca told you I was coming?"

"Sure did. Almost got my hand bitten off for asking why."

He gave a nervous laugh but seemed more relaxed. "Yeah, I almost lost my ankle."

"Hudson gonna be okay with you gone?" I blurted the question out before thinking.

Devin shrugged. "He's gonna have to be, I guess. Malik's working with him. He'll survive." Then almost defensively he added, "I'm not sure why you're asking. Hudson doesn't need me for anything."

You two are totally fucking. I kept that thought to myself as I nodded. "Alright. Well, you can grab another loaner bike if you feel comfortable riding on your own."

As everyone got situated and mounted up, I spotted Astarte

on the apex of the garage roof. The dove and I only stared at each other. I didn't even have to ask a question. She knew I was wandering into something blind and wouldn't give me a clue as to what it was.

Remember what I said, were the only words of wisdom I got.

I could only imagine what she'd be referring to. The goddess had said plenty of things to me over our time together. What stuck out to me in that moment was what she had told me in a dream the night before all the nightmares started.

This will be the hardest battle you, or any living human, will have to face. And you cannot afford to lose it.

With that happy reminder, I began a slow acceleration down the driveway. Once I confirmed my team was behind me and the open road in front, I hit the throttle and tore out with a roar.

It was all I knew how to do.

7

TORRANCE

Rori's dust had barely settled by the time I started checking my phone for updates. Logically, I knew it was pointless to worry. She wouldn't be Rori if she couldn't handle herself. With Santos, Val, and LJ with her, there was nothing that could stop them.

All of this, I knew to be true. But what I couldn't shake was the sight of her in bed this morning. Watching her struggle to breathe, thrashing around like she was trying to escape a captor. The only time I'd been more scared was when I saw that she'd gotten shot.

My woman was strong. But was she strong enough to fight a god? One who was wearing her down and depriving her of sleep? Who knew what those cult elders could do once Rori came upon them?

Not to mention that weirdo, the Saint, made me uneasy as all hell. She was trying to keep an eye on him, see if he was up to anything nefarious, but I still didn't like him in her proximity without me around.

"Astarte and Tezca better be putting in some overtime," I

grumbled, walking back up the gravel driveway toward the houses.

I'd drive myself crazy with worry if I didn't keep myself in check. And the best way for me to do that was to hit the weights.

The workout areas in the courtyard were pretty much cleared out, most of the guys bullshitting elsewhere or having lunch. They'd be getting antsy soon. We needed a real ride, some kind of battle plan after Rori got back. These fighters, whether they were born that way or molded into it, wanted blood. Our one rescue mission was nowhere near enough to sate that desire.

A thought hit me as I changed into workout shorts, leaving my shirt off to keep cool, then headed back out to the courtyard. I wondered if the Sisterhood was arming themselves, getting ready for battle, or if they expected their goddess to handle everything. We already knew some of them were armed, but the vast majority were not.

Another thing to talk to Rori about when she's back, I thought as I chalked up my hands. Either situation needed to be dealt with carefully. The cult members needed to be dealt with, but we'd never stoop to the level of massacring a bunch of unarmed people.

I began with squats, the most difficult and taxing of all lifts. Always best to get them out of the way. I started with sets of lower weights to warm up, gradually adding more to the makeshift barbell. Eventually, I found the perfect mental zone of focus. Or rather, it found me.

That was how lifting always was with me. Once I hit a certain threshold of weight, the mental fortitude snapped into place like a suit of armor. If it wasn't there, I'd be likely to hurt myself.

Time ceased to exist as I pushed my body to the limit. Maybe I had spectators, maybe I was hogging the squat rack while someone else waited. I didn't know or care. My whole world was reduced to adding more weight, seeing how much more I could take.

Lifting used to be a fight to the death with myself. I constantly strived to be stronger, better. Because when I could always lift more, it meant I wasn't enough yet.

Never strong enough. Never good enough. That's why they left you to die. That's why Rori's family had to take you in like a stray dog.

The exertion was a punishment as well as a reward. I got stronger over time despite feeling like I was going to die after every workout. It became an addiction, a punishment I craved and sought out. Like my parents' abandonment of me wasn't punishment enough.

But now I had Rori who believed I was good enough. She loved me. *Actually* loved me.

Was I really though? When she'd told me countless times since we got together that she loved me? When she came back for me and Santos, made me her VP, listened to my advice, had been there for me through thick and thin over the years? Was I really good enough if I couldn't bring myself to repeat the same three simple words to her?

Why did it have to be anything but easy for me? Three single-syllable words held the weight of my whole heart, which felt heavier and more dangerous than the plates on this fucking barbell. The risk of saying those words out loud felt like dropping all that weight right onto my toes.

I knew it was dramatic. It was my subconscious drawing on fears from my childhood. Shit, maybe I needed to talk to Malik more than Rori. She'd never been afraid of putting her heart out there. And I knew, even though I continued failing at expressing what I really meant, she'd never give up on me.

All my shortcomings as a partner made me damn glad she

had Santos to make up for it. He was like her, fearless about loving wholeheartedly with no hang ups about saying it. Even after seeing the worst of humanity, of women especially, none of that stopped him from falling headfirst for her and letting her know it. I could learn a thing or two from him.

By the time my legs were screaming, I felt mentally lighter. I was a constant work in progress and the one Rori had left in charge. Sometimes it wasn't good to stay stuck in my mental hamster wheel all the time. What a concept.

Motion caught my eye as I set the barbell on the catches, and I looked over while I caught my breath. *Well, speaking of hamsters in enclosures.*

Hudson had not only left his room but the house. He was outside, in the open.

Trying not to stare, I wiped the sweat off my forehead with my arm. He was using another barbell rack to stretch his shoulders, from the looks of it. He had a T-shirt and athletic shorts on, and the vast majority of his skin was covered in tattoos. Good ones too. The kind that rivaled the quality of mine, done by Rori's dad.

My curiosity piqued even more when he reclined on the bench under the rack, scooting and adjusting it for his reach. After a few warm-up reps with just the barbell, Hudson rolled up and added two plates to each side.

My eyebrows shot up. Two plates. Two hundred and twenty-five pounds. It wasn't an enormous amount of weight, but definitely a lot to start out with. Especially for a guy who didn't look like he weighed two-twenty-five and had spent years confined to a single room.

"Hey." I headed over before I could think twice. "Hudson, right?"

He could have been squinting in the sunlight or glaring at me, it was hard to tell. "Yeah?"

"You want a spot?" I gestured to the bar.

He shrugged like it didn't make a difference to him. "If you want to."

I went behind the rack as he reclined on the bench, his head near my knees. Once he found his grip, I braced myself, ready to stop the barbell from crushing his Adam's apple once he realized it was too much damn weight.

To my surprise, the lower and lift of each rep was incredibly smooth and controlled. As was his breathing and his form. The guy knew what he was doing, maybe even better than me.

He did a set of ten like it was warm-up before setting the bar back on its catches.

"Well, shit." I laughed as he rolled up. "You had me worried when you loaded those two plates, but guess I underestimated you."

Hudson shrugged and brought his arms behind him to stretch again. "I used to compete a little bit, just amateur stuff. It was a hobby."

"I mean, it's a hobby for me too but I've never warmed up with that much." I came around to the front of him, sticking my hand out. "I don't think we've formally met. I'm Torrance. Everyone calls me Torr."

Hudson hesitated, staring up at me for a moment before clasping my hand. "You're the second in command. To her."

"That's right."

Hudson rested his hands on his thighs, elbows flared out in a pose that looked a little defensive. "Gotta admit, I'm surprised you offered to spot me instead of bashing my head in with one of those plates. Or is that still on the table?"

I crossed my arms, taking my time to answer. "I'm not interested in bludgeoning you to death, no."

"And the woman?"

"Her name is Rori. And no, she's not interested in killing

you either. Which is pretty damn reasonable, considering you tried to kill *her*. But we're all very sympathetic to your situation, in case the free food, housing, clothes, and other amenities," I gestured to all the workout equipment, "doesn't show that already."

Hudson lowered his head, shoulders rounding down slightly while his eyes remained connected to mine. "I am appreciative. Of all of it. You've noticed I haven't tried to kill anyone else since I got here."

"That's a low bar of gratitude, but we'll take it."

He huffed out a breath, which almost sounded like an attempt at laughter. "It's a nice day out," he remarked after a few seconds of silence.

"Yeah." He wasn't lying. It was just warm enough with a bit of a breeze and a clear sky. It would've been a perfect day for riding if I didn't have to keep an eye on things.

"I almost didn't leave my room when I found out Devin was leaving." Hudson rested his forearms on his legs. "But then I found out the--uh, Rori was going. And the other woman, I don't know her name. Dark hair, blue eyes."

"Valorie," I informed him. "She's Rori's cousin, goes by Val."

"Right, yeah. So I've been able to see this yard from the window. And I figured, if there's less people around, I could see if I still got my technique, you know?"

I didn't fully understand why he was telling me all this. Maybe because I was the only person around to talk to? Whatever the reason, it seemed important to listen.

"It's good to get out of your comfort zone," I said. "Break down those barriers you set up in your mind."

Hudson nodded. "Malik and I talked about that. What's familiar isn't always what's right, even if it feels better to stay within those barriers. Doing what's uncomfortable, taking that risk, that's how I stop being the person I was before coming here." He leaned back, straightening. "So, that's why I decided to leave my room and try some lifts, run the risk of talking to someone, like you."

I studied him, my feelings somewhere between surprised and amused. Damn it, I might actually end up liking this guy. "And how does it feel?"

"Feels..." Hudson paused to consider that, head tilting slightly. "Feels good," he said with a definitive nod. "Yeah. I'm glad I came out here."

I wondered if he'd feel the same way if Rori and Val were around. Or if the mere sight of them would send his hackles up, shutting himself back in his room like a cornered animal. Either way, I didn't need to push it now. We'd find out when they returned. For now, at least, the guy and I were getting along.

"Well, you clearly don't need my assistance with your lifts," I said. "I'll leave you to your workout. Nice talking to you—"

"What's she like?"

The abrupt question threw me off-kilter for a second. "Who? Rori?"

Hudson nodded. "I know what Devin thinks of her. He tries to be very straightforward and objective, but everyone has bias. Especially when it comes to other people. How do you feel about her?"

Well if that didn't make me curious as hell about what Devin said about her, but I smothered that thought with an awkward laugh. "Shit, I don't even know where to begin. I've known her for thirteen years."

"So you know her well."

"Better than most. Doesn't stop me from being biased, though. Your best bet is to get to know her yourself."

"I can't do that yet." Hudson shook his head, blowing out a long breath. "I'm not ready to speak to a woman face-to-face. So

I'm trying to learn from those around her. And anyway, your biases are different from Devin's."

All valid points. "Well." I rubbed my jaw. "She's the most loyal friend anyone will ever have. That shit runs deep with her. No one is a casual acquaintance with Rori. You're either a stranger to her or you're practically family. And she's someone who will ride into battle for the people she cares about, no questions asked."

Hudson made a snorting sound and shook his head.

"What?" I demanded.

"So why'd she run in to save me, then?" He met my eyes again, challenging me. "She didn't know me, so what you're saying makes no sense."

"She did it for Santos," I snapped. "Because she loves him and *you* were important to him. 'Til you tried to kill her, at least." Hudson opened his mouth to argue, but I cut him off. "And even if you hadn't been tight with Santos, if we'd have found out about you another way, she'd still want to rescue you because what they did is fucked up. Sexual slavery is wrong, and you didn't deserve that, no matter who you are. It's not that fucking complicated. If something fucked up is going on, any decent person will want to stop it. That's the normal, expected thing to do."

Hudson and I stared at each other for a few tense seconds before he broke eye contact with a sigh. "I definitely don't know what's normal or expected anymore. It's like I need to recalibrate my sense of reality."

My temper ebbed away, and I found myself leaning against the barbell rack. "I can't imagine what that's like. Sorry I got defensive."

"You're really protective of her." Hudson's eyes flicked up to mine again. "They don't call you the Guard for no reason."

"Look, Rori isn't perfect," I said. "In fact, she's a massive pain in the ass sometimes. Stubborn as a bulldog with the bite to back it up. But I'll put my life on the line for her because I know for a fact she'd do it for me."

Hudson chuckled dryly. "You're lucky. I can't say I ever had someone that would do that for me."

"Rori will," I told him before I could think better of it. "You just have to give her the chance."

Before he could respond, a motorcycle rumbled to life. I looked toward the garage, noticing an ex-gladiator straddling one of the loaner bikes, which wasn't unusual. With all the free time the guys had, many of them practiced riding.

The rider turned out to be the Bull, and he gave me a little wave as he noticed me watching.

"Be right back," I said to Hudson as I started toward the man on the motorcycle, some instinct poking at me to stay alert.

"Hey, VP," the Bull greeted me as I came closer. He seemed eager to leave, with one foot already off the ground and his hands twitching on the handlebars.

"Hey, Bull." I meandered casually to the front of his bike, blocking his way. "You headed somewhere?"

"Nah, you know. Just want to hit a couple of practice runs." His eyes darting to the road behind me told a different story.

"Hey, why don't Hudson and I join you?" I glanced back at the man still sitting on the weight bench. "It's about time he learns to ride, and I could keep an eye on both of you."

The Bull ground his teeth. "No offense, VP, but I'd rather do this one alone. Want to clear my head a bit. Next time, though?"

I smiled at him, trying to keep a calm facade while reading into his body language. "Seems like you're in a hurry. You got somewhere you need to be?"

"No," he huffed. "What's with the interrogation? I thought we weren't prisoners anymore."

"You're not, but you also don't know the area. It's not safe to ride off alone."

"Not trying to be disrespectful, but I really need to blow off some steam."

"Why, what's got you riled up?" I pressed. Damn, sure wish I had Santos to check my six.

"None of your business, to be fuckin' honest."

"Hey, no need to have a tone with me. If you need to blow off steam, take a walk. Lift some weights. Shoot some targets around back. But you can't just ride off on a bike that isn't yours."

The Bull snorted out a big breath like his animal namesake. He seemed to relax for a moment, complying with my request. Then he jerked the handlebars and started the bike, kicking off as fast as he could in an attempt to go around me.

Too bad he didn't know motorcycles like I did.

I reached over his dash and hit his killswitch, stopping his ride dead in its tracks. Then I lunged, grabbing the lapels of his jacket to swing him off the bike. He hit the ground, but the ex-gladiator wasn't going without a fight. A meaty fist swung and crashed into my temple, knocking me off him while the world spun.

He scrambled for the bike again, but I grabbed his foot, bringing him back down to the ground with me. He rolled before I could successfully pin him and kicked me in the stomach with his free foot. I doubled over and got clocked in the head once again.

Fucking hell, I really needed backup. Rori had to take all the good people with her. The only one I could really trust here was the Hunter, and he was probably horizontal with Paige right now.

The Bull had knocked the wind out of me and my vision was dotted with stars and black dots, but I held onto anything I could. His jacket, his pant leg. I could not fucking let him get on that bike.

"Gotta warn them," he muttered to himself as he tried to shake me off.

"Warn who, asshole?" I crawled up the backs of his legs, trying to get on top of him so I could get an arm around his neck or something, but he flipped over, pinning me beneath him.

His tailbone pressed directly into my stomach, painful and making it difficult to breathe. I bear-hugged around his torso and tried to get my legs around his, but none of the angles were right. I should have done more of those jiu-jitsu classes with Daren, but that was his thing, not mine.

"Let go of me!" The Bull tried to unlock my hands from their grip, but I held on. "They're keeping her safe! I can't let them, ugh, get to her!"

I couldn't fully process what he was saying, not when my sole focus was preventing him from getting away. But it hit me then as one hell of a delayed realization that we might've been suspicious of the wrong person.

The Saint was weird. Eccentric for sure. But this man, grappling on the ground with me right now, was without a doubt disloyal to us. Maybe the Saint was too, but I couldn't worry about that now.

Despite his size, the Bull managed to wriggle around enough to drive an elbow into my gut. He must have hit a nerve because the pain made me black out for a second and also loosen my grip around him.

He rolled away, and I found myself staring at the sky and part of the garage roof. I tried to find the strength to move, to grab a foot and trip him again, to yell for help, anything. But I should have known better than to fight one-on-one with a former gladiator.

All my limbs moved too slowly and my lungs couldn't inhale

a full breath. Fuck! I couldn't let him get away, couldn't let Rori down. Rolling to my forearms and knees felt like it took a full minute, and the Bull was already grasping the side of the motorcycle, pulling himself up.

Hudson moved faster than either of us could perceive. In the time it took to blink, he stood between the Bull and me, hands on the other man's shoulders as he forcibly threw him off the bike.

The Bull was lying prone next to me, palms splayed out and eyes blinking like he couldn't figure how he'd ended up on the ground. Hudson was on his back in the next instant, bringing his arm to lock around his opponent's throat.

The Bull's face started going red and then purple. He gasped for air as he clawed at Hudson's forearm but was quickly losing the fight.

"Don't kill him," I rasped, finally finding air in my lungs. "We need to question him."

"I'm not. He'll just pass out soon." Hudson was calm as he answered, his chokehold rock steady on the other man.

Within another minute, the Bull's eyes rolled up and his body went limp. Hudson released him, and the color immediately began returning to the passed-out man's face.

"Holy fuck." I rubbed the tender spot on my stomach where I'd been elbowed. "Thanks for the assist."

Hudson nodded, his face remote. "We should get him restrained before he wakes up."

"Yeah. Help me take him to the basement?"

As we dragged the traitor across the ground, I could only hope Rori was having an easier time than me.

8

RORI

I t was three days of riding before we found them.

Aside from the general direction of south, we didn't know exactly where the four elder women were headed. For all we knew, they could have doubled back and returned the direction they came from. But that would have come from the assumption that they knew they had been watched, which LJ would not have allowed. The only other reason for changing course would be paranoia, and while this cult had that in spades, they also had a staggering amount of arrogance.

Whatever this split-three-ways plan was, I was counting on them being confident in it.

LJ and Val had triangulated their most likely positions based on the main road taken by the RV, and the estimation of where they'd end up based on distance covered and potential routes taken. So many of the roads out here hadn't been maintained for decades, since before I was born, probably. We eliminated most potential routes due to the sheer impassibility of them, all over-grown, cracked, and potholed to hell. It'd be suicide to travel those roads in something as bulky as a van, not to mention one carrying supposedly precious cargo.

"You think they'd avoid these towns?" Val pointed out a few settlements on the map. "Because, you know, *men*."

"I didn't see them pack much food," LJ said. "They'll need to stop for supplies, men or no. Safe to assume they'll avoid men if they can, though."

"Here." I dropped my fingertip to a dot marked Portisville. "This place has one of those self-serve stations. You grab what you need and then leave cash or goods in exchange. No need to interact with anyone."

LJ lined up his ruler on the map, muttering under his breath as he did the measurements in his head. "The distance fits within our time frame. If they kept a steady pace, they'll have been there today or yesterday."

"Let's go." I headed for my bike, trusting everyone would follow. "They're not likely to stay in one place for long."

I pulled out my phone the moment I lowered into my rumbling seat. Again, no service, just like every other time I checked. Sometimes I'd barely get a bar of reception that would only disappear in the next second. Regardless, I wrote a quick message to Torr, fully aware of the low chances he'd ever see it. *Connection's bad, but we're fine. Love you.*

Shoving the phone away, I went for the handlebars and hit the throttle, accelerating on the road with a roar. A glance in my mirror showed Santos just to the right and behind me. He looked relaxed on the bike, a complete natural. It wasn't lost on me that he was in Torr's usual spot, my right hand.

I returned my attention to the road with a smile, pleased that my men's formation on the road was just as seamless as it was off. Santos and Torr knew how to cover each other as if on instinct. When one had to stay behind, the other naturally stepped into his place at my side.

Devin hung a few paces behind Santos, and he also seemed at ease with the formation of our small group. More so than I expected, considering it was Tezca who said he had to be part of this mission.

My gaze shifted to the side, looking for the big cat running alongside us at a speed no regular jaguar could maintain. Tezca didn't like running on the road, so my peripheral vision caught the cat-shaped shadow keeping up with us through the brush, shrubs, and rocky terrain along the roadside.

Somewhere in the sky, Astarte watched over us too. The companion gods stayed with us, keeping us in sight while they remained out of reach. Their steadfastness was the only real confirmation that we were going more or less the right way. It wasn't like they were alerting us to the contrary, which by this point, I figured was as much as we would get.

Portisville stood on its own in a neutral zone, not currently part of any particular territory. At first, it was surprising that a nearby territory hadn't absorbed it, considering the one-stop-sign town had the most well-stocked service station for miles and was just off of a major roadway as well. You'd think some governor would be frothing at the mouth to levy taxes on all those goods. But once we crossed into the town's limits, it became clear why that wasn't the case.

The service station was at the center of town, easy to see from the road leading in. And it was surrounded by armed guards.

"Shit, is there a bank vault in there?" Val mused, parking next to me in the lot.

"No," I answered. "Just the only fresh food, water, clothes, and gasoline for miles."

"If you don't count the safe houses," she chuckled. "What do you want to do, Pres?"

I glanced at her. "We could use a restock for the road. You and I will go in, grab some stuff, and check out the inside."

Looking at the guys, I said, "You all stay here. See if you spot our targets or the van."

"And if we do?" the Saint asked, a smile coming to his lips.

"Do not engage. Wait for Val and me to get back."

With that, Val and I headed toward the entrance. If it weren't for all the guns posted at the entrances, it would have been a routine supply run. But the mere presence of those guards had me twitchy, on edge, even if they were there just to make sure no one made off with stolen goods.

"You seein' what I'm seein'?" Val muttered under her breath.

"What?" My handgun felt heavy at my hip and I tried to keep my arm relaxed, resisting the urge to reach for it.

"They're all chicks."

Every one of the guards was armored from head to foot, covered in steel toe boots, bullet and knife proof padding, multiple guns, knives, ammo, and with either helmets or beanies on their heads. From far away, it was near-impossible to tell gender. But getting up closer confirmed that every single guard was a woman.

And they each had a patch on the arm of their dark fatigues. Some symbol that looked vaguely familiar, though I couldn't quite make it out.

"Don't stare," Val hissed at me. "Be cool."

I tore my eyes away, focusing straight ahead. I could feel the guards' eyes on me as we passed through the front door, but they moved out of the way to let us through.

"Fuck, that was tense," my cousin sighed. "Alright, what do we need?"

I looked around, actually impressed by the neat aisles, produce displays, clothing racks, and bank of glass-doored refrigerators. This must have been one of those warehouse-sized supply centers from before the Collapse. There were so few now since such a large space with perishable food required a fuckload of electricity, and most grids weren't stable these days.

"Water," I told Val. "And food. Let's see if they got any whole chickens. Also wouldn't mind an extra blanket or two."

We wandered through the aisles, checking out the supplies while looking around for four older women with a baby carrier. Nada. More armed guards patrolled the inside, as if the ones at the entrances weren't enough.

After gathering our supplies, we made it to the collection box near the entrance. Under the watchful eye of a woman with bandoliers of ammo making an X across her chest, I deposited an estimated amount of currency into the box. Many neutral zone towns still bartered for goods, so prices weren't exact.

"May the Dark Mother protect you," muttered the closest guard as we headed for the door.

Val just about froze in her spot, but I grabbed her arm and pulled her along. "Be cool." I repeated the advice she gave me when we walked in.

"Well, that explains a lot," she huffed once we were out of earshot. "Good thing the guys didn't come in."

"Yeah, that wouldn't have gone well."

Santos, the Saint, LJ, and Devin were huddled in a semi circle when we returned to the bikes, their heads bent low.

"Y'all comparing dick size? What are you looking at?" I said when we walked up.

"This." Devin was the one who thrust the piece of paper at me. "There's a few of them stuck to trees and poles around here."

I glanced at what looked to be an event flyer for some stargazing thing. "'This week, Virgo will be the brightest all year.' That's cool, I guess. I think my little brother is a Virgo."

"You think?" LJ snorted.

"Do I look like I know horoscopes?" I shoved a jug of water

at his chest. "Stash this in yours, you got the biggest compartments."

Val laughed. "Typical Scorpio."

"Shut up." To the guys, I asked, "Did you all see anything out here?"

"Just the flyer, President," voiced the Saint.

"I didn't ask you all to look for a flyer, so I guess that's a no."

"You really don't know what Virgo is?" Devin pinned me with a stare that made me want to squirm with discomfort.

"No. Should I?"

"It's the constellation of a woman. A maiden, or virgin."

Silence fell over the group as that information sank in. "You think our targets will be at this thing?" I pointed at the flyer.

"Shit, the whole town might be," Val said. "The flyers are everywhere, and the guards back there said something about the Dark Mother's blessing. The cult probably owns the damn place."

"Where's this stargazing thing happening?" I scanned the paper. "LJ, how far is this from here?"

"About an hour's ride, maybe," he said.

"Let's go there now." I threw a leg over my bike, wasting no time. "We'll scout the location before it gets dark and see if there's a covered place we can watch."

Everyone followed without another word, LJ pulling up next to me since he knew the way. My stomach flipped with anxiety as we hit the road, the complete unknown threatening to make my thoughts spiral. I missed Torr badly right then. His strong, solid presence was always able to ground and calm me.

But I needed to beat my self-doubt now more than ever before. I didn't know what I was riding into, what I was leading my people, my family, into. Regardless, I needed to be their president and stand tall on my own.

9

RORI

The directions on the flyer brought us to a series of hills that looked like a miniature version of a much greater mountain range. The stargazing event would take place on the highest one, and we could already see groups of people settling in with blankets and food.

We parked our bikes at the base of one of the smaller hills, making sure to hide them in the brush, then hiked up the hillside farthest away from where the action was happening. We noted other people parking vehicles at the base of the tallest hill before making their way up, but there was no van that we could see.

What if this is all a waste of time? I wondered. *The Virgo thing could be a total coincidence and the Sisterhood has nothing to do with this. They could be getting farther away, or closer to the safehouses to do fuck knows what.*

I pushed on harder, putting more speed and power into my legs as I hiked up the hill. The ache in my muscles and lungs helped to keep the thoughts at bay, kept me here and focused. No wonder Torr used exercise as a coping mechanism.

We were here, so we might as well see it through.

A flapping of wings brought my attention upward, but in the fading daylight, the white dove was a dim blur.

Remember what I told you, Astarte had said.

She said to trust my instincts, to look deep into the divine part of myself, below the surface of anxiety and what-ifs.

I took a deep breath, still pushing onward as I tried to quiet my mind.

We were in the right place. Deep in my gut, I fucking knew we were in the right place.

Everyone spread out once we crested the hill, keeping low behind the cover of boulders, shrubs, and trees. We had an unobstructed view of the neighboring peak where everyone was gathering. Voices drifted over, all feminine. People chatted and laughed, sounding relaxed with an air of excitement. Someone started a campfire, which slowly grew as people fed it dry wood. After a few minutes, it was a roaring bonfire, lighting up every-one's faces with an orange glow.

"Look." Val nudged me. "The two on the left. They were at the service station."

I nodded at her observation. "Did you happen to see what their patches were? The black ones on their arms."

"Oh yeah. Looked like the female reproductive system. The uterus, tubes, ovaries, all that. Just stylized to look cool on a patch."

"Jesus," I muttered. "Real subtle, aren't they?"

Our whole group seemed to collectively hold a breath when four figures appeared on the opposite side of the bonfire. We could only see their silhouettes through the flames, but there was no mistaking them. They stood together, solemn and poised while everyone else looked like they were there to party. And the dead giveaway was one of them holding a large, bulky object with a handle, which could only be a child carrier.

My gaze was fixed on them, unable to look away. I couldn't

erase the feeling that they could see me, even through the cover of darkness and our hiding places, and were staring right at me.

Do you know I'm watching you? I wondered. *Did you want me to follow you and see this?*

A hand on my shoulder jolted me out of my trance-like state. "It's just me," Santos said when I startled. He frowned with concern at whatever he saw on my face. "You okay, paloma?"

"Yeah." I blinked and rubbed my eyes, already feeling the strain from staring at the bright fire. "Yeah, I'm good."

His mouth tightened, but he didn't comment further. "What's the plan? Just watch? Or do we engage?"

"Do not engage." I carried my voice to make sure everyone heard. "We're just watching. If we can isolate the four we know are from the cult, we'll go after them. But everyone else might be innocent. We don't want anyone caught in the crossfire."

With that order, everyone settled in for the show.

Stars emerged as the sky darkened. People started pointing up, assumedly at the constellation they all came to see.

I never had much interest in the stars and planets. That was my little sister's thing. On family camping trips, Lucia would have her telescope and book of star charts ready the moment the sun set. She would then map out the planets and constellations, pointing them out to everyone until she nodded off from tiredness.

She would have loved something like this. A bonfire on the top of a hill, gathering with people who shared the same interests as her. Lucia was popular and always making new friends.

A bolt of rage struck through me, surprising me at how quickly it came on. It pissed me off that the Sisterhood would use things like this most likely to recruit and brainwash members. Impressionable kids like my teenage sister.

They probably ran fundraisers that looked like they were

supporting women's shelters. Probably gave talks about empowering women and giving them back control of their lives. All things that looked wonderful on the surface but were rotten and evil underneath. My anger rose like a pot of water boiling over, that they could target my sister, or some other girl who was vulnerable and actually needed help. They made it so easy to fall into their trap. By the time they revealed what they were actually doing to men, it was probably too late to get out.

So if their goddess gave them some supernatural ability to see me, I hoped they could read my mind as well.

I'm going to kill you all, and I won't stop until every vulnerable girl, woman, boy, and man is safe from you.

All at once, the chatter on the high hill stopped. Only the crackle and pops of the fire reached our ears. The four figures raised their arms and an eerie chanting began.

"What the fuck?" someone near me whispered.

I was too transfixed by the sight to say anything. The middle one held the child carrier between her hands, high above her head.

The chanting was nonsensical. It wasn't English and didn't sound like Spanish or anything else based in Latin. It was just rhythmic vocalizations repeating over and over.

It was hypnotic.

I could feel myself getting drawn in, my body starting to sway from side to side just like the rest of the bonfire attendees. Their voices started to join those of their leaders, amping up the vibrations and volume through the air.

Something dark passed in front of me, the fire no longer visible. Two hands fell to my shoulders and shook me violently.

"What the—what?" I demanded, feeling disoriented like I'd just woken up from a deep sleep.

"Snap the fuck out of it, Rori." Devin's face hovered in front of me, his dark eyes narrowed in a glare. It was his hands on my shoulders, now digging in with an unforgiving grip. "You start doing that again, I'm gonna slap you. And then Santos is gonna kill me."

"Doing what?" I smacked his hands away, feeling almost...ashamed? Like I'd been caught doing something bad.

"You had joined in, chanting and swaying. I watched you for a full minute." Devin sat back, giving me space. "Whatever they're doing is getting to you."

"Fuck, I'm sorry." I rubbed my eyes, scrubbed my face. It really felt like I had just woken up from a deep sleep. "You don't have to slap me, just pinch me or something." I looked around at my group, finding everyone's face in the orange glow of the fire. "Was anyone else affected?"

They all shook their heads slowly at me, even Val.

It had to have been because the Dark Mother had touched me already, had access to my mind, just like with the nightmares.

Devin moved warily to the side, letting me have a view of the hill again. I watched just in time to see the woman holding the carrier swing her arm and throw it into the fire.

We all let out collective gasps and curses of shock. The chanting and swaying continued as if nothing had changed. But now, black smoke rose from the fire, a dense floating mass that looked like it held more weight, more substance than ordinary smoke.

It hovered above the fire, shifting and writhing in midair. The smoke, or whatever it was, kept its form. It never floated away, never dissipated into the atmosphere. It stayed in place, hovering a few feet above the licking flames like a malevolent spirit.

Suddenly all of the chanting stopped, creating an eerie silence that felt more like a vacuum of sound. I couldn't hear the fire crackling anymore. Couldn't hear my own breathing or my riders if they were saying anything.

Then the floating black mass started to move.

It floated toward me, its dark, ethereal form almost shimmering. It looked like a swarm of bees heading my way.

Every instinct told me to run, but I felt frozen in place. I might as well have been sitting in the middle of a road, watching the headlights of an eighteen-wheeler head straight toward me.

Something touched me, and that was when my self-preservation kicked in. I sprang to my feet and turned, running across the crest of the hill and heading down the other side.

Some president you are, turning tail and leaving your people vulnerable to that thing.

I jerked my head around at the thought and saw the black floating mass heading straight for me. It crossed from the bonfire hill to this one in no time at all. Through it, I could see my riders chasing after it at a much slower pace. Their mouths moved, shouting something. My name, probably.

Facing forward again, I kept racing down the hill. The dark mass from the fire wanted me, not them. Somehow, I'd known that from the moment I saw it rise up from the fire.

And it was gaining on me. I didn't have to look behind me to know that. It started to not only surround me, but absorb *into* me. The sensation was like sandpaper on my skin, tiny pinpricks being pushed into my pores and hair follicles. Every time I dragged a breath in, it felt like I was inhaling sand.

Fuck, this is my dream, I realized in a panic.

I ran harder, even though I could barely see through my eyes feeling sandblasted with pain. I was choking now, my throat working to remove the foreign bodies forcing themselves into me and cutting off my air.

I must have fallen because I was rolling on the ground now,

trying to cover my face, my mouth, my eyes. It hurt so fucking bad, and I felt like I was going to pass out from lack of air.

The last thing I saw was Astarte, the dove the only clear object in my blurry vision.

Remember what we told you, she said.

* * *

As soon as I woke up, I started coughing, my throat seizing up from the dryness. I rubbed violently at my eyes, desperate to get the sand out.

"Hey, hey. Take it easy."

Someone pushed a thermos into my hands and I drank the water from it greedily, gulping it all down in a few swallows. Someone else's palm made circles on my back, soothing me as I returned to rubbing at my eyes.

It took a few seconds to realize my eyes felt normal. Nothing but the usual grittiness from sleep. I blinked and looked around, meeting the worried faces of my crew illuminated by the morning sun.

"Uh. Hi, guys." I scanned all the faces again, noting someone was missing. "Where's Santos?"

"Right here, paloma," said a husky voice near my ear. He was the one rubbing my back, sitting behind me with his legs on either side of me.

"You scared the shit out of us, Pres," LJ grumbled.

"What happened?" I leaned back, letting my head rest on Santos' shoulder. My throat was dry. My legs and feet ached a little, probably from running and climbing the hill. But otherwise I felt...fine. Normal.

"You took off running out of nowhere." Val's blue gaze bounced all over me like she was examining for injuries. "And then you just collapsed. Crumpled to the ground like someone cut your strings."

"It was the smoke! Or the cloud, swarm thing. It was coming straight at me."

"The what?" the Saint tilted his head. It was probably the first time I ever saw him look confused.

"They threw the carrier in the fire and this black smoke rose out of it. Only it wasn't like smoke, it was...it seemed like it was alive."

"We saw them throw the carrier in," Devin said. He was next to me and must have been the one who had given me water. "And there was smoke for a bit, but that was all. Then you took off running like someone was after you with a chainsaw."

The realization hit me with a cold sense of dread in the pit of my stomach. "None of you saw it." I looked at Val, who was frowning with just as much confusion as everyone else.

"Fuck." I rubbed my temples. "Did I dream it?"

No. There was no doubt in my body or mind that it had been real. I had *felt* the grains of sand digging into my skin like thousands of tiny needles. I felt the exertion in my body as I tried to get away, the burning in my lungs as I had struggled to breathe. It was entirely too vivid to be a dream. And minutes ago, before I had woken up, there had been nothing. No dreams at all for the first time in over two weeks.

"Are you okay, Rori?" The question came from Devin, but everyone stared intently at me.

I must have gone quiet for a few minutes while trying to decipher dreams from reality.

"I...think so," I said cautiously. Then more firmly, "Yes. Yes, I'm fine."

It was one thing to let my guard down in front of just Santos, or even my family members. But right now, these were my riders, my Vengeful Gods, and I was their president. I couldn't look like a wilting flower in front of them.

"Sorry to worry you guys." I forced a smile. "But I feel good now." Physically, anyway. At least I was partially honest. "So where are we? Base of the hill?"

"Yeah," Val confirmed. "We didn't want to risk moving you after you passed out. So we just camped out where you dropped. Your vitals were strong, so we figured we'd give you a few hours to wake up."

"I wanted to get you a doctor immediately," Santos muttered.

"In an area that's clearly unfriendly to men," Devin tacked on. "Great idea, that was."

"Well, it all worked out. I'm awake and feeling fine." I planted a kiss on Santos' still-frowning lips before climbing to my feet. "What happened on the other hill? Did someone keep watching?"

The Saint nodded. "Not much happened after they threw the carrier in. They kept chanting for a while until the fire died down, then everyone left."

"I saw the direction the van went," LJ added. "We can keep pursuing them if you want."

I thought for a moment, then shook my head, my head swimming for a moment and my vision becoming disoriented. Rubbing my temples to get clarity, I heard LJ speak again.

"You don't think they—" LJ stopped, his voice catching in his throat.

"Spit it out, cuz." Val squeezed his shoulder, encouraging him to go on.

"Burned a baby," LJ continued, his face paling. "Would they just murder a child like that?"

"If it was a boy, they wouldn't blink." Devin walked over and clapped a hand down on his other shoulder. Even in my state of trying to decipher reality from dreams, I was still pleasantly surprised that Devin seemed to be getting along with the whole group.

"It could have been a new type of male sacrifice for them," the Ghost went on. "But we had no idea what they would do and were too far away to act." His hand dropped from my cousin's shoulder, looking at him sympathetically. "There was nothing we could have done."

"We're not even sure if a child died," I said. "Let's check the fire. If we find remains, we'll give it a proper burial."

"If not a baby, then what was in that carrier?" asked the Saint.

No one answered, but I remembered part of a dream right then. When I thought I had a daughter but it turned out to be a faceless, fleshy mass that moved and writhed.

* * *

EMBERS WERE STILL GLOWING in the bonfire's gray ashes when we crested the neighboring hill. We all found long branches and got to work, sifting and poking through the fire's remains.

Pieces of the carrier emerged quickly. Mostly plastic parts that had melted and then cooled. A few metal bits like washers, bolts, and screws. Even a piece of charred fabric from the seat itself emerged. But nothing that resembled human remains.

No bone fragments or even teeth. It was a big fucking fire, but there would have been something more than dust left behind.

We kept searching until we scraped the unburned ground directly beneath the fire pit.

"There was no child in that carrier." I dropped my stick and wiped my ash-covered hands on my jeans.

"So what then?" Santos asked. "Was it even a sacrifice?"

How was I to answer that? Was there even a name, a term for that fleshy blob thing? Was that the god that had spoken to me, inserted itself into my mind and now possibly my body?

I folded my arms over my stomach as if to protect myself. "It might not have been a sacrifice," I said, more to myself than anyone else. "But an awakening."

10

SANTOS

The ride home was long, tense. We left the remains of the bonfire feeling like we had accomplished nothing on this trip. Like we may have been too late.

The closer we got to the safe houses, I became increasingly more worried about Rori. She seemed quiet, withdrawn. On our last day on the road, she also appeared sick. Her complexion was pale, and she began slumping over her bike instead of sitting tall like she usually did.

"Ride with me," I told her on our last rest stop, less than two hours away from home. "You look like you're about to fall over." I pushed a canister of water into her hands.

"So sweet of you to compliment me," she cracked. Despite her fire being diminished, she still had some energy. "I'm fine, just tired," she added.

"You look half dead," I retorted. "I'm genuinely concerned about you being able to drive."

"Don't be." She waved her hand dismissively. "I can ride in my sleep. Besides, I'm not going to abandon my bike out here."

"Val can get it with her truck later. I'm worried about you, paloma. You really don't look well."

I cupped her cheek, which felt too cold against my palm. Touching my lips to her forehead, her skin was cold there too. And clammy.

Rori sighed, leaning her face into my palm as she gazed up at me. "I don't feel so good, but I *have* to lead us home. I'll rest when we get there."

"I'm telling you that you don't have to. You can rest now."

My stubborn woman shook her head, lifting her cheek from my hand. "On the road, I have to be the president. It's only two hours. I can make it."

It was my turn to sigh. There was no fighting her when she was this determined. "Fine, but I'm going to be on your ass the whole way home. If your tires wobble once, I'm running you off the road and tying you to my bike if I have to."

Rori laughed, the sound genuinely amused despite being soft and weaker than usual. "Don't threaten me with a good time."

"I'm serious, paloma."

"I know." She lifted to her tiptoes and kissed under my jaw. "I love you."

"Love you." I let my hand trail down her arm, to her back, then her waist as she walked away.

She walked with purpose, a general leading her troops as she re-mounted her bike. It couldn't have been easy for her, putting on the image of a strong leader while she felt like shit.

Making her life easier was my job, as far I was concerned. Torr would see to the club while she recovered at home, and I would remain at her side for her every need. We just had to make it there first.

It felt like an eternity on the road before our tires crunched on the gravel driveway leading up to the safe houses. And Rori, with her superhuman grit and resolve, did not wobble once.

Torr waited for us in front of the garage. His face looked

grim, even before he saw the condition Rori was in. When she pulled to a stop in front of him, he looked just as worried as I felt.

"Welcome home. How did it go? Oh shit!"

Torr ran up to Rori before anyone could answer, because she was pitching over the side of her motorcycle. All of us that had been riding ran up to her in a concerned rush. Most of them hadn't noticed how bad of shape she was in until now.

"Rori? Rori!" Torr cradled her upper body in his arms while LJ and I carefully removed her legs from their straddle position on the bike.

Once Rori got her feet under her, she started to stand. "Sorry, I'm okay. Feet fell asleep, and I'm a little lightheaded. Just been on the road too long."

"Why are you so pale?" Torr cupped her cheeks, much like I had. "Are you sick? What's wrong?"

Just like with me, Rori waved away his concern. "No, no. Just tired. I'm fine, really."

"You're wobbling like a newborn fawn," Devin pointed out.

"You need to lie down," Val agreed. "With your feet elevated. And you're probably dehydrated."

"You all don't need to fuss over me," Rori snapped. "But I will rest so you all can stop worrying. We'll brief everyone on the mission tomorrow."

Torr leaned down to pick Rori up, much to her grumbling dismay. With her secure against his chest, he turned toward the house. I followed him while everyone else dispersed to go their own ways.

While Torr took Rori up the stairs, I started rummaging through the kitchen for something to feed her. She'd barely eaten the last couple of days, only taking small sips of water on our rest stops. When she'd walked off to take a piss, I'd also noticed her dry-heaving.

I found a sleeve of saltine crackers and an empty water pitcher with a built-in filter. I filled the pitcher, grabbed a glass and the crackers, and headed upstairs with them.

Torr had gotten Rori out of her riding clothes and was tucking her into bed when I entered the room. "This should help settle your stomach," I said, setting everything up on the nightstand.

Torr frowned. "What's going on with your stomach?"

"Nothing." Rori glared at me.

"I saw you dry-heaving," I admitted to her. "I know you wouldn't want anyone to know while we were out there, so I didn't say anything until now."

"What, now you're motion-sick?" Torr asked.

"Maybe, I don't know." Rori begrudgingly accepted a cracker from me and nibbled on it.

"What happened out there?" Torr demanded when she didn't say anything else.

"I thought we were leaving it for tomorrow," Rori grumbled.

"Not with me, you're not."

"Tell him what you told us," I said, holding out another cracker. "What you saw that none of us did."

Torr got laser-focused on her as soon as I said that. "Better start talking, Ror."

"Or what? You'll spank me?"

"I am not fucking kidding around. Start. Talking."

While I could understand her wanting to use humor to deflect, I stood with Torr on this. As her VP, and the one who knew her better than anyone else, he needed to know.

Reluctantly, Rori relayed the night of the bonfire to him. She held nothing back, not even the vision of the hovering, black swarm that had chased her. After she had first told us what she saw, she immediately clammed up. Like she was afraid we'd think any differently of her if she saw things we didn't. I couldn't speak for the others, but I believed every word.

The Sisterhood's goddess had spoken to her, infiltrated her dreams. She was the one being targeted by the enemy's deity. And now my biggest fear was that the enemy had succeeded.

"So you started feeling sick after this cloud thing had caught up to you?" Torr asked.

"No, I felt fine when I woke up. It's come and gone in waves, actually. Like right now, I feel good." Rori sat up in bed, leaning against the headboard as if to prove her point.

She did look better, with more color to her face and her eyes more alert than she had been.

"Why didn't you go after the four women?" Torr asked her. "That was the whole goal, right? You want to eradicate this cult, so why didn't you go after the ones who we're all but certain are the leaders?"

Honestly, I had the same question. LJ had seen the van leave and suggested giving chase. Rori had just woken up then and still seemed a little out of it, but she'd shaken her head and adamantly refused to go after the cultists.

Rori frowned now as she stared at Torr. Then she blinked, looking confused and saying nothing.

"Paloma?" I prompted, worry stabbing through my chest.

"I, um." She ran a shaky hand through her hair, the color once again draining from her face. "I don't remember making that decision."

* * *

Rori's fatigue took over soon after that, so Torr and I left the room to let her sleep. But that didn't mean either of us felt better about the situation.

"Something's happened to her," he said, pacing the living

room downstairs. He was a pacer when he was worried. I was trying to calm my nerves by cleaning my machetes.

"The Rori I know would not have let those cultists get away. It's the whole reason she's out here! She's fucking bloodthirsty for them."

"I agree," I said with a pass of a whetstone over my blade. "But I'm not sure what we should do now."

Torr stopped pacing and stared at the ceiling as he sighed heavily. "I'm not sure either."

A few seconds of silence passed while I finished my first blade and picked up my second. "How was everything here while we were gone?"

His shoulders tensed and he rubbed his jaw. "Something happened here too. But...I don't know if I should tell her about it. Especially if she's got gaps in her memory." He started pacing again. "If it seems like she's there when she's actually not, who am I really talking to?"

"Fuck." I dropped my machete and my tools on the coffee table. "You make it sound like she's..."

"Possessed," he finished for me. "Like Tezca and Astarte have animal vessels. What if..."

"No." I shook my head. "Dude, she can't be. She would never let that happen."

"I'll bet that's the real reason why she was having all those dreams," Torr went on. "To make her sleep-deprived and weaker. To break her down so she would be easier to control."

Fuck me, that was horrifying. It all stemmed back to the night that we rescued Hudson. Their deity must have touched Rori the moment she spaced out.

And had its claws in her ever since.

"Has Tezca said anything to you?" Torr asked. "About how to stop it? How to help her?"

"Not a word," I said with an apologetic shake of my head.

Torr dropped into an armchair like he couldn't handle pacing anymore.

"Want to tell me what happened?" I asked after a few moments of depressing silence.

Torr rubbed a hand over his hair, his gaze staring at nothing. "We had a situation with the Bull. I've got him locked in the basement." His eyes flicked over to me. "How was the Saint on the trip?"

I shrugged. "Fine. His normal, weird-ass self. What'd the Bull do?"

"Tried to leave without anybody noticing. Got all cagey when I started asking questions." Torr rubbed his chin. "I think he was going to the Sisterhood to give them information about us."

"Why?" I asked, my gut roiling with disgust. "Why would he keep any kind of loyalty to them?"

"Dunno. Maybe they have some leverage over him."

"Rori would want his head on a spike," I growled. "And rightly so."

"The real Rori would, yeah." He nodded grimly before pointing to the ceiling. "But I'm not entirely sure Rori is up there."

"You're the VP, you can act in her stead," I reminded him. "And maybe if this Dark Mother has one less minion doing her bidding, it will weaken her hold on Rori."

Torr drummed his fingers on the armrest. "I'm hesitant to do this without Rori's input. Or if she really is not in control, someone's opinion that I trust."

"You trust mine?"

Torr drummed his fingertips some more. "You want to come talk to him and see what you think? He denied everything to me, but maybe he'll talk to a fellow ex-gladiator."

"We were never close in the pit, but sure."

I sheathed my weapons on my belt, which drew a raised eyebrow from Torr.

"You will not be using those. Not until I or Rori give the order."

"Consider it an extra security measure." I rested my hands on the handles, my grip loose and relaxed as I stood. "Shall we go?"

"You're a deadly enough motherfucker without those but fair enough."

Torr stood and headed for the basement door while I trailed behind him. It was the same room where Nella was kept and then ultimately killed by Devin.

The door swung open and Torr had barely taken a single step down the stairs when he froze. He brought his hand up with his index and middle finger extended. I'd also heard what he had and touched my fingers to his to show that I understood.

There were two people in the basement. Voices from down below had hushed as soon as the door opened.

Torr started down and I followed, drawing one of my blades. He was a strong fucker but didn't have a weapon. There was also no other way in or out of the basement, and they already knew we were coming. If we had more room on the stairs, I would have slid in front of Torr so my machetes would be the first things in the room. But our way down was narrow, barely containing the width of our bodies in single file.

We hit the basement floor, and I moved in front of my friend to protect him if necessary. The sight before us wasn't entirely surprising, but it didn't mean there was no threat.

"Saint," I said, eyeing the man sitting on a stack of crates next to the Bull, who was cuffed and tied to the support beam in the middle of the room.

"Butcher," the Saint returned in a bland tone. "And the Guard," he said with a nod at Torr.

"What are you doing here?" Torr stepped around me to address the Saint head on, apparently unbothered by the dagger the other man casually twirled between his knees.

"I came looking for my old friend." The Saint straightened, regarding the Bull with a look I couldn't read. "When he wasn't in the main house, I had a feeling he'd be down here. And I was right."

The Bull ignored us, instead staring at the fighter next to him. "So, you gonna cut me loose so we can kill these assholes and go or what?"

"You two aren't going anywhere," I hissed, drawing my second blade and stepping in front of Torr again. He needed to grab a shovel or whatever else was down here, because no fucking way he'd be running upstairs for a gun at this rate.

"Shut the fuck up, Butcher. You're so deep in her cunt, you don't see what's really happening." He glared at Torr. "Same for you. And fuck you for putting me down here."

"What the fuck are you talking about?" Torr asked with a surprising amount of calm.

"The Bull and I made a pact in the chaos at the coliseum before we left with you," the Saint said, his eyes on the dagger twirling in front of him. "We go way back, he and I. Before the gladiator pits and the prison they dragged us from. We came up on the street together, didn't we, Bull?"

"That's right," the other man said with a metallic clink of his cuffs.

"Once we were captured, we got used by the Sisterhood a few times, didn't we? Tested out to see how well we'd breed them."

"Yeah." The Bull gritted his teeth. "They gave me a daughter."

"And a beautiful girl she was." A faint smile touched the Saint's lips. "When was the last time you saw her?"

The Bull's head dropped, shaking sadly. "Probably about 3 years. I wasn't there for the birth or anything. They just let me see her for a second; I couldn't even hold her." He gave a dry laugh. "She looked like a little old man."

"But they promised you something, didn't they?" The Saint stopped twirling the dagger, his whole body going still as a predator.

"That I could see her again, be present in her life." The Bull's eyes lit up with joy for the first time that I'd ever seen. "I could teach her things, you know? Be an actual fucking father."

"In exchange for what?" the Saint pressed.

"Always remaining loyal to the Sisterhood," the Bull said without missing a beat. "That I would deliver them any traitors of the Dark Mother, male or female." His gaze snapped to the Saint, who had risen to his feet, the dagger gleaming next to his thigh. "And you agreed to do the same. We made a pact! I showed you a picture of my girl, and you said she was worth destroying everything for."

"And she still is." The Saint moved so fast, I'd barely registered what happened until I felt warm droplets of blood speckle my face.

I blinked and saw the Saint holding the Bull's head up by the hair, the red line on the Bull's throat weeping blood.

"Your daughter can still be saved but not by a father like you," the Saint said calmly. "I had a child by them too, a son. You know what they did right after he was born?" He leaned in close, directly next to the dying man's ear. "They smothered him to death. Right in front of me!"

Though he had been calm, the Saint was shouting at the top of his lungs before he was done. Torr and I could only watch as he clamped a hand over the wound he'd made in the Bull's throat.

"Oh no, you don't get to die yet. Not until I've told you

everything." The Saint was shaking with rage, adrenaline, grief, and who knew what else. "I didn't tell Aurora about our little pact because I wanted to kill you myself. I didn't expect to have an audience, but here we are."

He didn't even glance at Torr and me as he said that. "After everything we'd been through together, swearing we'd always have each other's backs, you threw it away on *one* false promise from the people who enslaved us. Did you really fucking believe they would let you see your daughter? Did you?"

There was only a gurgle from the Bull as the life drained from him, choking on his own blood.

The Saint pulled his hand away, wiping it on his pant leg as his friend's life continued to fade.

"You wanted to please their Dark Mother so badly, I hope you rot in hell with her." Those were the Saint's last words to the Bull before the ex-fighter's head dropped forward and all motion left him.

With a resigned breath, the Saint looked at us, and Torr and I glanced at each other like we couldn't believe what just happened.

"Well," the VP said. "That was unexpected."

"This kill was not authorized by the president, I know." The Saint straightened, lifting his chin. "She may punish me as she sees fit, but I hope she understands this is proof of my loyalty. And that it was necessary to our cause."

"I'm sorry about your son." It was the first thing I could think of to say. "I can't imagine anything worse."

The Saint's eyes flicked to me, and he nodded slowly. "After it happened, I was on my way to tell him." He jerked his head toward the corpse. "I was so broken, shocked to my core, and I didn't really have anyone else, you know? Then, before I can get a word out..." The Saint swallowed, his face tightening into anger. "He tells me, all fucking excited, that he has a daughter, and they will allow him the privilege to be a father to her." He scoffed, shaking his head at the body of his dead friend. "He was always a self-absorbed bastard, but he was so goddamn happy that he didn't even notice I was a fucking shell of a human being."

Torr cleared his throat. "I won't say you're not justified in this kill. But when you're in a club, that's not something you can do independently anymore. You should have come to Rori or me first."

"I know this." The Saint turned his back on the dead man and his face was calm, if even serene. The very picture of that saying, *out of sight, out of mind.* "It will not happen again. I will accept whatever punishment Aurora sees fit for me. She is the one who saved me, saved all of us. Even if she casts me out of the club for this, she has my unwavering loyalty." Resolved, he jerked his chin down, planted his feet wide, and brought his hands together behind his back. "Take me to her. I will tell her everything I told you."

"This has to be resolved later," Torr said with a shake of his head. "She's resting from the ride."

The Saint's brow furrowed. "The ride wasn't that strenuous, especially for her. Is she not well?"

"She's just resting," I said to back up Torr's point. "She'll deal with you when she's ready."

The Saint's face broke out into a grin. "She's pregnant, then! Well done, such a blessing."

"She's not—" Torr's mouth snapped shut before he went on. I guess we didn't really know, did we? "Anyway, clean this up. Get someone to help you if you want."

"At once, Vice President." Back to his eccentric self, the Saint gave a slight bow and started rummaging around for a tarp as Torr and I went up the stairs. We could hear him whistling cheerfully before closing the door.

"What do you think?" Torr asked the moment we were out of there.

"Honestly? Good riddance. He just did what Rori would have done sooner." I let out a soft laugh. "I almost wish she had seen that."

"Same." Torr smirked. "Do you believe everything he said?"

"I do, actually." I checked myself over for blood before sitting down on the couch. "I think his weirdness is a mask, a coping mechanism maybe. When he was talking about his kid, he dropped all of that. I think that was the real him."

"I agree." Torr sat next to me, sinking down heavily. "Poor guy. Malik would have a field day with him."

He leaned his head all the way back, suddenly looking weary with his eyes on the ceiling. I followed his gaze, knowing exactly what he was looking at, thinking about. Our whole world was up there.

"She's gonna be okay. Right, Torr?"

It took him a long time to answer. "Fuck, I hope so."

11

RORI

My sleep was fitful and restless. I went from feeling like death to perfectly fine and back again. I had cold sweats and a roiling stomach, and then I became exhausted and dehydrated.

But my physical symptoms weren't the worst of it. I heard the same voice that had haunted my dreams for the past two weeks. Only now, it was while I was awake.

Just accept me, Aurora. You'll feel so much better if you quit fighting.

"Can't stop fighting," I mumbled. "Have to hold on to...myself." My stomach protested violently, and I leaned over the side of the bed to retch into the trash can someone left me.

I had thrown up those saltine crackers hours ago. At least, I think I did. My sense of time was all distorted, and there were gaps in my memory. I recognized the bedroom at the safehouse but barely remembered riding home.

"What the fuck is happening to me?" I groaned into the sweat-soaked pillowcase.

I think you know, Aurora.

"Stop." I clasped my hands to the sides of my head, balling

them into fists as I tugged at my roots. "Get the fuck out of my head. I don't want you here."

Oh, you will. Once you see what we're capable of together. Enough with this ragtag group of men *you've collected. Don't you want to be worshiped? By thousands, no, millions of women? Women we have saved.*

"No!"

I rolled in an attempt to escape the voice that followed me everywhere and landed on a hard surface, probably the floor. Crawling my way to the chair where my clothes were, I fumbled around for my holster.

Now, now, the voice chided. *We're not doing that.*

I blinked, and then suddenly I was back on the bed. Some time had passed, and it was now dark outside. Another black-out.

"Fuck!" I cried, sitting straight up.

Santos and Torr weren't in bed with me, but a massive, dark shape with golden eyes was.

"Tezca." I reached to the jaguar for comfort, instantly soothed by that velvety pelt and the rumbling purr that started up.

"I'm scared, Tezca," I confessed. "I don't know what's happening to me."

Yes, you do, the jaguar god said mournfully. *And I'm sorry, daughter. I wish I could prevent this.*

My hands froze on his back before they started to shake. "What do you mean?"

I know you can make it out through the other side. He head-butted my hand, then licked his sandpaper tongue across my palm. *Be brave. Don't lose sight of who you are. Remember those you love.*

"I can't—I don't—" A migraine hit me like a punch to the

jaw. Pain radiated up my jaw, exploding behind my eyes. My stomach roiled again, spasming around nothing.

The next thing I saw clearly was Tezca, not on the bed with me but on the ground. His back was arched, fangs bared with a low, constant growl emanating from him. When I reached for him, he hissed and swiped a huge paw at me, claws extended.

"I should make a rug out of your pelt, useless male."

My palms clapped over my mouth in horror. I said that. Not *me*, the voice leaving my mouth was not my own. It was the one I always heard in my head. The one that first spoke to me in the Sisterhood's village.

Are you understanding now, Aurora?

"No. No, no, no, no."

I ran to the bathroom on wobbly legs, slamming the door against the wall as I crashed through it. Holding onto the pedestal sink for support, I glared into the mirror.

"Get out." My horror had given way to rage. My own, familiar anger felt good, felt like me.. I drew on it as a source of strength, a connection to myself. I hated this cult, and I would not allow its fucked-up deity to take up residence inside my skin.

"Get the fuck out," I repeated. "I'm not your fucking vessel."

"Mm, but you are," my reflection said cheekily back to me. "You're the perfect vessel, Aurora Wilder. I've waited decades for you."

"I didn't consent to this," I growled. "I don't want you. How are you better than a man, huh? Invading my body like a fucking parasite?"

"I'm a deity, child. I exist outside of the boundaries of time and space. Your limited senses can't perceive existence like I do. But if you allow me, you can. Don't you want to be divine, Aurora?"

"No!" I screamed.

The mirror cracked, and I slumped to the floor. I didn't know if it was the Dark Mother or me that did that, but I felt truly in control for the first time since I woke up after the bonfire.

Only I knew something was different.

I had control for now, but that rotten deity was still inside me. She had retreated for the moment, but she would come back and fight me. For control of my own body.

I rubbed at my arms, curling into a ball on the bathroom floor. I'd never felt so utterly violated in my life. My own skin was not a safe place to be.

I couldn't let her win, couldn't let her have full possession of me. But she had been right. My human body had limits, and it already felt like I was there. I was exhausted, weak, and felt so small. A kitten scratching at a full-grown lion.

There was only one solution my exhausted, pain-addled brain could think of, and it brought tears to my eyes. No, there had to be another way.

"There isn't," I whispered aloud to myself, looking out the bathroom door to the gun holster in the chair I'd almost reached.

The Dark Mother wouldn't let me do it. She'd stop me again. No one in my club would, especially not my men. Devin might've been happy to once upon a time, but things had changed between us. We were practically friendly at this point.

Even if I explained what was happening, if I said this was necessary to prevent the Dark Mother from gaining a vessel, they either wouldn't believe me or wouldn't be able to bring themselves to do it.

There was only one person who could do it. And he would be the only one willing to.

I climbed shakily to my feet, again grasping the sink for support. I avoided looking in the mirror as I splashed water on my face and rinsed out my mouth. Then I pulled on some clean clothes, as well as my holster with the gun still in place.

Tezca had disappeared, and I felt truly alone as I left the bedroom. The house was quiet as I reached the ground floor, but there was activity out front.

It sounded like a barbecue, with the sounds of conversations and the sizzle of something cooking on the outdoor grill. Through the window, I saw Santos throwing a football to someone. He was smiling, laughing, then running to catch the ball as it was thrown back to him.

Torr was at the grill, idly snapping a pair of tongs as he talked to LJ.

I ached to go out there, to greet their smiling faces with a grin of my own. To accept embraces and kisses, to be pulled into conversations and maybe even a touch football game. I watched it play out like a movie. Like I was outside of my own body, a ghost of my former self.

I couldn't bring myself to go out there. I wouldn't be able to hide the heartbreak of what I was about to do, the sorrow of never seeing them again. I couldn't subject them to that. I should just let them be happy.

I turned away from the scene in the driveway and headed for the back door. Going through, I closed it as quietly as I could behind me.

It was an unseasonably warm night, probably why everyone was outside.

I looked at the back porch of the house next door. He was standing there, looking up at the stars with his tattooed forearms on the railing, a beer bottle dangling from one hand. The fact that he was the only one out back solidified the belief that this needed to be done. And I needed him to do it.

"Hudson," I said, stepping off my porch.

His head snapped over to face me and he straightened, guarded and stiff at the mere sight of me.

"I'm not going to hurt you. I promise." I lifted my palms as I approached. "Can we talk?"

He didn't answer. His jaw was clenched tight, as was his grip on that beer bottle. Sharp blue eyes fell to the weapon holstered at my hip. Of course, my open palms meant nothing.

Moving slowly, I kept one hand raised as the other went for my gun. I placed it, barrel facing the woods, on the railing in front of him, and then walked away from the weapon. "That's my only firearm. You can hold onto it if you want."

His gaze flicked to the gun, though he didn't touch it. After a few seconds, he unclenched his jaw enough to mutter, "What do you want from me?"

I took a deep breath, trying to ease the tension in my chest. "I need a favor from you."

Hudson flinched like I'd physically touched him. "I don't do things for women anymore."

"It's not like that," I protested. "I don't have much time to explain but I..."

Oh God. Would I even be able to say it?

"I need you to take my gun." My voice shook as I nodded at the weapon between us. "And..." I closed my eyes and forced the words out. "Shoot me. Shoot to kill."

Hudson's eyebrows slashed down with confusion. "Why the fuck would I do that? What are you setting me up for?"

"I'm sorry. Really, I'm so sorry to pin this on you. To put you in this situation." I blinked back tears and sniffed. "But you have to. Please, Hudson."

He just stood there, staring at me like I was speaking nonsense.

"Please just get it over with," I whimpered, letting the tears fall. "Before I have too much time to think about it and back out."

He didn't move a muscle. "Why do you want to die?"

"I don't *want* to, I *have* to," I sobbed. "Or it's gonna use me to destroy everything."

"What is?"

"Their goddess. The Dark Mother." I was full-on crying now, so afraid that I didn't care what I revealed. "Their deity is...inside me. She's trying to possess me, and I can't let her, Hudson."

12

HUDSON

Holy shit, was she really asking me to do this? To finish what I intended to do the first time I saw her?

I looked at the weapon she put in front of me, then slowly picked it up. The gun fit comfortably in my hand, the weight of it dense and satisfying. With the grip nestled into my palm, I let the barrel rest on the fingers of my opposite hand.

Guns used to excite me. I'd nerd out about the mechanics and specs of various models. It wasn't even so much about the power or damage potential for me, but how the weapon was built. What kind of recoil did it have? What made one weapon feel like an extension of my arm while another felt clunky and awkward?

This one, Rori's, was nice. I knew immediately I'd be comfortable shooting it. My aim would be accurate. But as I held that weapon in my hands, there was none of that excitement from years ago. It was just a tool, a means of causing irrevocable harm. Harm I had no desire to do, but that was exactly what she was asking of me.

I didn't know how much time had passed before I looked up

at Rori again. She stood there, waiting, shaking like a leaf and with tears streaming down her face.

"Please." She hugged around herself and took a shaky breath. "I can't let her control me. She'll use me to hurt Santos and Torr, all of you. Please, Hudson. I can't ask anyone else."

"What's to stop her from taking over someone else?" I struggled for a moment to recall the names of the other women. "Your cousin, Valorie. Or the Hunter's woman. If you're gone, wouldn't she just take over one of them?"

"I don't know, maybe. But doing this might buy us some time. Kill me, and then warn the others. Tell them what you did and why."

"Are you fucking mental?" I hissed. "They'll kill *me* as soon as they know what I've done! Did you think this through at all?"

A sob choked out of her as she wiped tears from her face. "I don't know what else to do!"

Her display of emotions was so jarring and strange to me. Everyone talked about how tough this woman was, that she was a natural born leader and nothing could faze her. I found that hard to reconcile with the terrified woman standing in front of me, pleading with me to murder her.

I felt...bad.

No, bad was too bland of a word. I felt terrible for her, and that in itself was one hell of a shock to my system. I was feeling sympathetic. Toward a *woman*.

I hated that she felt this was the only way forward, a premature end to her life that was so full of promise. I hated that she was scared. Scared of death, scared of hurting the ones she loved, scared of losing the life she would never have.

And I hated that she'd come to me for this. Because I was the woman-hater who had tried to kill her before. I hated that she saw me that way. I was...ashamed of it. I didn't know when the change in me had occurred, but I didn't want to kill her. I didn't want to use this gun, and I didn't want to see her cry.

So I pressed the magazine release on the gun and caught the slide as it fell out. Then I set the two pieces on the porch railing and stepped away from them.

"I'm not going to shoot you."

Rori let out a noise of despair, rubbing her eyes angrily. "You *have* to! Think of what she'll make me do to you. You don't deserve that, Hudson!"

Images of my past captivity flashed through my brain for a moment before I shoved them away. Malik taught me some refocusing techniques today, and I was already finding them useful.

"I don't want to hurt you," Rori continued. "I don't want her to use *me* to hurt you."

"That's not going to happen," I found myself saying as I stepped off the porch toward her. For some reason, I wanted to ease her and reassure her, make her less afraid. It was almost like a compulsion to be strong for her while she was falling apart.

"It could," Rori argued. "If she gets control of me, that could be the least of what happens. They want war, Hudson. They want to kill or enslave all men."

"And you want to prevent that?"

It might have been a weird question to ask, but some nagging feeling needed to hear it from her mouth. I might have grown more tolerant of being in her presence, but I still found it hard to believe she was truly different from the women who had abused me.

"Of course I do," she said, exasperated and without hesitation. "I *love* the men in my life. I love Santos, Torr, my fathers, my brothers, all the men in my family, even my grumpy-ass Grandpa Finn. I like the Hunter because he's funny and he treats Paige so well. I like and respect all the ex-gladiators who want to ride and fight with me. Shit, I even like Devin! I just want all of you to have happy, fulfilling lives like everyone else."

She started crying again, and I let free the weird impulse that had been gnawing at me since I first saw her tonight.

I came down from the porch, walked right up to her, and put my arm around her.

Rori resisted when I tried to pull her toward my chest. She looked up at me, her face tear-stained and confused. "What are you doing?"

I wasn't sure how to answer, so I said, "I don't like seeing you cry."

She continued to stare up at me, then let out a little scoff and muttered something like, "Whatever, fuck it," and let her forehead fall to my sternum.

Her hair smelled nice, so I lifted my face away in order to not be weird and inhale more deeply. My arm rested across her upper back and shoulders, and she leaned into me until her chest was against mine. My other arm itched to wrap around her waist but I kept it at my side.

At some point, Rori's arms went around my waist, palms resting on my back. She gave a gentle squeeze and sighed.

"We'll figure this out," I said. "But killing you is definitely not the answer."

She gave a little snort of laughter. "What changed your mind on that?"

"Well, I got pulled out of a brainwashing cult and into the real world. That tends to fix your perspective a little."

"You're already a completely new person," she said. "I mean, this is the last thing in the world I expected." Her fingers lifted from my back and tapped down again.

"Me too," I admitted.

My thumb rubbed over her shoulder. The embrace felt nice, different from the affection I'd started exploring with Devin.

She was taller than I expected, her hair almost tickling my chin. The slight weight of her leaning against my chest felt good, grounding, like a heavy blanket.

We stayed like that for a while, not speaking. A shaky breath escaped her after some time, and she seemed to lean on me a little more.

"I'm glad you told me no," she whispered.

Before I could think about it, my hand passed over her upper back, rubbing up and down until I stopped abruptly with a realization.

"Have faith," I told her. "We'll find another way." Apparently, I was including myself in that *we*.

"Faith? Are you religious?" She glanced up from my shoulder.

"We all are somewhat, aren't we?" I leaned back from our embrace to meet her gaze. "We have them." I nodded at the jaguar, barely visible at the dark treeline. "Our vengeful gods."

Rori looked toward the big cat, her arms still around my waist in a loose hold. "Does he talk to you?" she asked, her tone curious.

"Just once," I said. "While I was in there. He told me to hold on, to not give up. That my suffering was ending soon."

Rori looked at me, her expression brighter than it had been all night. "He came through for you."

"I guess. He made sure you did, anyway." I rubbed the back of my neck with my free hand, the one that wasn't still around her upper back. "It's given me a lot to think about. How fortunate I really am. So many never got rescued."

"Did you see them?" Rori's voice went low. "The sacrifices?"

"Some of them. They'd drag me out to watch sometimes. I heard pretty much all of them." The look in her eyes wasn't pity but commiseration. "Did you see one?"

She nodded. "Got a bird's eye view." Only then did she step back, bringing her hands to her hips as she looked thoughtfully at the woods. "I want justice for them too. And the gladiators that died. Everyone who's been hurt by the cult since the beginning."

"There's too many to count," I told her with a shake of my head. "Not just men, either. Women who have tried to run away. The blood bags, the—"

"What?" She cut me off. "What are blood bags?"

"Men that they keep alive just to cut them so they bleed. It's how they indoctrinate the young girls. Once they start their period, they cut the blood bag and make him bleed every day they themselves are bleeding."

Rori's mouth fell open, her face going pale. "You mean, like..." She trailed off, swallowed, and tried again. "It's a bunch of shallow cuts all over their body?"

"Yeah, usually avoiding areas with big blood vessels to prevent permanent damage. Nothing on the neck, wrists, the chest near the heart, but everywhere else is fair game. They want him to stay alive. That's his whole purpose, to bleed."

I hadn't told anyone about the blood bags yet, and it felt good to get it off my chest. When I occasionally saw those men covered in thousands of tiny slashes, both old and fresh, I sometimes wondered if my position was better or worse than theirs.

"God fucking damnit." Rori raked her hands through her hair before balling them into fists.

"Sorry," I said. "I probably shouldn't be so graphic."

"No, it's fine. I'm glad you told me." She gave me a weak smile, but her eyes still looked haunted. "I'm...pretty sure I know someone who was a blood bag."

"You do? Here?"

"No, someone from back home. A family member. He's, well, older than us."

DEATHLESS

"How much older?"

She shrugged and wobbled her head. "Fifties."

My eyebrows shot up. "Damn. He must have been one of the first, then. How'd he escape?"

"I don't know. He never talks about it. Not to me." She crossed her arms, frowning. "I suspected he'd been a victim of theirs after I started to learn more, but I had no idea it was...like that."

"It's a fucking nightmare," I agreed.

She glanced at me. "You've been having nightmares?"

"Oh yeah. They're routine at this point." I shrugged. "Talking to Malik is helping. So is waking up next to Devin."

A slow, knowing smile spread across her face. "So that's happening, huh? You and Devin."

I hesitated before answering. He and I never talked about keeping our 'thing' a secret or being open with it. I suspected he had a crush on Rori, so maybe he didn't want her to know? He wasn't the type to sneak around, though, unless he was being the Ghost and putting knives in people's throats.

"I had my suspicions," Rori said in my silence. "He did mention feeling something for you, from before."

I gaped at her. "He did?"

Rori's eyes went wide, and she placed her fingers over her mouth. "Oh. Maybe I wasn't supposed to say anything."

"Whatever." I waved it off. "It's out there now."

She cleared her throat. "Well, I'm glad you two are making each other happy." She sounded a bit stiff but otherwise genuine.

"Thanks." I glanced down at my hands, unsure where else to look. "Maybe one day, I'll be able to be with a woman again, but not for a while."

"Oh yeah?" Her eyebrows went up in surprise. "So this thing with Devin is temporary?"

127

"No. I mean, I don't know. I don't want it to be, but I don't know what *he* wants. I'm a mess mentally, and with everything going on...we haven't really talked about it."

Rori nodded, a smile touching her lips. "Well, I hope you two are together for as long as it makes you both happy."

Footsteps crunching over the ground made both of our heads snap to the side.

"Paloma, there you are." Santos approached with a big smile of relief on his face. "Torr and I have been looking for you." Once he realized who she was standing with, his smile disappeared and he hurried to her side. "What's going on?"

"Nothing."

"Nothing."

Rori and I blurted out the word at the same time, only making ourselves look more suspicious.

"We were just talking." She turned into him, accepting being tucked under his arm and leaning against his chest, closer than she had been with me.

"Talking?" he repeated like he'd never heard bigger bullshit in his life. "*You* two?"

"Yes," Rori insisted with a glance back at me. "We're actually getting along alright. Aren't we, Hudson?"

"Yeah," I agreed, nodding my head under Santos' hard glare. "I don't mean any harm to her, or anyone."

"Then why is there a fucking gun right there?" Santos jerked his chin at the forgotten weapon lying next to its removed ammo on the railing.

"I brought it," Rori said before I could answer.

Santos looked at her, his confusion mounting. "Why?"

Rori opened her mouth to answer just as someone pushed the sliding door open behind me and Devin's husky voice floated to me.

"The hell are you doing out here?" One arm came around

my waist, the other over my shoulder to stroke my chest. His teeth had just barely nipped my shoulder when he noticed Santos and Rori. "Hey guys. What's going on?" He went stiff when he too noticed the gun and clip of ammo. "What *the hell* is going on?"

"It doesn't fucking matter." The voice came from Rori, but it wasn't her speaking.

She pushed Santos away with so much force that he lost his balance, windmilling his arms and eventually landing on his ass.

He returned to his feet just as Rori turned her gaze on me. Devin's grip tightened around me as he muttered, "Fuck," in my ear.

Fuck was right. Rori's eyes had gone completely black, no irises or sclera visible at all.

"Oh, now she's fighting me hard." The strange voice from Rori laughed. "Making quite a racket up here." She tapped an index finger against her temple. "So protective over these *men,* that's her biggest flaw. But don't worry. I'll make her *perfect.*"

"Shit," Santos gasped. "It's taking over her."

"Hey!" Torr was jogging toward us now, and I didn't know if that was a good or bad thing for the deity gaining control of Rori. "You found her." He slowed, confusion hitting him as he took in me, Devin, Santos, and then Rori's demonic black eyes.

"You were right," Santos told him quickly. "She's being possessed."

Out of nowhere, Rori crumpled to a heap like a marionette whose strings had been cut. Santos and Torr ran toward her, and Devin released me to do the same. Her eyes, their normal dark green color, snapped open with a gasp of breath.

"You have to get away from me," she said in a panicked rush. "All of you, everyone. Get them out of here. She's taking control of me, and I can't stop her!"

"We're not leaving you," Torr insisted. "We can keep you restrained. We can—"

"That won't work!" Rori screamed in his face. "You can't win against a god! Get everyone to safety before she makes me kill you all."

"There has to be something—" Santos started.

"Yes! Killing me," Rori cried. "I came here to ask Hudson to do that, but he wouldn't, and now it's too fucking late." She stared straight at Torr, darkness creeping into her eyes before she blinked the inky blackness away. "If you love me at all, you will either shoot me right now or get the hell away. Those are the only ways we keep going."

"Hudson." Devin took hold of my arm, his feet moving like he was trying to lead me away.

But I was transfixed, held in place by some kind of grim fascination. I'd seen lots of terrified expressions, my own included. The brain moved the muscles of the face to express fear and terror all in similar ways, whether that was fear of death, torture, or the unknown. And yet, Rori's fear was unlike anything I'd ever seen before.

She was rapidly losing control of herself to something already inside her. I saw her hands working like she wanted to grab her men for comfort, yet she refused to draw them any closer for their own protection. Even now, consumed by her fear, she was only thinking of them.

"Don't be fucking idiot heroes and try to save me," she said. "I'm done for. Go save everyone else."

"Fuck everyone else," Torr spat. He reached for her, she backed away, and he only advanced closer. "You're all that matters in this."

"You're not fucking listening!" Rori screamed. She dropped to the ground again like a ragdoll and sprang back up before the guys could get much closer.

130

This time, Torr and Santos backed away, their eyes meeting Rori's soulless black ones.

"Are you really surprised, Aurora?" The entity used Rori's mouth to speak as she went to the porch railing and picked up the gun. "Men never listen." She slapped the loaded magazine into the grip. "Not when we say 'no, stop, it hurts'." With ease and proficiency that could only come from Rori's muscle memory, she pulled back the slide. "When we're smarter than them, they ignore us or steal our ideas."

Her eyes were black as tar now, without a flicker of the real Rori left.

She was really gone.

And the thing animating her body held a loaded gun.

"Hudson," Devin hissed, tugging at my shirt.

Everyone tensed as Rori lifted the gun in the air, a sinister smile on her face as she pointed the barrel at the sky. "Maybe you'll listen this time. *Run.*"

The gun fired and, like the start of a race for our lives, we scattered.

13

DEVIN

The moment she raised that gun, my only instinct was to cover Hudson. I shoved at him, forcing him to start running while I stayed on his heels. Another shot fired and that kicked up our speed, our heads ducking low. The bullet never touched us, but it was close enough that I could smell it in the air.

"We've got to get everyone out!" Torr yelled, drawing his own gun which he aimed behind him as he ran.

"No, don't!" Santos grabbed at his arm, trying to wrestle the gun away.

Torr kept the weapon out of his reach, pushing on Santos' chest with his free hand. "Stop. It's not her anymore," he told the Butcher.

Santos started faltering. He couldn't stop staring at Rori, who was advancing on us at a leisurely pace like she had all the time in the world.

"She's still in there," he protested weakly. "We can't abandon her like this."

"Santos, listen to me." Torr clapped a hand on the other man's nape, dragging him along to keep him moving. "We *will* get her back. But that thing is going to kill us all if we don't get out of here right the fuck now."

Another shot rang out, making Torr and Santos jump as a small dust-cloud erupted at their feet.

"Keep running," the odd voice called from Rori's mouth. "Run as far and fast as you can. You can't escape me."

Torr looked at me. "Evacuate the frat house, no time to pack anything. Double or triple up on bikes, I don't care. Just get everyone to leave. We're taking the main road out."

"Okay."

That was all I said before shoving Hudson again, forcing him to take a hard left toward the front door of fighters' house.

"You get everyone in the common areas. Open up the garage and get the bikes started," I said. "I'll go room to room."

We entered the house together and immediately parted, him yelling at the men lounging around the kitchen and living room while I hoofed it up the stairs.

I didn't bother knocking, just blasted doors open with my foot or shoulder, screaming at the top of my lungs that we needed to move. Thankfully no one was delaying too much, and the commotion I heard from downstairs indicated that Hudson's evacuation was working as well.

I opened the final bedroom at the end of the hall, expecting it to be empty, but stopped dead at the sight before me.

Rori held a fighter with an arm around his neck, her gun barrel pressed directly into his crotch. He struggled like hell, grabbing at her forearm to pull it away from his throat, while his lower body jerked and spasmed as he tried to get away from that gun. Apparently, possession came with superhuman strength.

The thing wearing Rori's body grinned at me, wild and maniacal. "I was hoping for an audience," it said in that strange voice.

Her finger curled around the trigger, and it went off before I could so much as say, "Stop."

The fighter's scream hit my ears painfully. Rori released him, leaving him slumped over to bleed out as she went out the open window. I heard scratching on the exterior walls, the groaning of the gutters and siding as she climbed.

She's getting on the fucking roof? I could barely process anything, not the possession that just happened or the poor, bleeding man on the floor.

I dropped to my knees, crouching over him as I withdrew a knife and cradled the back of his head with my free.

"I'm sorry," I told his wide-eyed, shocked face. "I'm so sorry. Go peacefully, friend." Fuck, what had he been called again? The Iron. I hadn't known him well, but he was a solid man, as far as I knew.

I brought my knife around the back of his head, and with a few quick motions, severed his spinal cord just below his skull. He went limp and quiet, and I closed his eyelids as I released him.

Severing his brainstem was the most painless, swift death I could give him. I hated that that was the last kindness he ever got, and right after something so horrible. He trusted Rori, believed in her and chose to follow her. Now that he was no longer confined to his body, I hoped he understood.

"I'm sorry," I said for a final time before getting up from the floor and heading back downstairs.

Hudson had successfully cleared out the lower part of the house, and I heard the distinct sounds of multiple engines running in front of the detached garage.

I burst out of the front door, sprinting toward the fleet of vehicles. "She's on the roof!" I yelled. "Fucking go now!"

Three shots rained down, making everyone duck and scramble. Several people were in the bed of Val's truck, which tore off down the road with a roar of the engine. I saw a riderless motorcycle and went for it, throwing my leg over and gripping the handlebars like my life depended on it.

"Hudson!" I called. "Where's Hudson?"

A weight settled behind me as a pair of arms squeezed around my waist. "Go, go, go!" he yelled in my ear.

I started down the gravel road with a jerk forward and could only hope everyone else was making it out too.

Some nagging impulse told me to look back, and in my mirror I spotted Rori on the roof of the fighter's house, her gun trained not on anyone escaping on the ground, but on the horizon.

I wrenched the bike over, turning it to the side. Ignoring Hudson's screaming at me, I followed Rori's line of sight to the white dove, flying away like a ghostly apparition.

I tapped into all my instincts, my practice, my muscle memory, because something told me I had never needed it more than this moment right now.

I let a knife fly at a distance I'd never thrown before. I put all my strength into that throw, hoping my force would resist gravity just long enough to...

The blade stabbed Rori through the hand, forcing her to drop the gun just as the shot fired. Hudson was now silent as Rori locked eyes, pure black soulless eyes, with us. She pulled the knife from where it stuck her, squarely in the back of her palm, and the wound instantly seemed to close back up.

Like waking from a dream, I jerked us into motion again, turned onto the road and sped to catch up with the evacuating fleet of vehicles. It wasn't long before I came up on a bunch of red brake lights stopped on the road.

"What's the hold up?" Hudson demanded, his grip tightening on my waist.

"They're talking to the guard at the checkpoint." I had to

stand on the footpegs and crane my neck over Val's giant-ass truck to see. "They're basically dragging him into the truck."

"They need to hurry up."

It would almost be funny if the situation wasn't so dire. We were escaping for our lives from a sadistic deity set to enslave or kill half of the human population, and we were caught in a traffic jam.

The vehicles finally started moving just as a thought hit me. Where could we even go? It was the only coherent question in my mind as we drove through the night.

* * *

NEAR DAWN, our fleet of vehicles drove up to what looked like a warehouse and a few trailers in the middle of nowhere. I was bleary-eyed and exhausted beyond belief but managed to follow the flow of traffic into the warehouse and park the motorcycle in the available spot.

Engines shut off and the large space was filled with the echoing shuffle of people getting off bikes and the low murmurings of conversation. The guy who had been at the checkpoint, he went by Slick or something, broke away from the crowd to address everyone.

"The trailers don't have much, but there's bunk beds, sleeping bags, maybe some air mattresses you gotta blow up. But before you go." He raised a hand and scanned the crowd like he was looking for someone. "Someone needs to tell me what the hell is going on and where the hell Rori is."

"We can do that." Torr walked up to him with Santos at his side. The two of them looked beyond exhausted. They looked haunted.

I nudged Hudson's shoulder. "You find a place to sleep. I'm gonna back them up, and I'll find you later."

He shook his head stubbornly. "I'm coming too."

Slick led us all to a sectioned off area of the warehouse. There were folding tables and chairs set up to make it look like a small break room or office.

The older biker wheeled around on Torr. "Start talking any time," he said, crossing his arms. "Starting with, where is my niece?"

Torr let out a big breath that seemed to deflate all his strength. "Rori's been taken."

"By who?" Slick demanded.

"A cult that really likes to murder people, especially men."

"And you chose to bring all these former gladiators *here* instead of fighting to get her back?"

Torr was silent for a while, as were the rest of us. We were waiting for his cue, knowing that he didn't want to just tell anyone what we were really up against.

"You were with the Demons, right?" Torr asked quietly.

"Still am." Slick lifted his chin proudly. He was in his late forties maybe, but only the graying at his temples and in his beard showed it. "What's that got to do with my niece?"

"You were there?" Torr pressed. "During the war that saved Four Corners, you *saw* what the enemy did?"

"Yeah. Some kind of entity that had a bunch of people under mind control. Craziest fuckin' thing I ever seen. Thousands of people moving in perfect sync, like some kind of hivemind."

"That's what has Rori," Torr explained. "She's under the control of this...deity that the cult created. It has her, and it's going to use her to lead them."

Slick went silent for a long time, his face draining of color. "You're telling me it's back?" he whispered.

"We think it's something new," Santos spoke up. "This thing

has never possessed a human before. It wanted Rori. Like it was...waiting for her."

Slick's eyes snapped to him, then scanned over all of us. "You all saw this?"

The four of us nodded. "Rori had been fighting it for a couple of days," I said. "But it had been breaking her down over weeks, giving her bad dreams so she couldn't sleep."

"Fuck." Slick tilted his head back, eyes closing wearily. "We have to tell the Steel Demons."

"I'm sorry, I disagree." Torr lifted his chin, meeting the older biker in the eye.

Slick glared back, the two of them looking like they were getting ready to square off. "She's their *daughter.*"

"I know. Exactly why we shouldn't call them," Torr said. "They're going to rush in to save her, all four of her fathers. Probably her mom and brothers, too. And wouldn't this cult just *love* that? At least four, maybe six, men to kill, abuse and torture. All while Rori has a front row seat to it all."

"They won't be rash," Slick argued. "We're all far more seasoned in war than you. We've seen our loved ones taken, tortured, controlled, and been forced to keep a cool, strategic head about it. You're the one not thinking this all the way through, Torrance. You just don't have the experience under your belt yet."

"But we do." I stepped up next to Torr and Santos did the same, the two of us loyal soldiers. "We've seen it all in the gladiator pit," I went on. "And we support Torr. For their own safety, Rori's family should not get involved. Not yet, at least."

"This is our fight anyway," Santos added. "The Steel Demons have done their part. Let the Vengeful Gods finish what they started." Slick eyed each of us, even Hudson, who had come up to stand by me. I'd have to tell him later how much his quiet support meant to me. He didn't have to be part of this at all but was choosing to be.

"Alright," Slick finally relented. "Come up with your plan then, and quick. I don't want to tell my brothers you left their daughter behind to die."

With that, Slick walked off. He still wore a Steel Demons cut, the old leather soft and worn, his patches faded and fraying. I tried not to think of that grinning horned skull on his back as mocking us.

14

TORRANCE

The warehouse and accompanying trailers turned out to be a temporary shelter for Valkyrie Network riders and refugees. I half-expected to see Rori's cousin, Carter, but he wasn't present among the small crew who was running things. I would have loved to get his advice, because I felt utterly lost.

I was president now, until we got Rori back. It was never supposed to be this way. I was supposed to support her, be her right hand. The fearless Aurora Wilder was never supposed to be taken out of the equation. And now that she was...

I stood from the bench, heading over to the barbell on the ground to do another set of deadlifts. My few hours of sleep had been broken and fitful since we'd arrived. My stomach was a block of cement, so I'd barely eaten any of what was rationed out.

I was not mentally, nor physically, well enough to lift such heavy weight, but it was the only thing I *could* do. My solace and my punishment.

The last thing Rori had said to me was that I wasn't listening. And that was so painfully goddamned true. Two people lost their lives because we didn't evacuate fast enough. Devin told me about the guy he had to mercy kill. Another fighter got attacked in the mad scramble for motorcycles. He'd been shot in the leg from the roof, then pulled off a bike and dragged away behind the garage. I could still hear that laughter coming from Rori's mouth, that unsettling inhuman sound that was not her at all.

Was she present during everything that happened? Could she see and feel what her own body was doing while she wasn't in control? I hoped for her sake that she wasn't there for any of it, that she wouldn't have to deal with the horrifying recollections that 'she' had murdered two people she had promised safety and refuge to. Controlled or not, she would never forgive herself.

I did deadlifts until my lower half was jelly, then I let my ass plant on the concrete floor of the warehouse. Sitting there in that moment of total physical exhaustion, the one thought I had been avoiding slipped to the forefront.

Would I have to kill the woman I loved?

My stomach turned on itself in protest, and my palms slapped the hard floor as I doubled over to fight the dry heaves. My skin broke out in a cold sweat, and that stubborn beating muscle in my chest squeezed with a painful ache. Every cell in my body rejected that thought, hated it.

I couldn't do it. It didn't matter if I had a guarantee from the gods themselves that it would eradicate the cult for good. I didn't care. I was not sacrificing her for some greater good bullshit.

Not only that, I'd prevent anyone else from doing it too. I'd kill Santos, Slick, anyone who tried to say it was the only option. I'd let the cult enslave every man in the world before I lost Rori for good.

I was getting her back alive and whole. The only question was how.

How the hell would I expel a god from its vessel without harming the vessel?

Once my legs got stable enough to support me, I worked my chest and arms. The repetitive movements became a blur, nothing but white noise to my thoughts going around and around again.

If Rori were here, we'd bounce ideas off each other. We'd just say what was on our minds, no matter how ridiculous it sounded.

We'd be serious, devolve into stupid jokes, then get serious again. We'd offer counterpoints to the other's ideas, things we never would have thought of on our own. She and I had completely different thought processes from each other, but together we could form a complete picture.

At some point, I stopped moving and just let my arms dangle. Staring up at the ceiling, I found it ironic and cruel that figuring out how to get Rori back alive and well was the moment I needed her feedback the most.

I needed her toughness, her compassion and level headedness. I even needed her anxiety, those racing 'what-ifs' and worries that she never shared with the rest of the club.

She was alone, lost, and it killed me that I couldn't be there for her, couldn't talk her through her fears and reassure her that it would all be okay.

It might never be okay again.

A side door opened, the hinges loud and squealing. Footsteps approached me that I recognized as belonging to Santos.

"Hey," I said without looking at him.

"You couldn't sleep or eat either, huh?" I felt his weight lean against one side of the rack.

"No. It all feels like a waste," I admitted. "Like every minute

I'm not thinking of how to get her back is just time being pissed down the drain."

"She'd call you all kinds of names for saying that." He chuckled. "Talk about how rest and fueling yourself is important and you're an idiot for not doing that."

"Of course that applies to everyone but her," I replied. "You know how she keeps going until she's about to drop dead."

"Yeah," he said quietly. "I know."

After a few minutes of silence, I asked, "So what have you been up to instead of eating and sleeping?"

"Begging Tezca for answers," he admitted. "You'd think having a companion god would mean something now more than ever, right?"

"So I take it you didn't get much out of him?"

"Nothing." Bitterness hardened Santos' voice. "He kept saying I'm asking the wrong questions, asking for the wrong thing. Tried going to Astarte and got the same shit. Now I know why Rori was so annoyed with that bird."

I sat up from the bench, narrowly missing getting hit in the forehead by the barbell. What Santos had said alerted me to something, ringing some kind of bell. I just didn't know what exactly.

"What did you say?" I demanded. "Tell me exactly what you asked Tezca."

Santos frowned, confused. "Everything I could think of, really. Why this was allowed to happen. Why Rori, of all people. What did we need to do to get her back. How are we supposed to fight a god without hurting her. I mean, I kept going until I was literally out of questions to ask."

"And he said you were asking the wrong questions?"

"Yeah. I can't even imagine what that would be, though."

"So he *did* want you to ask something specific." I rubbed my temples. I was too sleep-deprived and hungry to be thinking about this, but I was onto *something*. I just didn't know what it was. "Did he say anything else to you?"

Santos scratched his head. "No, but Astarte said something like, 'To ask, you must also give'. What the hell, right?"

"To ask, you must also give," I repeated, thinking on it hard. "We need to ask some specific question, and in doing so, give them something in return."

"Like what?" Santos asked. "A sacrifice? An eye for an eye kind of thing?"

"No, that's not it. They've never asked us to do anything like that before. That's what sets them apart from the cult goddess. We've never needed to prove our devotion to them."

"Because they're much older," Santos said. "Tezca was worshiped by the Aztecs. Rori told me Astarte is even older than that."

"Yes, but they also weren't born out of ideas like revenge or hatred." I felt like we were straying from the original point, so I tried to refocus, despite a headache building in my temples. "I feel like the answer is right in front of our faces. What are we missing?"

Santos unsheathed his machetes and rolled out his wrists, making the twin blades dance in the air. I got the sense that he leaned on those blades like I did on weights. They kept him honed, focused.

"What's something that you give when you ask for something?" he said, more to himself than to me.

"I keep thinking of that expression, better to ask for forgiveness than permission." I shook my head. "I'm not sure if that's the right train of thought, though."

"Asking for forgiveness is also giving...what?" Santos began juggling his machetes, and I was forced to look away. "Giving someone another chance to trust you?"

"That's not yours to give, though," I pointed out. "The other person has to decide whether or not to trust you again. That's their gift when you ask forgiveness."

"Okay, what about permission, then?" He stopped juggling, and I breathed a sigh of relief. "Same thing, right? You ask permission and someone else has to give it."

"Yeah…" Something about that nagged at me. The answer was right in front of us and we were dancing blindly around it. "Permission is another word for consent," I mused.

"Uh-huh." Santos went back to twirling his blades, the sharp metal becoming a silver blur.

"What if you're not asking for permission to *do* something, but asking for something to be done *to* you?"

Santos' blades stopped abruptly, then he turned to me. "So by asking for this thing to be done, you're giving consent."

"Yes!" I jumped up from the bench. "That's it! The asking and giving at that same time."

"I still don't get it," he admitted. "What are we asking for? And giving consent to?"

I looked him squarely in the eye. "We're becoming vessels for the gods."

15

RORI

I t was such a weird sensation, being unable to use my own body. I felt like I was floating through space, weightless and adrift. I would have preferred to have felt bound by rope or even chains. At least then I would have felt something.

But I didn't even feel my toes inside my shoes or my hands shoved into the pockets of my jacket. When the Dark Mother used my lungs to breathe, I couldn't smell the trees, couldn't get a sense of the air my body pulled in to stay alive.

I could still see and hear, but I got the feeling that was only because she allowed it.

Despite all the nothing I was able to do, I kept fighting. I willed my body to punch and kick. And because I had no use of my physical throat, I screamed endlessly inside my own head.

Get out! Getoutgetoutgetout! Get the fuck out of my body!

She ignored me, but I knew she heard. She was like a parasite that had infiltrated my brain. A squatter coming in to make themselves at home where they were not welcome.

It was the morning after she had taken full control, and we stood on the front porch of one house, watching RVs and Jeeps pull into the cul-de-sac where my motorcycle club once stood.

147

All the motorcycles were gone now, even mine. Someone must have taken it in the chaos of the evacuation, which was good. I didn't want anyone in this cult touching my ride, not even if it was my own hand controlled by someone else.

The door to the biggest RV opened and a woman probably in her sixties came out, her gray hair spilling loose over her shoulders. She wore dark red robes that looked almost priest-like, with details in gold thread on her cuffs and lapels.

"Mother..." she whispered in awe, taking hesitant steps toward me. "It worked. Goddess in all of us, it worked!"

"I told you it would," her goddess answered using my mouth. "Come here, daughter of mine." She extended a hand, *my* hand, and the woman eagerly came forward. The Dark Mother held the woman's shoulder and bent forward to kiss the top of her head from our elevated position on the porch.

I felt none of it. Not the solidness of a shoulder under my palm or the woman's hair against my lips.

"You've done well for me, daughter," the Dark Mother praised. "So well that I have a gift for you."

"A gift?" the woman parroted. "Dearest Mother, seeing you in the flesh is the greatest gift of my life. I could not possibly ask any more of you."

"Even so," her goddess answered with a chuckle. "I've secured a man for a sacrifice tonight."

The woman's eyes lit up while dread filled my soul. "A sacrifice, how wonderful! We'll make it the biggest celebration yet. For our new home and your new form."

"See that you do," my voice said, as if such a thing was to be expected and a human fucking sacrifice wasn't absolutely barbaric. "This is far from over. They will attempt to take back these homes and this body."

I was screaming all kinds of obscenities and wordless rage, but my parasite ignored me like I wasn't even there.

The woman nodded sagely. "Should we wait before bringing the children, then?"

"Yes. Keep the children where they are for now. The men will try to reclaim their home and bring bloodshed, as they always do. And we must keep our future secure."

Folding her hands in front of her, the woman made a noise of agreement. "Where is the sacrifice, mother? I'll start preparations for tonight's rituals immediately."

"Come with me, daughter. I'll take you to him."

I felt something then. Not a physical sensation but a feeling being pushed at me so strongly, it felt like a smothering blanket. The Dark Mother was feeling smug, superior, and she wanted me to know it.

What is this? I wondered as she led the woman into the house. *How can you have a sacrifice? He already died.*

This one didn't, she answered me for the first time, heading for the basement.

She must have allowed my sense of smell to reach me, because the air was thick with the tang of blood. The woman following had no reaction, like she'd been here hundreds of times. How many sacrifices had this woman overseen to have no reaction to human suffering and to manifest a goddess that controlled a human body?

Heavy lengths of chain wrapped around a man's torso, tying him to the support beam in the center of the basement. There was a dark stain on the concrete under him, like a massive puddle of blood that had been cleaned up. What the fuck had happened here? The man's head jerked up as soon as we came down the stairs, and the hopeful look on his face broke my heart.

"Rori! President! Thank God you're here."

The thing in my body reached up to grab a chain and pulled it, turning on the bare bulb and casting the whole basement in an eerie yellow light.

Immediately the man shrank away. "President, what happened? What's wrong with your eyes?"

Ignoring him, the woman hummed approvingly at my side. "He'll do nicely."

The ex-gladiator looked at her. "Do nicely for what? Who are you?"

"I shot him through the shoulder and bandaged the wound, so his damage is minimal. He should last a while through the ritual."

The fighter's brow furrowed in confusion. "You're the one that shot me? And dragged me off the bike? What the hell is going on?"

I screamed the whole time and was ignored like I was in a soundproof cage. My anger became panicky and I was begging, even bargaining for the man's life. I screamed at him to run, to fight, save himself. But no one heard a word.

Why don't I remember him? I wondered. *I remember the other guy she shot, but I don't remember this one.*

Because I wanted to surprise you, the Dark Mother deigned to answer me. *You thought all but one of your men escaped, so I just allowed you to keep thinking that. But don't worry, you'll watch the entire ritual too.*

Please let him go. If I had control of my face muscles, I would have been sobbing. *I'll...I'll get the others not to attack you, just don't kill him.*

I won't. My followers will, in devotion to me. And they will make sure it lasts the whole night.

Please, I begged. *Just stop all of this. I saved these men. Please, I'll do anything you want.*

You're already doing just that, the deity said gleefully.

I'd never felt such hopelessness before. Not even when Santos and Torr were captured. At least I was in control of my actions then. But now? This cult would find my men, kill and abuse them, while I could do nothing to stop it. Even worse, their fucked-up goddess would make me watch.

We left the basement as the man cried out and called for help. The house was filled with women now, moving in and out of bedrooms, poking through the kitchen, and rearranging things like a bee colony taking over a new hive.

You can't do this, I protested weakly. *None of this is yours. You and your fucking cult have no right to be here!*

The houses will be well-maintained and taken care of, the Dark Mother replied with false reassurance. *They would have looked like landfills in another month if you'd continue to let men live here. Consider our occupation a favor.*

These are safe houses for people who need refuge! I screamed. *My family built these so people could escape from things like you.*

And now they'll provide refuge for the victims of those you housed here. Poetic justice, isn't it?

You're insane. How can you be so powerful and have your logic so twisted? My men were your *victims!*

Your human perspective is so limited. Of course you don't understand.

She had walked my body outside again to help with some of the unloading. A woman with a modest baby bump, probably early in her second trimester, was carrying in a basket of laundry when we approached her.

"Dear daughter, let me take that from you," my mouth cooed, taking the basket from the stunned young woman.

"Oh no! Dark Mother, please! It's no trouble. You shouldn't bother yourself with things like this."

"And you shouldn't be carrying things when you have back pain," the deity chided gently, taking the basket. "Get off your feet, dear one. Take some time to connect with your daughter."

The woman's face lit up with joy as her hands fell to the

gentle rounding of her stomach. "It's a girl? Oh, thank you, Dark Mother! I've been praying."

"I can't reveal what is not meant to be known." My lips curved with a smile that felt like someone sticking their fingers in my mouth and pulling my lips apart. "But all things are either a blessing or a lesson. I know you will be ready for what comes."

My feet turned away, walking back up the porch with the laundry basket, when I came to a realization.

You don't actually know, do you? I said. *Being a god doesn't make you a fucking ultrasound machine. You don't know if she's having a girl or boy, and you can't control if that happens because even you can't fuck with how biology works.*

It's just as I told her. The Dark Mother set the laundry basket down in an armchair. *She will be blessed or she will be tested.*

You're really gonna make her kill her infant if it's a boy? And you don't see how fucked up that is?

I allow some males to live. The smugness in her voice returned. *Like your father. Like Torrance. Really, you should be thanking me. Neither of them would have been in your life if I hadn't allowed them to live.*

The confirmation that Shadow had been a victim of her cult was heartbreaking enough. But Torr's name was the last thing I'd expected to hear.

What's Torr got to do with you? I demanded.

His mother was a failure. Her tone became disappointed. *She was recruited too late and could not see the truth. She snuck away multiple times to see a man who was not one of our breeders. At our colony, she pretended to use the breeder but never did. When her pregnancy began showing, she led everyone to believe she had conceived in our way, the only approved way.*

I thought back to what Torr had said about his early life. He barely remembered anything before he was twelve years old. If he did, he never mentioned it.

She went to be with her man to birth the child, the Dark Mother went on. *Girl or boy, she would not have raised her child with us.*

Good for her, I declared. Whoever Torr's birth mother was, I was insanely proud of her in that moment. She probably couldn't leave the cult voluntarily, but she did what she could to keep her baby safe.

I was a mere spark of consciousness back then, but I could see all. I knew what she did. The Dark Mother sounded spiteful. *I let her think she could keep up her double life for ten years. As my power grew, I inspired my true daughters to interrogate her. They worked her over for hours, but the bitch didn't crack. She was released just to use the bathroom, but she made a run for it. She hit one of my daughters with a crowbar and stole a car, then drove straight to her man and son.*

And they evaded you. I couldn't help the glee in my mental voice, the pride and pain I felt for Torr's mother. How I wished I'd known her. *For at least two more years, right?*

Oh, I let them believe they did. Every so often I would ransack Rochelle's mind and give her terrible nightmares. It was how I learned to perfect you as my vessel.

You've got a knack for that shit, I'll give you that.

Eventually, she caught on that I was real, I was in her mind, and I would never let her escape me. So she talked her husband into leaving their son behind, because she was afraid of what I would do to him through her.

Smart woman, I thought.

I was not capable of taking a vessel at the time, and even if I had, I never would have chosen her.

I wanted to roll my eyes at how much this deity was sneering like a high school mean girl.

But I was capable of fucking up her mind, so that's what I did.

I hesitated before asking. *Is she still alive?*

Wandering the streets of Blakemore with extremely advanced dementia at only 52 years old, but yes.

If only I could close my eyes to squeeze out some tears. If only I could hit something, feel the ache in my chest that I knew was there, scream until I felt a satisfying, painful rawness in my throat.

You're so fucking cruel, I said with despair. *How can you really believe you're making a better world?*

Because I'm rooting out true evil and everything that enables it.

She just wanted to keep her son safe!

And let him grow up in a world where he can take what he wants without consequence, simply because he's a man. She would enable him, no matter what he did, because he's her little prince who can do no wrong. Sound familiar?

The need to cry and scream was building up inside me with no outlet. Yelling inside my own head was nothing like being able to use my body to express my rage. There was no catharsis, no way to process all this emotion. I was stuck in an endless loop, tied up and shut away while someone else took the wheel.

Men can live alongside women one day. The deity said it like she was conceding a point to me in a debate. *But that day is centuries from now, when all of their current programming is long removed. Their violence and oppression will be long forgotten, and they will revere women as the divine beings we are. Only then can we permit men to exist with us.*

I didn't know why I even bothered to argue. This being didn't care, didn't see reason or ethics at all. She talked about the divinity of women while puppetting my body, while telling me about how she tortured a woman to the point of dementia. She called infanticide a test and a lesson.

Nothing to say? the Dark Mother taunted me. *Good. I was waiting for you to be quiet. The less you think, the faster this goes.*

Faster what goes?

The binding of myself to this vessel. The longer I'm in this body, the more your physiology adapts to my being here. Your skin, bones, and blood will become my permanent home.

And what happens to me?

Oh, you're coming along for the ride, Aurora, she informed me gleefully. *I could shut you down and end this swiftly for you. But I enjoy your amusing little head noises too much. For as long as you're with me, you will bear witness to my new world. You will be deathless.*

16

SANTOS

Torr only told his plan to three of us—me, Devin, and Hudson. What he proposed was shocking, and yet somehow made total sense. It felt right. As he spoke it aloud, it cemented into my mind as the only answer. This was what we had to do, what was meant to happen.

"Only the four of us can go." Torr's voice was steady, a general confident in his battle plan. "No one else gets involved. We don't even tell anyone else about it. This has to be us, because we were chosen for this."

Hudson, the only one of us who seemed unsure, scratched the side of his head. "I understand you three, but why me? I'm not part of your little group. I barely even talked to her last night before it all went down."

"And it was a pretty significant conversation, wasn't it?" Torr said.

"I don't know. I mean, I guess."

"You're also good with a gun," I reminded Hudson. "So you and Devin will be our backup with the more traditional weapons."

Torr looked across the table expectantly at me. "Are we ready?"

"In a sec." I looked at Hudson. "Can I get a word with you?"

He looked surprised but nodded.

"Make it fast." Torr rose from the table, his footsteps echoing over the warehouse floor. "The sooner we get that thing out of Rori, the better off we'll all be."

Devin followed after Torr, but not before giving Hudson a reassuring squeeze of his hand. Without another word, my former friend and I went to stand by a stack of wooden pallets for relative privacy.

"So, what's up?" Hudson tried to sound casual but there was no hiding the eagerness in his voice.

I pulled in a long breath, gathering my thoughts before speaking. "If you can promise me now, and mean it, that you will never seek to harm Rori, or any other woman, again, I can maybe forgive you for trying to kill her."

He opened his mouth to reply, but I held up an index finger. "I'm not done." Abruptly, his mouth closed and he nodded, waiting for me to continue.

"It doesn't matter if it's with a gun, your hands, or your fucking words. You are somehow important to all this, so I gotta deal with you being around. It's really fucking inconvenient to hate you if I gotta see your face all the time, so that's why I'm extending this olive branch. But only *if* you can guarantee that women, especially mine, are safe around you. I don't care what kind of relationship you have with Rori, if any. But if you even break her shoelace, I will banish you myself. That'll be the end of her hospitality. Got it?"

Hudson just stared at me for a while, then blinked a few times. "Yeah. I got it, but—"

"Good. I'm glad we could have a productive conversation after what happened."

"Santos, my dude." He huffed out a laugh. "You realize she's not exactly the damsel in distress type, right? She can boot me out herself if she wants."

"She can." I rested my hands on the hilts of my machetes. "But she shouldn't have to. She shouldn't have to raise a finger to exile the man who shot her on sight."

"I am sorry about that." All humor dropped from his expression. He looked and sounded sincere, the regret weighing heavily on his shoulders. "I really am. It was wrong."

"Why?" I wanted to hear the reason from his mouth.

"Because she was innocent. She was helping you guys rescue me." He shrugged. "She had done nothing to warrant me almost killing her. I realize that now, and I regret being so reactionary."

I took several seconds to inspect him, sizing him up from head to toe like I would an opponent in the fighting pit. "You're really different in such a short time," I observed. "That's a good thing. You look better, more alive. Well, even."

Hudson shrugged. "Devin's been the biggest help, honestly."

"Devin?" I noticed the flush that creeped up his neck. "How's that going?"

"Um, good." He blushed darker, avoiding eye contact with me.

"Just good?"

"Fuck, Santos." Hudson dropped his forehead into his hand and groaned. "I think I'm falling for him. Hard."

"Nothing wrong with that," I said. "I fell hard and fast for Rori. If you two are happy, then—"

"I think *he's* in love with Rori."

My mouth fell open and nothing came out for a long beat of silence. "Oh."

"And it's like, I can't even hate her for it." Hudson ran a frustrated hand over his head.

"Wait, what makes you think he feels that way?" Now I was confused. "They're either at each other's throats or ignoring each other."

"I dunno, it's just a feeling I get. He's...really, really good to me. But I'm a fucked-up mess, you know?"

"Who isn't a fucked-up mess?" I countered. "Even if the three of us hadn't been through the shit we had, we'd be a mess in some other way."

Hudson shook his head. "Just sucks when you're so fucked up that you're not enough for someone."

"Has Devin told you that?" I argued. "Or done anything that would make you believe such a thing?"

"Well, no, but—"

"Then it's not fucking true. It's your own brain telling you lies." I put a hand on his shoulder and squeezed. "You deserve to be happy, dude. Is that so hard to believe?"

He let out a long sigh. "Sometimes, yeah."

"I get that." I said with a release of his shoulder. "But try to let yourself be happy with Devin, as long as he's good to you. The longer you're there, the more you'll believe it."

"But what if I'm right?" He looked at me with a hard expression. "What if he wants to be with me *and* Rori?"

I thought on that for a moment. Devin in our dynamic wouldn't be so bad. In the rare moments that he and Rori got along, they had some chemistry. But I couldn't see him doing that if it was detrimental to Hudson. Devin had essentially appointed himself Hudson's caretaker, and it was a role I knew he took seriously. He wouldn't let anything interfere with Hudson's emotional progress, especially not if romantic feelings were involved. It could get messy though, I had to admit.

"That's a bridge we'll cross if we come to it," I said. "Rori will be the one who ultimately decides. And believe it or not, she wants you to be happy too."

"I do believe it, actually," Hudson said softly. "When we talked before you showed up last night, she was...nice. I might even like her."

"Well, holy shit." I crossed my arms, unable to suppress my grin. "If that isn't progress, I don't know what is."

"Yeah, well." He was blushing again, a small smile playing on his lips. It almost seemed as though he more than liked her. Hudson had a crush. On a woman. *My* woman.

No wonder he had all kinds of conflicting feelings.

I initiated this talk with him feeling skeptical, but now my fears were completely assuaged. He was far more likely to kiss Rori than kill her. And I wasn't worried about him with other women either.

"You'll be alright." I gave him a slap on the shoulder. "Thanks for talking with me."

"Yeah." He smiled as we headed to where Torr and Devin were waiting. "Not to get all mushy or anything, but I'm glad we're friends again."

I grinned at him. "Me too."

Torr and Devin were just outside the open warehouse door, next to the motorcycles we rode in on. Tezca sat off to the side while Astarte was perched on Torr's handlebars.

"We doing this?" I asked Torr, then glanced at the animals.

"Now or never." He looked at the dove, who cooed and stretched out her wings.

Likewise, I stared at the jaguar, unsure of what I was waiting for. "Uh, do we do this at the same time? Is there some kind of procedure?"

Just ask what you need to ask. Astarte sounded like she was sick of our shit. *We can't do anything until you ask.*

"Okay, well, you've given us no direction or help, so thanks for that," Torr grumbled.

You sound like Aurora, Astarte griped back. *As I've told her before, we cannot interfere with your decision-making. You must make these decisions on your own, with no influence from us.*

"Alright, I'm going." I kneeled in front of Tezca, meeting those golden eyes that seemed to carry all the wisdom in the universe. He returned my stare calmly, waiting as I braced myself with a deep breath.

"I'm asking you to possess me," I said to the jaguar god. "I give my consent for you to use me as a vessel."

For what purpose? Tezca's voice breezed over my skin and spoke directly inside my head.

"For the purpose of killing a destructive god," I answered. "And to return Aurora to us safely."

A new sensation came over me then, one that was strange and a little uncomfortable, but not painful. Something pricked my skin, like it was trying to get inside of me through my pores. Something entered my mouth, funneling its way down my throat. The same thing entered my sinuses, then my brain. I felt a gentle pressure on my eyeballs, and then blinked at a gritty feeling like sand or dust.

My occupation of you is temporary, Tezca said, now entirely inside my head. *I will only control your functions and perform my abilities when necessary. Even with me along for the ride, your free will remains intact.*

I blinked several times until the grittiness cleared from my eyes. My palms were planted on the ground, as were my knees. Like an animal, I was on all fours on the ground.

I sat back on my ass, meeting Devin and Hudson's bewildered expressions.

"Well, that was the freakiest shit I've ever seen in my life," Devin remarked.

"What happened?" I demanded.

"Tezca disintegrated into, like, this smoky form, and you basically absorbed him." Hudson nodded at Torr. "Same for him."

Torr and I looked at each other, then looked around. The dove and the jaguar were nowhere to be seen.

"How do you feel?" Torr asked.

"Alright. You?"

"Yeah. Pretty much the same." He placed his hand on his chest, then cocked his head like he was listening to something. "Astarte's like, 'What did you expect? This is real life, not a movie.'"

"Hah." I did feel normal, if even good. I felt sharp, alert, strong. Like right before a good fight in the pit.

There was something else there, a subtle presence other than myself if I paid close enough attention.

"I can feel Tezca in here." My hand came to my chest, much like Torr's gesture. "He's quiet, though. Almost lurking."

Torr snorted. "Astarte is *not* lurking. She is making her presence very well known. No wonder Rori can't stand her." He brought a hand to his temple and squeezed his eyes shut. "Okay, okay, okay. Sorry, geez." He didn't elaborate on what the dove goddess had said, probably for good reason.

"So that's it, then. We good to go?"

Devin and Hudson nodded. "Ready when you two are."

Torr and I gave one last look at each other. "Let's get our girl back."

And eliminate this unhinged god killing our sons and daughters. A low feline growl rippled over my mind. It took a moment to realize it was an audible, physically made sound too, not just in my head.

"Whoa, Tezca." Devin held a palm up. "Easy."

I rubbed my throat, wondering how he was able to make

that noise through me. "This vengeful god's ready to kick some ass."

With that, and a final nod from Torr, the four of us mounted up and hit the road.

Stay strong, paloma. I focused the thought toward the horizon as we sped toward our destination. *We're coming for you.*

17

TORRANCE

I t was fucking weird, having a god just hanging out with me under my skin. The best I could describe was that sense of someone sitting near you, maybe behind you or just over your shoulder. You couldn't see them but you could *feel* them there. That was what it felt like, only inside of me.

Although she was a smartass when she spoke, Astarte was a quiet passenger for most of the ride. I got the sense that she was thinking hard about what was to come.

"Do you know what's going to happen?" The rushing wind over me and the motorcycle stole the volume of my voice, but I didn't need to be loud for her to hear me. "Like, can you see the future?"

The future doesn't exist for me. Neither does the past. Time is...well, it's not something that applies to me.

"But do you know?" I pressed. "What will happen when we get there?" It was the best way I could ask if we had a snowball's chance of getting Rori back without losing my shit.

I can see several outcomes. The end result will depend on the choices you make.

"Helpful as always."

You are welcome to fight this other deity yourself.

"No need to get sassy."

Astarte actually didn't reply with a cutting remark to that, keeping silent instead. Could gods be nervous? Because that was the sense I got.

"So you've seen all of human history, pretty much?" I wasn't sure why I felt so chatty, but what other time would I be able to ask questions like this?

Not all, but a sizable portion of it. I've seen genocides, wars, and the rise and fall of many civilizations.

"What's your favorite thing about humanity?"

An odd sensation tickled my nervous system, and I got the sense that Astarte was laughing.

What are we, on a first date?

"I'm just curious." Could gods even have favorites?

Your tenacity is astounding, she said after a while. *It's almost paradoxical, your ability to carry on and adapt. You keep surviving but pass on your trauma and coping mechanisms to your children, whether or not you realize it. It's fascinating how the youngest generations carry the wounds of several generations past.*

"By fascinating, do you mean sad?"

Sometimes it's sad. But also fascinating.

"Do you know about my birth parents?"

For years, I'd convinced myself I didn't care about them. They left me, so why should I care? I'd just lift to get strong as hell, sleep around, and keep my heart out of anyone's reach. No one could hurt me because I was emotionally untouchable.

But ever since Mystic Canyon, when Rori and I broke down our long-standing walls, I started to figure out that I *did* care. I wanted to know why. Why did they leave? Why didn't they want to keep me? All my life it had been eating at me and I shoved it down, pretending like it didn't affect me. But everything I did, pushing my body to the extreme and never letting anyone get too close, was a direct result of that hurt.

I see them, yes. Astarte's tone was low, almost mournful.

"See them?" I repeated. "They're still alive?"

You can't afford to be distracted, Torrance, she chided me. Then more gently, *Your past isn't going anywhere. You can meet it when you're ready. But if you want Rori in your future, you need to focus.*

A future with Rori was all I wanted. I still needed to man up and tell her I loved her.

Don't fight me during the moments I must control you, Astarte added. *Trust that I will not harm you as my vessel.*

"And Rori?" I asked.

The deity was silent for a while. *I will do my best.*

* * *

Dawn approached when we entered the valley where the safe houses were hidden. I didn't know exactly where to go, but Astarte guided me. Not like she was giving me directions but gently steering my body and therefore bike in the right direction.

I brought the bike to a stop at the first checkpoint on the road leading up to the houses. The little guard station was now empty, but it seemed as good a place as any for a final pep talk.

Angling the bike to address the others, I waited until Santos, Devin, and Hudson drove close enough to hear me.

"I don't know what we're getting into, so use basic common sense," I said. "If they're armed, shoot them. If they surrender, keep them detained. If they run away, follow them. Injure them if you must, but try not to kill anyone who's not trying to kill you." I paused to level a stare at Hudson, who stared back impassively.

"And if it's Rori that's intent on killing us?" Devin asked.

Santos' eyes went completely black, much like Rori's had when she got possessed. From Santos' mouth, Tezca thundered, "We will deal with Aurora and the parasitic creation inside her."

Santos' eyes returned to normal and he shook his head as if clearing it. "Fuck, that's weird."

"But can you make sure she survives?" Devin demanded, his jaw clenched.

It wasn't the first time I'd seen him so concerned about Rori. He was the one who bandaged her leg and carried her out of harm's way when Hudson shot her. The guy didn't make his concern for her obvious, except in the ways that counted most.

Astarte used my mouth to answer him while my mind processed those thoughts. "That depends on how far gone Aurora is already. We can extract the parasite from her body without causing injury. But until that happens, there's no telling how much of her is left." Devin's face hardened even more, a muscle feathering in his jaw. "What are we waiting for, then?"

I turned my bike to face forward, accelerating on the narrow dirt road to what had once been our home.

"What are the chances?" I asked Astarte. "That we'll get Rori back?"

I don't know, the deity answered. *She was possessed violently and without consent after being broken down for weeks already. I'm sorry, Torrance. The chances aren't good. Even possessing you as we are now, done in a way that is minimally invasive, is damaging long-term. The prophets of your ancient times were not stable because they had been possessed by their deities for too long.*

"Huh. Well, that explains a lot." My fist clenched on the throttle. "Rori's a fighter. I know she's still in there. She hasn't been possessed for long. She'll be okay."

I didn't know what the fuck I was talking about. But believing the alternative was not an option.

As we pulled up, the safehouses looked the same as when we left them. A couple of idyllic, two-story cabins with a detached garage between them, an open gravel driveway in the front, with trees surrounding the sides and back.

Only this time, a couple of RVs sat parked in front of the garage. Instead of motorcycles filling the driveway, there were Jeeps, pick-up trucks, and vans.

We parked the bikes and headed for the house on the left, all four of us on a single-minded mission. Santos was at my side, his steps falling into sync with mine. I couldn't quite tell if Astarte was in the driver's seat as our boots ascended the porch or if it was a mix of us. Either way, I felt like a well-oiled machine sent out to do my one purpose.

I shoved open the front door, making it bounce off the wall with a loud bang. The few women inside, maybe three of them, scattered, diving behind furniture with shrieks. Santos and I moved through the house which had once been so familiar but had already changed so much. Hudson and Devin fanned out behind us while we headed for the back door, as if pulled to the area behind the house on instinct.

We only took a few steps through when the women opened fire. They hadn't dove out of fear, but to grab hidden weapons that were stashed.

Devin and Hudson disposed of them quickly, without mess or fuss. A single shot of returned fire and the quiet, wet sound of a blade slicing open a throat.

We went through the back door, where we found the rest gathered in the wooded area before a grisly scene.

"Shit," Devin muttered from behind me.

Twelve women sat in a circle around a central figure, who wore a flowy white dress. The garment clung to a feminine body, thin fabric hugging hips, a waist, and breasts that I knew. That I had held, worshiped, and adored.

Santos sucked in a breath of shock beside me before a low, rumbling growl began emanating from his throat. Tezca was pissed, as was Astarte.

The remaining details of the scene filtered through in slow motion, like my brain needed extra time to process everything I was seeing. The lower half of the white dress and the figure's hands and forearms were stained dark red with blood. Behind the central figure was a man's body, strung up between two trees. And the ground was soaked with so much blood, I could see the reflection of the tree branches in a small pool of it.

But nothing shook me more than that easy, careless smile on the central figure's face. Because it was Rori's smile, Rori's face. It was Rori, walking barefoot through the bloodsoaked ground toward me and holding her bloodstained hands out in a welcoming gesture.

"I'm so glad you boys could make it," Rori said in a voice that wasn't hers. "You just missed the first ritual, but don't worry. We'll take volunteers for tonight."

"You will sacrifice no more of our children," Astarte said through me. "We're here to put you down. Cull you like the bad seed you are."

The grin on Rori's face faltered for a moment, her all-black eyes flickering like a lightbulb going out. And just as quickly as it happened, the maniacal expression returned.

"This is no place for old gods," the Dark Mother said flippantly. "Go back to your crumbling tombs and dust-covered idols behind museum glass. You are no longer relevant."

"You are no god," Tezca snarled, turning Santos' eyes fully black. "You are fanatical obsession with a voice and a body that you stole. You are murdering our sons and daughters because you have no true devotion, no real power."

"I've gathered more devotion in decades than you have in millennia. My people called me forth because they *needed* me. Where were you during the humans' Collapse? Didn't your sons and daughters need you then?"

"You're as short-sighted as a child," Astarte sneered. "You know nothing."

"And you," the Dark Mother raised a bloodstained finger to point at Santos and I, "are too late, old gods. I'm what today's people need. I'm creating a new world."

"This world is already here," Astarte replied. "And it doesn't need you."

Right then, my control was yanked away. Astarte had been true to her word that she'd only control me when necessary, and that time was now.

I lost all feeling in my limbs, all sense of space and balance, though I could still see and hear. Energy hummed through me, creating a pulsing pressure that wasn't entirely unpleasant.

Tezca had gone behind Rori, Santos' form visible over her shoulder. I lost track of Devin and Hudson and could only hope they were handling the other women as planned.

Rori took off running at an impossible speed. Astarte surged after her, the trees whipping past us in a blur, as if we were in a moving car. Tezca was on her as well, nearly on her heels. In a puff of dark smoke, Rori vanished.

"Are you tracking her?" Astarte immediately asked Tezca.

"Yes." The jaguar god stilled, only turning Santos' head as if to listen. After a few moments, he drew one of Santos' machetes and hovered his free hand over the blade, muttering something under his breath.

He held the weapon out toward Astarte, and I watched my own hand hover over the razor-sharp blade. My mouth moved and made sounds that I couldn't begin to decipher. The pulsing energy that I'd felt before seemed to find an outlet through my palm and went into the machete.

Internally, I started to panic. *Don't kill her. You said you wouldn't hurt Rori!*

This will not harm her physical body, the goddess answered me. *This will sever the connection between them. Rori's parasite will be forced to leave and no longer maintain a physical form.*

Relief filled me, but only briefly. *Rori will need to regain control for this to work,* Astarte went on. *It only needs to be for a moment so we can seize the deity and cut it from her, but Rori has to be aware of herself and fight like hell.*

She will, I insisted. *She'll do it. I know she can.*

Astarte was quiet for a while. *I only hope there is enough of her left to fight. I will give you control of your voice. Tezca will do the same with Santos. If she hears you two, it might rally her strength just enough.*

And if...there isn't enough of her left? To fight? I was terrified of the answer but still had to know.

We can still extract the parasite, but the vessel will have to be destroyed, Astarte answered gravely. *Aurora will die.*

"I found her," Tezca announced before I could reply.

He made some kind of gesture in the air, fingers curling into a fist, and then made a pulling motion with his whole arm. Rori's form appeared before us again, and the two gods taking us for a ride didn't hesitate.

With inhuman strength and speed, they each took an arm and pinned her to the ground.

The Dark Mother kicked and thrashed so hard, she was creating a human-sized crater in the ground. Pushing and fighting to get free against two other gods gave her the strength of an excavator in a human woman's body. Tezca and Astarte used that same superhuman strength to keep her down.

Now, Astarte instructed me. *Use your voice to reach her.*

172

"Rori!" I called out. "Rori, it's me. It's Torr. I know you're in there, creep."

My woman's body surged hard against her restraints. She kicked a leg out and hit me in the thigh. The force of it would have broken my femur if I didn't have god-armor on. Astarte dropped my leg on top of Rori's pinning her down flatter.

Keep trying, Astarte encouraged. *Keep talking to her.*

"Come back to us, paloma," Santos urged, his voice aching and desperate. "We need you." Bravely, he lowered down to Rori's struggling form, brushing his forehead against hers. "I need you."

The Dark Mother spit in his face. "Fuck you, *male.* Get away from me!"

"Rori!" I yelled to draw her attention away from him. "I know you're not weak. Take back control of your body right the fuck now."

Something flickered in those empty black eyes, and another surge of pulsing energy filled my limbs.

It's working. Her awareness is rousing, Astarte said. *I can sense her, but we need more. She needs to fight harder.*

"Rori, we need you to fight harder." I hovered over that pissed off, snarling face with the soulless black eyes. "You need to kick this rotten cunt to the curb right now."

"Toss her out on her ugly ass," Santos chimed in. "You're strong enough. She wouldn't have chosen you for a vessel if you weren't a fucking badass. Show this bitch how strong you really are."

Rori's head threw back and let out an animalistic cry of fury.

Fuck. For the first time, Astarte sounded truly worried. *I can feel her fighting, but she's not getting the upper hand. What little control she has is slipping. I'm sorry, Torrance, but she's almost gone.*

A new kind of desperation overtook me now. A sense of

such utter helplessness, knowing that what little I had left to give wasn't enough. And still, I'd offer it up anyway, because it was all I had left.

Give me one of my hands, I said to Astarte.

That isn't a good idea. Strong as you are, it's not enough to—

Just give me one of my fucking hands! Let me touch her before I lose her, for fuck's sake.

There was a moment of hesitation before I felt control return to the palm and fingers of my right hand. I used that hand to cup Rori's cheek. Her face turned toward me with surprising ease, those soulless eyes somehow amused in their lack of expression. Leaning down, I touched my forehead and nose to hers as Santos had earlier.

"Listen, Rori." My throat was impossibly tight with a choking knot. I was all but saying goodbye to her and had to get the words out.

"Listen, you need to come back." My thumb stroked over her cheekbone, still so warm like she was very much alive. "You need to come back not because you're strong and we need to save the world or some shit, but because I—" I swallowed, but the knot wouldn't loosen. So I forced the words out. "Because I'm too weak to go on without you." Something about saying it out loud made the floodgates open, and the rest came pouring out.

"I need you to come back because I can't fucking handle you leaving me, okay? Not you. You swore you wouldn't. You asked me to trust you, and I did. You said you loved me, that you'd never leave. So don't become a fucking liar, Rori. Don't you dare fucking leave me like they did."

Nothing else registered as I closed my eyes, unable to look into that face that was no longer hers. "I love you too much to let you go."

18

RORI

A young man sat next to me. He was handsome with russet brown hair, green eyes, and a cheeky, dimpled smile. Some of his features, like the shape of his nose and chin, reminded me of my father Reaper.

"Hey, kiddo," he said quietly.

"Uncle Daren?" I tried to look around but couldn't get a sense of where I was. I wasn't even sure I had a head to turn. "Am I dreaming?"

"In a sense."

"Am I...dead?"

"No. It would feel like a mercy if you were, but it's not your time to die yet. Hades told me himself."

He was speaking words that I recognized but had trouble making sense of. I tried to lift my hands to see them, to stand up, to look around and observe my surroundings again. But the more I tried, the more it seemed like I didn't have a body.

"Where am I?" Panic frayed my voice, even though I couldn't physically feel any anxiety. "If I'm not dead, how can I see you so clearly?"

"It's alright, Rori. Just listen carefully." My uncle's face was solemn as he spoke to me. I'd never met him before, he'd died before I was born. But ever since Reaper told me about his younger brother, I'd felt an inexplicable bond to this man. Another father figure whose spirit guided me through dreams.

"You're not in control of your body right now," Uncle Daren told me calmly. "Someone else has taken over, so you've retreated to a safe place." He gave me a lopsided smile. "Turns out, that's with me."

His words began to make sense, and I nodded as the memories returned. "I always did feel safe with you. When I had nightmares as a little kid, you told me to come find you so the monsters wouldn't get me."

"That's right." My uncle smiled. "I figured, if I couldn't be around to protect my nieces and nephews in the physical world, I'd protect you in your dreams."

"Well, a real-life monster did get me." I tried to run my hands through my hair but felt nothing. It was trippy not having a body. "So, is this it for me? You and me, hanging out in Dreamworld?"

"No, Rori." Uncle Daren's smile disappeared, his stoic expression reminding me of my father again. "Your story is not over. But you have to fight your way back, harder than anyone ever has. It will hurt. You will be confused and disoriented, but if there's one person on earth badass and stubborn enough to fight off a god's possession, it's you."

If I had corporeal hands, I would reach for his. I would hug him in an attempt to seek comfort and strength. But all I had was this ghostly, detached feeling.

"Come with me?" I asked, despite knowing the answer.

Uncle Daren shook his head, the hint of a smile returning. "I have no body to return to, sweet niece. My place is here."

"I don't know if I can do it alone."

"You're not alone, Rori." A gentle sensation of pressure

wrapped around me, and it felt like this was my uncle's way of hugging me. "You've got those men who love you on the other side. Your whole family. Fuck, every person alive right now wants you to win, whether they're aware of it or not." His non-corporeal squeeze became a little tighter. "And you've got at least one not-alive person rooting for you too."

Never before had I wished I could cry so badly. I wanted to make myself small and let him rock me until I was soothed.

"You'll still come see me, right?" I said. "When I'm dreaming, after this is all over."

"Hell yeah. We'll do the impossible stuff we can only do in dreams, like ride motorcycles over the ocean and shit."

I laughed despite my fear. His sense of adventure and fearlessness was infectious. What I would have given to ride with him while he was alive.

"You ready, Rori?"

With my nod, the pressure of his embrace released me, and I felt myself floating away. "See you soon, Uncle Daren."

His smiling face became smaller, like I was actually traveling a physical distance. "Knock 'em dead, daughter of Demons."

* * *

I STARTED to rouse as if waking up from a deep sleep. Some noise was breaking through the thick fog that had settled over me like a suffocating blanket. The sound was muffled at first, fuzzy and muted. Slowly it grew sharper. Clearer.

"Rori!"

I tried to blink, tried to wipe away whatever was blurring my eyesight, but neither my hands or eyelids moved. Where was I? *Who* was I?

It felt like I was at the bottom of a muddy, murky lake,

looking for the surface. There were ripples and distortions, and everything was so dark, so unclear. I thought I could make out a man's face but wasn't sure.

Why couldn't I feel my body? Was I dead? Somewhere between life and death?

"Hello?" I tried to call out, but I didn't seem to have a voice.

Shut up! A harsh voice reprimanded me that seemed to come from everywhere. *Just be quiet, Aurora.*

Aurora. Was that my name? It was pretty.

"...back to us, paloma..."

Paloma. Was that also me? A nickname? It meant something in another language. How did I know that?

Memories and thoughts tickled at me with the more questions I asked, the more I became aware of myself. The answers were there, just out of reach. But as I woke, I stretched and grasped for them. Who called me paloma?

Santos! I realized with a start. My sweet fighter, the Butcher. A brutal killer by necessity and my loving, eager-to-please partner by choice. He was here. He was trying to reach me.

"Rori!" Someone else called my name, and an overwhelm of emotion flooded me at the sight of Torr. My first love, the one I never believed would be mine. He'd come for me too.

I tried calling out to both of them, but the fog blanketing me darkened and became heavier. It dragged me down like an anchor, and the faces of my men became murky again.

Wait, who were they?

Torr! Santos! Voicelessly, I screamed out their names, trying to reach them while also keeping them in my mind, my memory. But they were slipping away so easily, like water through my hands.

I was grasping at hundreds of tiny, fragile threads, trying to keep everything together without losing again. My own name.

My men. Who I was. My family. What happened to me. What I was fighting for.

Hold onto yourself, Aurora. Another voice that seemed to come from everywhere, but different than the first one. This one was masculine, warm. Somehow incredibly powerful and gentle. *Hold onto yourself. Do not lose sight of who you are.*

Who are you? I tried to scream into the silent, empty void pressing in all around me.

Louder. Use your voice. A third person was talking to me, feminine and familiar. This person had made me feel...annoyed. Frustrated. And yet I had immense respect for them. *No matter what she tells you, do not stop fighting. You're a daughter of Demons, so give her hell.*

"I don't know what's happening!" The sound of my own voice was shocking to me. I could hear myself!

At the same time, I felt myself pulled down further, the oppressive weight on me even more restrictive. My memories, my loves, and my awareness were further away than ever.

Look at his face, this man you love, the third voice commanded me. *Don't lose sight of him. Don't you dare forget him, Aurora.*

He was barely visible through the fog and the vast distance between us, but I saw the tension in his brow, the slope of his nose. His lips trembled as they moved and I strained to hear him. A tear tracked down his face. Why was he crying? Who was he, again?

"...don't become a fucking liar, Rori. Don't you dare fucking leave me like they did."

A tear dripped from his nose onto my lips, and holy shit, I could *feel* it.

"I love you too much to let you go."

"Torr!" I cried out with all the strength I could gather. "I'm

179

never fucking leaving you, meathead. You're mine. I love you. I will never be someone who abandons you."

It felt like trying to push a house off my chest, but I fought against that oppressive force holding me down with renewed vigor.

Torr's face became clearer, his heartbroken beautiful face. One day I would roast him for crying over me, but I needed to reach him first. He thought he was losing me, and I couldn't put him through that. I needed to kiss those tears away, hold him and tell him I was here, I was coming. And I would never leave him.

The more I fought against the current trying to drag me down, the more I remembered. The more of myself I regained.

I'm Aurora Wilder, president of the Vengeful Gods MC. I'm the eldest daughter of the Steel Demons MC. My twin brother is Daren. My two lovers are Torr and Santos. A deity has possessed me against my will, and for that, I'm one pissed off bitch.

For every new piece of myself I remembered, the invasive force inside me tried even harder to drag me back under.

Your vessel is mine. You are my prisoner, Aurora!

"Fuck you!" I screamed back. My throat, my actual physical throat ached from the scream, and it felt good. "Get the fuck out of my body!"

You can't get rid of me! You are mine.

"Go cease to exist, you rotten cunt! Fuck the hell off!"

I was *just* there. I could feel cool dirt beneath me, felt the weight of limbs pinning me down. I moved my own eyes, my own head, and I could see my men's tense faces.

"Torr! Santos!" I screamed so loud, my lungs ached. "I'm here! I see you!"

But something was wrong. Santos' eyes went completely black and Torr's completely white.

Over my body, which seemed to be lying face up on the

ground, Torr held his hands out, palm up, as if offering something to Santos on the other side of me. In response, Santos raised his machete over his head.

"No, what are you doing?" I demanded, now overrun by fear. "It's me! Santos, I love you."

He brought the blade down in a smooth arc with no hesitation. I felt the blade tear through me and screamed at the blinding pain.

I felt like I'd climbed up the rocky face of a cliff bare-handed and maimed to reach them. I'd used all my strength, fought to hold onto every little scrap of myself, only for them to toss me back down, hurtling toward my death.

That machete severed the last tie I had. The final thing connecting me to the men I loved.

In a freefall, I hurtled through darkness until there was nothing left.

19

HUDSON

The sight of Rori was terrifying. She was every bit an evil apparition from a horror movie. The white slip dress covered in blood. Those empty black eyes. I felt the evil from her like the weight of a boot on my chest. She was pure hatred, not the scared woman who ran to me because she wanted to sacrifice herself.

Torr and Santos closed in on her while the circle of women jumped up and tried to scatter.

I fell back on my weapons training and my orders from Torr. A cluster of women darted to the left, and I raised my gun to fire warning shots a few feet ahead of them. They stopped short, lifting their arms to cover their faces as they shrieked.

"Come quietly and you won't be harmed!" Devin called out.

The women slowly lowered themselves to all fours, hands splayed on the ground in a clear picture of surrender. I relaxed, allowing my aim to lower, and that was when they struck.

One was faster than the others, pulling a gun out of seemingly nowhere and firing off a shot before Devin or I realized what happened. By the second shot, our brains had caught up and we went diving for cover, flattening ourselves against a tree trunk.

"Well, so much for that," Devin hissed. He had two knives in each hand, slotted into the space between his fingers like claws. "You alright?"

"Yeah, you?"

"Fan-fucking-tastic. I love it when guns are just hidden in the leaf litter on the ground."

My breath came hard out of my chest and I tried to quiet it, listening for footsteps, voices, any clues about where our enemy was located.

"Shoot to kill," Devin reminded me. "And don't let any get away. Pretty sure they're all armed at this point."

"I know."

A month ago, that would have thrilled me. How many times over the years had I fantasized about killing these people?

Now, there was no pleasure, no surging satisfaction at the prospect of taking lives from those who had taken so much from me. I only wanted to see this through, to do what was necessary to get through another day. And maybe see a future where this cult didn't exist.

"Hey." Devin was distracted, peeking around the tree, and didn't answer me. As he pulled back to cover himself, I made sure he paid attention.

The kiss was short, but I made it count. I took my fill of his lips, swiping my tongue against his, and pulled away before he could react.

He stared at me, surprised and a little breathless, before he smirked. "What was that for?"

I shrugged, re-checking the ammo in my weapon under his heavy stare. "Just good luck, I guess."

He slid a hand around my neck, squeezing my nape as he leaned his forehead on mine. "We'll celebrate properly when this is over." It was a promise of delicious things, of touch that felt good. Orgasms for pleasure, not as a means to procreate.

Devin was exactly what I needed, when I needed it. He was both a friend and a welcome reset of my sexual hardwiring. I never thought I'd be into men. And maybe I wasn't, generally. Maybe it was just him.

I thought back to the conversation I had with Santos before riding out here. The swirling mess of my thoughts over the last few days had culminated into that conclusion the moment I voiced it. The guy I was sleeping with also had a thing for Rori.

And...maybe I did too.

That conversation would have to come much later though, if Rori or any of us even survived to that point.

Devin and I took turns covering each other, shooting at our attackers. He was decent with a gun, though I was better. He wanted to save his knives for guaranteed kills, so they stayed in his spare hand while he shot with the other.

I was damn lucky to be with an ambidextrous man.

After exchanging fire for several minutes, a flurry of movement caught my eye on the far side of the house.

"They're up to something over there," I said to Devin once we back-flatted against the tree again.

"Gonna have to be a lot more specific." He peeked around and let a knife fly, dropping one of our attackers in an instant.

"Don't know, I just saw movement around a corner."

"Well, shit. We're pinned down here for a minute." He returned to our cover and glanced at me. "How do you think Torr and Santos are doing?"

"Hopefully better than us." The worst thing about a shootout like this, where we were outnumbered five to one, was that it was time-consuming. I had no doubt we'd win. We were the better shots for sure, but there were simply more bullets flying toward us than away. We had to be careful as we decreased that number and gained the upper hand.

So far we'd dropped three of the women shooting at us. Only seven more to go. I could tell they weren't particularly experienced or skilled, but they had more than a rudimentary introduction to guns.

"Did you hear that?" I could barely hear it over the ringing in my ears, but there was some new sound in the air.

"Yeah." Devin cast a worried glance toward where I saw movement earlier. "Sounded like a car starting."

Not even a minute later, a Jeep shot out from where it had been hidden on the far side of the house. There were two women inside, the driver white-knuckling the steering wheel as she drove onto the main road, heading away from the safe houses.

"Fuck!" I trained my gun on the tires, firing at those increasingly smaller targets as they got further away.

Bark and splinters exploded near my ear and I ducked on instinct, covering my eyes. Our shooters had taken advantage of the distraction.

"We have to go after them." Devin grabbed my shirt at the back of my neck to lift my head up. "You alright?"

I blinked several times. "Yeah." Probably got some splinters in my cheek and ear canal but my eyes were fine.

"We gotta run for the bikes," he said. "You with me?"

"Yeah, I'll cover you. On three. Ready?"

We counted together, then I sprang out from behind the tree, running as fast as I could while returning fire. One more woman dropped.

Devin reached the motorcycles, starting mine and then his own while I blocked their line of sight to him.

"I got you, let's go!" he hollered.

Putting all my trust in him, I turned my back to our

attackers to mount my motorcycle. All I saw was a flash of metal catching the sunlight before three more dropped dead.

He was already tearing off down the road, and I leaned down over my handlebars, accelerating hard to catch up. We were still being shot at, and I wouldn't put it past them to climb into another vehicle and pursue us.

As chaotic as everything was right then, we had to keep our eye on the prize in front of us.

I caught up to Devin, slightly behind and flanking him. We were driving through the dust cloud kicked up by the Jeep ahead of us, our targets a dark silhouette just on the other side.

"You shoot their tires!" Devin yelled. "I'll cover us from the back."

I nodded and sped up to get ahead of him. Dust and gravel were killing my eyes but I needed them. I didn't dare blink as I came within twenty yards of the Jeep's bumper. Driving the bike with one hand, I raised my firing arm and tried my best to take careful aim. I could not afford to fuck this up. They could not get away.

The car started swerving just as I fired. Yeah it sucked for my aim, but that would be a boon if they rolled that damn Jeep for us. Even better if they went into a ravine or something.

I kept steady, following their movement with my eyes and my gun. When a clear shot lined up for me, I didn't hesitate. I fired.

And heard the click of an empty magazine.

"Fuck!" I roared. I needed two hands to reload and didn't feel confident about going hands-free on the bike. Reloading would take a split second though, and I fucking *needed* these shots.

In the moment I lifted my hand away to reach into my pocket, a cry of pain had me wrenching around to look behind me. Devin was nearly facedown on his dashboard, clutching his shoulder, which was wet and stained with dark blood.

That was all it took for me to lose control of the motorcycle. Not thinking about anything else, I tried to turn my whole body. I forgot I was driving a vehicle at all and tried to *run* to the man who drew me out of the darkness, who showed me what it was like to be human again.

The ground hit me hard with a full-body slap. My back, my chest, my ass. I got hit all over as I went rolling. Eventually I stopped, but the world kept spinning. Still, I forced myself up, knowing we were still being shot at.

"Devin!" I called, scanning the wobbly landscape for any sign of him as I fought to get my feet under me.

A massive dark shape zoomed past me, kicking up a massive cloud of dust. Another car?

"Devin!" I spun around helplessly, a sitting duck for our attackers, but no way in hell could I function in this fucked up place without him.

"I'm okay!"

The relief took nearly all of the strength from my legs, but I stayed upright as I went toward the sound of his voice.

Devin was still straddling his motorcycle, his feet planted on the ground, engine at a low rumble as he breathed hard, gripping his shoulder.

"They got a lucky shot on me," he panted, grimacing with pain. "But I think it went all the way through, so there's that silver lining."

Once I knew he was okay, reality hit me like that fall I'd just taken. "I let them get away."

Together we looked at the horizon, where a now-distant dust cloud surrounded two vehicles shrinking on the horizon as they drove away.

"Fuck." My hands tore through my hair, which I wanted to rip out in frustration. "Goddamnit, I fucked that up so bad."

"We'll figure something out," Devin said wearily. "It'll be okay, Hud."

But I wasn't ready to stop being pissed off yet. I wanted nothing more in the world than to eradicate this cult. I was a sharpshooting champion in my teens. Sure, I was out of practice, but I was still fucking accurate enough to make hits. This should have been the easiest fucking task for me, and I fucked it up.

"You were worried about me." Devin could sense the anger pouring off me, it seemed. "I shouldn't have yelled like a little bitch and distracted you."

"Not your fault. Getting shot fucking hurts."

"You're telling me," he groaned, tentatively lifting his hand from his bad shoulder.

Guilt shot through me. Here I was, throwing a pity party for myself, relatively unscathed, while Devin had actually been injured.

"Come on, let's get that taken care of." I pulled off my jacket and then my shirt so he would have something to stem the bleeding with.

Once we had his shoulder wrapped up, I got on his bike and he settled in behind me, holding my waist with his good arm.

"Do you think they got Rori back?" Devin rested his chin on my shoulder.

"Guess we'll find out in a sec." I accelerated gently, heading back for the safe houses.

"She'll chew us the fuck out for failing if she is back," Devin said. "Thing is, I'm kind of hoping for it."

"Me too," I admitted.

Once I parked in front of the house, Torr and Santos came around the side, both of them looking as somber as pallbearers at a funeral. Torr held a limp, unresponsive Rori cradled to his chest.

"Oh God..." Devin trailed off mournfully.

I helped him off the bike, then we hurried over to the two men who looked like broken shells of themselves.

"Is she...?" I didn't dare finish the question.

"She's breathing and has a pulse," Santos said flatly, his eyes vacant. "But we don't know if she's...there."

Torr carried her wordlessly into the house, assumedly to bathe her and put her in bed. She was covered in dirt and leaf litter on top of the blood that had already coated her arms, legs, and dress.

"What happened?" Devin demanded. "Is Tezca still...in you?"

Santos shook his head. "The gods left us as soon as the deed was done. They drew the Dark Mother out and cut her away from Rori, but..." He pulled in a shaky breath, looking as if he was moments away from tears. "She fought so fucking hard. We don't...we just don't know if there's anything left of her."

"Can you find out?" I asked.

"If she wakes up."

"Fuck." I was saying that a lot today. "I'm so sorry, Santos."

He pulled in another breath, clearing his throat as he composed himself. "How'd you guys do? I saw some bodies. You get 'em all?"

"No," I said on a big sigh. "Two vehicles got away. I ran out of ammo, heard Devin take fire behind me and I just...couldn't keep it together."

Santos' head jerked toward Devin, as if noticing his injury for the first time. "You okay?"

"All things considered, yeah." Devin tried hard not to grimace. "I'll live."

Santos returned his focus to me. "How many people total got away?"

"I think five. There were two in the first car we chased. Then I'm pretty sure there were three in the one after us."

Santos nodded. "I'll let Torr know as soon as...you know, as soon as he's ready to think about something else."

"Yeah, of course."

"I'll see who I can call to get that looked at," Santos said to Devin before heading into the house, no doubt to check on his woman who may or may not be lost for good.

I turned to Devin with a sigh. "Let's find some clean gauze and alcohol until you can get some real medical attention."

"Sounds great."

We searched through the fighters' house, going through the motions while the big picture situation began to sink in.

The Sisters of Bathory might not have their goddess anymore, but they would regroup and, eventually, retaliate.

And we just might have lost our best weapon against them.

20

TORRANCE

R ori wasn't waking up.
I lost track of everything outside of her. It might have been a few days that had passed or a month. I didn't know. When I didn't keel over from exhaustion, I spent every waking moment staring at her face, willing those eyes to open, those lips to part.

I was only distantly aware of the movement around me. The club had moved back into the safehouses. I must have called them back at some point. Or maybe Santos did. It was all a haze outside of Rori.

Astarte returned in her dove form, as did Tezca as a jaguar. They often watched over her with me.

"Please tell me," I implored the gods. "Just tell me if I'm getting her back or not."

That's her decision, Astarte told me helpfully.

"Decision? She's fucking comatose; she can't make decisions!"

She has the power to return. She only needs to find and seize it, Tezca added, only slightly more helpful.

"So she *can* come back." I said. "If she can, then she will."

She is lost. She must find her way back.

I dropped my head into my hands, but that meant I wasn't looking at Rori anymore, so I lifted it up again.

"Come on, creep." I'd forgotten how many times I had repeated those words to her. "I know you heard me back then. I *know* you won't leave me."

Not a single twitch of movement on her face. Time passed. Santos entered and left the room. Motorcycles roared in the distance. None of it mattered.

At some point, I felt the weight of someone's hand on my shoulder, Santos' hand.

"Torr, you with me?" Apparently he'd been saying my name for a while.

"Yeah." I rubbed my weary eyes. "What's up?"

"A couple of guys just rode up. They say they're Rori's dad and uncle?"

I shot up out of the chair, panic lighting a fire under my ass, and stared at him. "What are they doing here?"

Santos shrugged. "I dunno, just coming to say hi, I guess."

"Shit." I rubbed my face hard. "Fuck. What do we tell them?"

"The truth, I assume." His eyes scanned over Rori as if looking for any changes in her condition. "They did this kind of thing back in their day, right? Maybe they can help—"

"First, they'll murder us for letting this happen to her," I groaned. "Although it's not like we don't deserve it."

This was going to be a shitshow. Aside from calling her aunt about the safe houses and supplies, then her dad about the logo for the club, Rori had been insistent that she did not want her family involved. Both for their protection and, I imagined, her own pride. She'd never admit it, but I knew she wanted to prove that she didn't need older adults for this situation.

Her family let her be independent, for the most part, but

they had always known about these safe houses. She hadn't checked in for a while, naturally, so they were probably doing the regular concerned parent thing and decided to swing by.

At least there was the small miracle that they hadn't shown up during the brief time this place was under the Sisterhood's control.

"Let's get this over with," I grumbled to Santos, moving past him to the bedroom door. "Should I get shovels?" he asked, following me down the stairs. "They're probably gonna have us dig our own graves, right?"

How he could muster up a sense of humor right now, I had no idea. But I was grateful for it, and a small snicker left my mouth. "Yeah. Better check the garage."

As I had feared, Shadow was the dad who'd decided to show up. Rori always said he was the biggest softie of her fathers, but from my outside perspective, I knew he was also the most protective of her.

Shadow's half-brother, Rori's uncle Grudge, stood next to him. Grudge was an OG member of Sons of Odin and one of Valorie's fathers.

The two older bikers sat astride their massive custom rides, relaxed and talking softly to each other as if they were guests waiting to be greeted. Grudge's hands moved in a fluid sign language while Shadow responded with his voice and an occasional gesture of his own.

Their bikes were shut off, and Shadow's had several compartments loaded onto his. Most of the fighters had made themselves scarce, unsure of what to do with these two strange men in the driveway.

Val headed for the front door just as I was, and she shot me a worried look that spelled out exactly how I felt.

"What do we tell them?" she whispered frantically.

"The truth," I answered, grabbing the front door and holding it open for her.

"Fuck," she muttered before stepping outside and plastering a huge smile on her face. "Heyyy, Dad! Uncle Shadow. What are you old farts doing here?"

Grudge made a disapproving grunting sound, then his face split into a wide smile as his daughter approached. "Is that any way to respect your elders, young lady?" he asked her in sign language.

"Shut up. You know I love you." Val laughed, signing as she spoke.

"Torr," Shadow said to me by way of greeting, holding his hand out. "You look like shit."

"Yeah, I'm—I, uh—"

While I stammered, hunting for the right words to say, he gave me a small punch on the shoulder as he dismounted his bike. "You haven't been lifting. I can tell," he added with a teasing smirk as he walked around me to greet his niece with a hug.

"What brings you guys here?" Val's eyes darted between the two of them, her voice taking on a higher, nervous pitch. "We, uh, weren't expecting you."

Shadow gestured to the compartments on the back of his bike. "I got your club gear. Finished the logo and made it into patches. Brought some leather cuts in a few sizes too, we figured not all of you would have them. And," he turned, making sure to catch my eye as well as Val's, "I brought my tattoo equipment."

"Wow," Val breathed, wringing her hands. "Everything to make us official."

"Rori deserves nothing less," Shadow said with a smile. "Where is she, by the way?"

"Can we see the logo?" Val said in answer. I didn't know if she was trying to stall for some reason or was just that damn nervous. Either way, Shadow was catching on that something was wrong.

"I really think Rori should be the one to unveil it." He turned to me, his scarred face hardening. "Is she okay? I figured she'd be out here talking my ear off by now."

"She's...I..." Even though I wanted to hold nothing back, hide nothing from this man I respected immensely, what could I say? How did you tell someone their daughter was technically alive but not with us?

"Torrance." Shadow growled out my full name in warning. "Where the fuck is my daughter?"

"She's upstairs. In the bedroom," I managed to spit out.

"And?" he pressed. "Is she sick? Injured? Down for a nap? You need to tell me what the fuck is going on."

"There was a battle," I forced out through the knot in my throat.

"Okay." The calmness drained from his voice. "So she got hurt?"

"No, she...she got possessed."

"Possessed?" Shadow's eyes sharpened with understanding. "By a god?"

"Yes. We got it out of her, but...she hasn't woken up in..." I glanced at Val.

"Today marks five days," she supplied.

"Who possessed her? Where the fuck are your gods? And who the fuck were you fighting?" Shadow's rapid-fire questions were the ones of a frantically worried father, and I fought to compose myself to answer everything for him.

"Our gods possessed us, Santos and I, to draw the one out of her and sever it. She was possessed by something called the Dark Mother, which is worshiped by an all-female cult called the Sisters of Bathory."

Grudge made a sound of disbelief and shock, while Shadow's mouth dropped open, his face going pale. "You did *not* just fucking say that," he whispered after a long silence.

I nodded. "We're all just waiting for her to wake up."

Shadow's gaze went somewhere else, focusing on nothing in front of him. He must have gone deep inside his own head, maybe even his past. Scrubbing one hand down his face, he traced the long scar cutting through one eye, the one that turned white, I assumed from said injury.

Rori had never gone into detail about what caused her father's scarred appearance. I got the sense that she didn't know the full story herself. Although with his current reaction to the cult's name, I could start to make some educated guesses.

"Fucking hell!" And just like that, Shadow was back, pacing around like a caged animal. "I told her. I fucking *told* her not to engage with them!"

"Shadow—" I started toward him, holding an arm out for...comfort, maybe? I didn't entirely know but was stopped abruptly by a large hand clamping down on my bicep and pulling me back.

Grudge leveled me with an expression that was somehow both calm and intense. He lifted his hands and signed to me, "Leave him be. He needs to process."

Of course Shadow's brother would have more insight into his emotional state, so I was inclined to listen.

Abruptly, Shadow stopped pacing. His massive chest and shoulders heaved with every ragged, strained breath. "I need to see her," he said and immediately headed for the house.

My own protective instincts surged. I was already distressed enough that I wasn't at her side at this very moment. "I'll come with you."

Shadow grunted disapprovingly but didn't argue. "Just don't get in my way, Torr."

What could I do but obey? Silently, I followed him through

the house and up to the bedroom. The moment he entered and saw her, his whole demeanor changed. His shoulders lowered on a long, slow breath, and his hands relaxed from their clenched position. He moved quietly to her bedside, as if taking care not to disturb her in sleep.

"Hey, Rormeister," he whispered, taking her hand as he sat next to her. With a quiet laugh, he added, "My stubborn, impossible daughter. Why didn't you listen to me? You need to do what your old man says sometimes."

He spoke to her softly for a few more minutes, then moved some hair off her forehead and bent to kiss her there. When he stood from her bedside and looked at me, the loving, doting father was gone. He was once again a hardened biker.

"Rori told me she made you VP," he bit out, crossing his arms.

"That's right."

"Since she's currently incapacitated and I'm one of the two most experienced riders here, I'm overriding that decision."

I stared at him. "What?"

"You're no longer in charge in her stead. Grudge and I are." He cocked his head, regarding me like I was mud scraped off his boot. "If you don't like it, you're welcome to challenge me."

Yeah, right. Shadow being thirty years older than me didn't change the fact that he was one of the deadliest assassins that had ever lived. He'd wipe the floor with me.

"You can't just override the position *she* put me in," I argued. "Rori trusted me, and you're going against her wishes."

"You are not worthy of the position she put you in," he answered coldly, then pointed to the bed where she lay motionless. "And *that* is precisely the reason why."

21

HUDSON

The whole atmosphere changed when Rori's dad and uncle showed up and decided they were in charge. Now, instead of just waiting anxiously for her to wake up, we were taking orders from a couple of strangers.

Torr made introductions, explaining who they were and that we could trust them. But the guy looked like the ghost of a dog who had been beaten all his life. With Rori still unresponsive and now being stripped of his VP title, he was a shell of his former self.

The day-to-day of being under Shadow and Grudge wasn't all that different from before, just more regimented. We worked out, practiced shooting and hand-to-hand combat, and learned more about motorcycle mechanics. The days were busy, but we still had free time to chill, talk to Malik if we needed to, or my preference, practice shooting some more.

When we faced off with the cult again, my shots needed to be guaranteed kills. I would not fuck up again.

I spent every available moment of daylight target practicing. Even when the sun went down, I'd go by the house's exterior lights until someone yelled that my shots were too loud and they were trying to sleep.

I'd gotten up before sunrise one morning and decided to try arranging the targets so the rising sun would be in my eyes. I had to prepare for everything.

I'd gone a few rounds with two different handguns when the low voice came from behind me. "You're a good shot."

Out of habit, I set the gun down and removed the magazine before looking over my shoulder. "Thanks."

Shadow stood watching with his arms crossed, the bright sun lighting up the hundreds of tiny scars criss crossing over his forearms and biceps. The biggest scar, which cut through his face, made him look especially menacing.

"Why are you shooting into the sun?" He didn't sound anything but curious as he came forward, squinting and shielding his eyes with one hand.

"Just trying to prepare for anything."

He made a small grunt of acknowledgment as he scanned the selection of weapons I had laid out to practice with. "It's good to challenge yourself, but staring into the sun will cause permanent damage. Let's clean these while we wait for sunset, alright?"

He had already opened a cleaning kit, sat on a tree stump, and taken one of the rifles across his lap. I had little choice but to follow suit.

Shadow waited until I was settled in on the stump next to him, cleaning a .40 caliber handgun, before speaking again. "Ask me what's been on your mind."

I froze, my hands holding two pieces of my weapon.

"Go on," he urged with a gentleness I didn't expect from such an intimidating man. "It's alright. I can talk about it."

I braced myself with a deep breath, praying to Tezca and

Astarte that I wasn't misreading him. "You were a blood bag, weren't you? For the cult."

"Yes, I was." He smoothed an oiled cloth down the rifle barrel with care.

"For how long?" Going off of how extensively scarred he was, I'd have to guess years.

"First twenty years of my life, give or take a few."

I dropped the pieces I was holding, feeling a strange mix of awed and horrified. "Twenty years? From childhood to..."

Shadow nodded, continuing with his calm, almost meditative cleaning of the weapon. "I was born into the cult and had just reached adulthood when I got out. At least, I think so. I never did find out exactly how old I am. They don't keep birth certificates for us, you know?"

The evidence sat right in front of me. He knew what a blood bag was, and that horrifying reality was all over his skin. And yet it didn't make sense with...*him*. This family man and father. This person who was calm and in control, whose presence held power and the confidence to use it.

Despite Shadow's scarred appearance, he was...normal. If even well-adjusted.

"How?" was all I could ask.

"You're going to have to be more specific." He reassembled one weapon with practiced ease, then took another one into his lap.

"How did you..." There wasn't one word or phrase that could sum up the transformation this man must have gone through. Survive? Heal? Escape? Get over it?

"It started with a very persistent woman." A smile pulled at Shadow's lips. He seemed to know what I was getting at. "She said good morning to me every day that she saw me. It...unnerved me. Made me suspicious. Defensive. But also curious."

"Rori's mother?" I asked.

"Yes." That single word from him was filled with pride and warmth. "To this day, I still don't know why she put in the effort to talk to me. But she changed everything for me because she *chose* me."

He paused, straightening as his face went solemn. "It wasn't easy or painless by any means. There were lots of setbacks and I almost lost her, multiple times. I can still feel the blades cutting me in dreams sometimes." He paused again, mismatched eyes focusing on me. "What I'm trying to say is, it's a long, hard road with many pitfalls. The love of a good woman wasn't the only thing that got me through it, but...I wouldn't have been able to do it without her. She was my reason and my strength."

"I'm happy for you," I told him with a nod. "But I don't have anyone like that."

"Sure, you do. You've got Devin, your whole club." He pointed a finger at my chest. "You were also an adult when you got captured, if I'm not mistaken, so you know this cult is batshit. You *know* they're not how the majority of the world is. You didn't have to learn that like me."

"I know. I know, but I—"

"No excuses. You can't take out your trauma on others. You're out now, you have to do the work to heal."

"That's what I'm doing. Why I'm practicing. I need to take them down because I need...closure."

Shadow's gaze fell from me to the weapon in his hands. "Yeah, maybe I do too," he muttered. Putting it aside, he added, "Are you willing to fight alongside my daughter and niece, even trusting them with your life?"

"Yes," I said without hesitation. "I don't know Rori that well, but the people I trust believe in her. She's only shown that she wants to do the right thing."

"Good man." Shadow nodded. "And listen, Hudson." He was quiet for a while before speaking again. "What they did doesn't define you. It's not part of you. It's not what you are. *You decide who and what you are, and no one can take that away from you. Remember that when you feel lost.*"

I nodded, unable to respond verbally with the sudden emotion that swept over me. I felt acknowledged and seen. Eventually I grunted out, "Thanks."

He nodded curtly and stood, quickly re-assembling and reloading his weapon. "Sun's down. It's good practice to shoot at dusk. Try the fifty-yard target with this one."

He placed the gun in front of me and just like that, we were back to business.

I shot targets under his instruction until it was too dark to see. Once we started to pack it in and head back inside, a door slammed forcefully. With rapid footfalls, a figure cloaked in shadow ran toward us.

"What's going on?" Shadow called, stepping in front of me as if to protect me.

The figure's face became illuminated under the porch light as he approached us, the Hunter.

He panted when he stopped. "Been looking all over for you...sir." Meaning Shadow, not me.

"I'm here. What happened?"

The Hunter's face broke into a grin as he delivered the news. "Rori's awake."

22

RORI

My eyelids were heavy as I blinked, fighting through immense fatigue to make sense of my surroundings. When I started to push myself up, someone grabbed me, bringing me to their chest in a crushing embrace. My senses were still coming online but it could only be Torr.

My arms went around him in return, the feel of him strange and unfamiliar. Had he lost weight? How long had I been out?

Lips brushed my cheek with a whisper of my name, and then I was kissing him desperately. I kissed him like I needed his air to live, the press of lips and stroke of tongues making me more alive than oxygen ever could.

The unfamiliarity didn't bleed in until we broke away. This mouth was different. The rasp of his beard was softer, the bristles longer than Torr's or Santos' stubble.

I pulled away to find Devin staring back at me.

The tenderness in his dark eyes gave way to full-blown panic.

"Shit. I'm sorry. Really, I'm sorry. I don't know what—"

He stood from the bed, backing away on clumsy feet to crash directly into Torr's chest.

The sight of him broke a dam of emotion that I hadn't even been aware of. A sob breaking through my chest was all it took for him to maneuver around Devin and take me into his arms.

Always so strong, the love of my life held me, rocked me as I shuddered out tears and ugly sobs. I cried for his parents, the childhood that I now knew thanks to that parasite that had been in me. I had no right to know, but I did anyway. I cried at the sheer bone-deep relief that he was here. Mine. My north star, steadfast and constant.

"I love you," he whispered repeatedly into my neck, stroking my hair and back with a heavy, comforting hand. "I love you, Aurora Wilder, and I will never let you go."

"Took you long enough," I said on a sniffle and shaky breath.

He laughed softly, pulling back to cradle my face in his hands and rest his forehead on mine. "It's so fucking good to have you back."

"I'm never leaving you." My hands drifted all over him, like I couldn't get enough confirmation that he was here, real and solid. And that *I* was in control of my own body again. *I* could touch him, feel him with my own hands.

"I know." He brought one of my hands to his lips and kissed my knuckles. "I know you won't."

A throat-clearing sound pulled my attention away from him, and I looked up, my mouth open with the intention of telling whoever it was to fuck off. The last person I expected to see looming in my doorway was my own damn father.

"Dad?" I choked. "What are you doing here?"

Shadow wasn't alone. He was flanked by Hudson on one side and Devin on the other. There was more activity behind him, like people were coming up the stairs to see for themselves that I was awake.

"Rori..."

My name, choked out in a rough whisper, was the only

warning I got before getting wrapped up in a tight hug that took me right back to childhood. Torr must have darted out of the way in a flash with how fast my father moved.

Shadow felt like an impenetrable shield surrounding me, his strength protecting me from all of the evils of the world. Worn leather and gunpowder filled my nose, and I burrowed into that safe, familiar place. After the hell I'd just endured, there was nowhere else I wanted to be.

All too quickly, he pulled away and straightened his spine. Subtly, he did the same to me, hands on my shoulders pushing back until I sat up tall enough to meet his eye.

"Welcome back, President," my father said, his gruff voice returning. "It seems you have a lot to catch up on."

* * *

"So the Dark Mother is gone?"

After being able to shower and eat, I was surrounded by my club just like in those early days that felt so long ago. Only now, Shadow and my uncle Grudge joined, watching us like judgmental chaperons overseeing a bunch of unruly kids.

Yes. The answer came from Tezca, sitting at the edge of the couch next to Santos, who all but held me in his lap. He and Torr were extremely reluctant to lose physical contact with me ever since I woke up. I could feel Devin's eyes on me like a physical touch too. His embrace and kiss remained imprinted in my mind, even lingering on my skin like an echo of what happened. But that was not where my focus needed to be right now.

When we severed the Dark Mother from you, we also severed her personhood. She is no longer a self-aware entity.

"So that's it?" The Hunter straightened in his chair, excitement brimming in his voice. "It's over?"

"Not until the cult is eradicated," I said. "Otherwise, they'll

209

be able to continue sacrificing men, rebuild their resort, and eventually bring their goddess back." I cocked an eyebrow at Tezca. "Am I right?"

You are.

"So there's still work to do." I scanned the faces of my people, my riders. Even now, after everything they'd been through, they looked as solemn and focused as soldiers awaiting orders. "Seems these old men have been keeping you all in shape while I've been down for a nap." I cocked my head toward Shadow and Grudge. "Are the Vengeful Gods ready for some action?"

A chorus of shouts rang out from the others, ranging from, "Fuck yeah!" to, "Goddamn, finally," along with a bunch of crotch-grabbing and obscene gestures. I laughed at the antics, realizing just then how much I'd missed my crew of animals.

"Grudge and I will be joining you," Shadow said when the noise ebbed. "You'll be in charge, of course. But this is personal for us too." He and my uncle shared a glance. "This will be...the closure that we've needed. An act of finally putting this behind us for good."

I nodded, the understanding passing between us silently. This was my mission, what I had been called to do. But my father and uncle also needed to be there. Maybe they had always meant to be. Only the gods knew for sure.

"We ride out in the morning, then," I decided. "No point in dragging this out. We've got guns, so do they. We're human, and so are they. Time to find out whose sense of vengeance is stronger."

"They also have children with them," Santos reminded me. "That's worth exercising a little bit of caution, right?"

"Their armed soldiers won't be the ones guarding the children, too much risk for a mistake. Those children are their future, so they'll be kept safe at all costs. We take out the armed guard first, then we find the kids."

"How do we know where to go?" someone else called out.

My gaze slid toward the window, knowing full well what I'd see. Astarte sat on the ledge, preening her white feathers like she was any other bird.

"We have eyes in the sky," I answered. "A guiding light."

23

RORI

"You okay?"

I kept my forehead on the windowpane while glancing back at Torr, who stood in the doorway. "Now why on Satan's scorched earth would you ask me a silly thing like that?"

He chuckled on his way over to me, his expression almost bashful. "Guess there's no easy way to ask how you're holding up after a coma and possession by an evil god."

"Guess not." I returned his smile. The sensation felt weird on my face, but I felt a little bit of joy returning. That easy comfort that we shared. "I'm okay, I guess. Just taking it minute by minute. I still get these moments where it suddenly hits me that I'm *me* again. And how hard I fought just to get back."

Torr gave me an uneasy look. "We don't have to ride out in the morning, you know. It's okay to rest, Rori. You're allowed to recover from this before putting on your president's cut again."

"No." I rolled my forehead from side to side on the windowpane. "I'll recover when this cult is wiped off the earth. I can't even start healing until they're gone." My head lifted from the glass. "I've reinstated you as VP, so your advice from now on better be good."

Torr chuckled again. "Just thought I'd try. And to think I was worried about you because you're not the staring-out-the-window type."

"I just might become one. Feels like I can think better with cool glass on my forehead." After a while, I turned around to face Torr, tucking my feet underneath me in the armchair. "Did you see Devin kiss me?"

He nodded calmly. "Yeah, I did."

"I thought it was you, at first," I admitted. "I thought you felt different."

"Is that what's got you staring out the window all longingly and shit?"

"Fuck you." After a few seconds, I added, "That's part of it."

"I'm fine with it, if that's what you're wondering."

"Fine with what?" I wanted to hear him say the words.

"You and him. Him being one of yours, along with me and Santos."

"He's with Hudson, though," I pointed out.

Torr grinned. "I think Hudson likes you too."

My knee-jerk reaction was to reject that notion, to hotly deny it. *Me? Hudson? Pfft, no fucking way.* But my clearest, most recent memory of him prevented me from saying that out loud. He'd talked me out of ending my life. He had hugged me, comforted me in the last few moments I had control of myself.

"He's alright," was the admittance I allowed.

Torr gave me an, *Uh-huh, sure,* look as he unlaced his boots. Wordlessly, he reclined on the bed, and I immediately went over to join him. Together, we shifted into a position that was as natural and familiar as breathing. My head on his shoulder and leg over his. His arm around my back until his hand nestled into my waist, with his opposite hand resting on my knee.

We let out a sigh once we found a place to settle, relaxing into each other for the first time in what felt like years. But even while nestled against him, my mind couldn't relax.

"Did you ever find out what happened to your birth parents?" I already knew the answer but had to start the conversation somewhere.

"No." Torr's thumb traced the dip in my waist. "Why, what's up?"

His patience was saintly as I worked up the nerve to speak. "She told me."

His thumb abruptly stopped moving. "The Dark Mother?"

"Yes." My fingers curled into his shirt. "I'm so sorry, Torr. I couldn't believe this cult had affected your life too."

"Tell me."

He was quiet as I relayed what the Dark Mother had told me. Like me, Torr's body became gradually less relaxed. His hand drifted from my waist up to my shoulder, which he squeezed almost painfully when I said where his mother was now, the condition she was in.

"They never abandoned you." I smoothed a hand over his chest, trying to read his expression. "They knew the cult would kill you or worse, torture you to set an example. They didn't have many choices, but they gave you the best possible chance of survival."

He might as well have turned to stone for how much he was responding, so I continued running my palm up, down, and across his torso. "And I couldn't be more grateful to them for doing that, for being brave enough to lead the cultists away from you." My hand stopped while I stared up at the side of his face. "Because if they hadn't, I might have never had you in my life."

After what seemed like an eternity, Torr brought his lips to my forehead. "Will you help me find them? After all this is over."

I hugged tightly around his waist and felt the crush of his arm against my shoulder. "You know how I am about family. I'll be happy to."

* * *

It was biker club tradition to throw a raging party the night before a long ride, or especially, a big battle. Said party would usually consist of, but not be limited to getting tattoos, drinking, and fucking. By sundown, I had started at the top of the list and planned to work my way down as the night carried on.

The kitchen table served as my father's tattoo station. I was sprawled on my back, shirt and bra straps pulled down and off my shoulders to give Shadow access to my chest, where he proceeded to ink the vengeful god, the icon of my club.

"It really needed to be this spot, huh?" Shadow grumbled over the buzzing of his machine as he traced the pen drawing below my collarbones.

"Don't be weird," I snorted. "You've inked tons of womens' titties."

"I'm nowhere near *that* area, daughter mine."

"All the more reason for you to not be weird about it." His brooding silence continued without answer, brow furrowed over his eyes, rapt with concentration on his work. "Are you mad at me, Dadow?" I asked in a softer voice.

He straightened with a heavy sigh, and the buzzing machine quieted as he lifted the needle from my skin. "I'm not mad, I'm—"

"Don't say disappointed. That's even worse."

He let out a dry chuckle while resuming his work, touching the needle down to my sternum. "I distinctly remember telling you to stay away from this cult."

"I didn't know who they were until after the whole thing

with the resort," I argued. "Besides, it's not like you gave me any context or reason. 'Watch out for the men-hating psychotic bitches' would have been a great heads up."

Shadow shook his head, eyes following the lines of his ink. "I thought I was being paranoid. I never thought you'd actually run into them. I never—shit."

He straightened again, setting the tattoo gun down as he started at some blank space on the wall.

"They were never supposed to touch you," he said after a long silence. "You were never supposed to know a world with this kind of evil. Fuck, Rori. I never wanted this to be *your* fight."

"But it is," I told him quietly. "This is what I was chosen to do. To finish what you started."

Stubbornly, he shook his head again. "We should have protected you from this. Years ago, Grudge and I should have done this ourselves rather than burying our heads in the sand."

"You didn't bury your heads in the sand, you were healing." I sat up, swinging my legs to dangle over the edge of the table. "You were being our dad, Mom's husband. Running your tattoo shop, taking care of your family. You did everything right, Dadow. By living so well, you told this cult, 'fuck you, right in the eyeball'."

He chuckled softly at that. "I wanted you and your siblings to have what I never had. We all wanted that. You grew so fast and we loved you so much, I never wanted to miss a single moment." His face darkened again. "But if I had taken a damn minute to consider the future—"

"You couldn't have predicted a damn thing. Seriously, Dad." I angled myself to face him head-on. "I really believe this was how it was all meant to play out. You were meant to escape them, to live and survive. To meet the love of your life and become a hero and a father. Then it was my turn to carry out the next phase. So that's what I'm going to do."

Shadow sighed heavily, but his eyes brightened and a smile played at his lips. "How did you become so wise?"

"Being possessed by a deity manifested out of hatred has a way of putting things into perspective."

He chuckled again, picking up his machine. "So you want your tattoo or not, President?"

"Yes, sir." I swung my legs to extend them along the length of the table again and reclined back into position.

"Don't underestimate them," he said as he resumed tracing a line. "Especially not now, so close to the end. They didn't have their goddess back in my day."

He didn't need to worry about that. Having the Dark Mother inside me had taught me more than I ever expected.

24

DEVIN

"I kissed her."

Hudson's expression didn't change. I almost thought he hadn't heard me. He sat on the porch railing, holding a beer on his knee as he watched some of the guys play a drunken touch football game in the driveway. Half of the shirtless team were proudly sporting their freshly outlined Vengeful Gods tattoos on their chests, stomachs, or backs.

At some point, I'd get mine as well.

I wasn't sure exactly when my loyalty to Rori became ironclad. Maybe it had always been there, an invisible motive hidden beneath my frustration at being attracted to her. Something that only came to the surface when I realized we could lose her, and then in the soul-shaking relief when she came back.

All of that was stuff I had to work through. But I also owed loyalty and honesty to Hudson.

If I were to gain something with her, I didn't want to lose him. It would kill me to do so. He felt a certain way toward Rori as well, and while it felt like a pipe dream for all five of us, Torr and Santos included, to end up a happy family, I remained clinging to that hope.

"Did you feel something?"

"Hm?" Hudson had finally spoken and pulled me out of my swirling mess of thoughts.

"Did you feel something when you kissed her?" he repeated.

"Yes," I admitted with a resigned nod.

"Similar to what you feel for me?"

"Similar but different." I yearned to touch him, to comfort and reassure him, but his posture was stiff and I knew he wouldn't be responsive. "It doesn't diminish what I feel for you at all. You're two different people, so what I feel is just...different for each of you."

I wanted to apologize for what I'd done, but it would be a lame attempt at absolving myself of responsibility and a lie on top of that. Hudson deserved better.

"I'm sorry for hurting you," I decided on instead. I was still an asshole, but at least that sorrow was genuine. "I never intended to go behind your back. I only wanted you to feel good."

"Jesus, stop."

I froze, taken aback as Hudson took a long pull of beer.

"We just decided to fool around. It's not like we got married. I never expected you to never want or touch someone else."

It took a moment for those words to sink in. "Oh."

"Honestly, I saw you falling for her from a mile away." He passed the beer bottle between his hands. "Probably since that night you all got me out, when you wrapped up her leg and carried her off like she was your bride."

"Well, she couldn't exactly walk."

"Right."

He didn't say anything else for a while, so I dared to keep going. "So you're not upset?"

Hudson pulled in a deep breath, his gaze still trained on the running, tackling, and laughing going on in front of us. "I almost want to be, but I'm not."

"Because...?" My worst fear in that moment was finding out he actually didn't feel as strongly for me as I did for him.

"Because I knew it was bound to happen." He set the now-empty beer bottle aside on the railing next to him. "Because I knew on some level, you started up this thing with me to distract yourself from her."

"That's not true," I protested. "I had always wanted you, since before her, before all of this. I won't deny that I was selfish. *I* wanted to be the reason you healed. I wanted to be the one who made you feel pleasure again, feel strong and confident again. *That* was what I always wanted. I...I didn't expect her."

Hudson let out a soft little laugh. "It's funny how the things we're meant for are the last things we expect."

I stared at his side profile, completely lost as to what to feel. "Are you saying I'm not meant for you?"

"What do you want, Devin?"

"What do *you* want?" I shot back. "You're a whole person, remember? You can make your own choices now."

He shook his head as he swung around, hopping off the railing to stand next to me. "I'm still too fucked in the head to really know what I want."

I moved closer to him. "Then I'll stay with you until you figure that out."

"But what do you *want*, Devin?" he pressed.

"I want you both," I admitted in a whisper. "I don't want to choose."

"What are you two doing moping out here?"

We whirled around to see Rori striding out onto the porch, a thick white bandage taped across her chest from her collarbones to underneath her T-shirt. Her face was flushed, probably still

riding off the adrenaline from her tattoo session. She approached us with a short tumbler of liquor in her hand, though her eyes were sharp as they darted between us. She looked battle-ready and not the least bit inebriated.

Even so, I couldn't resist poking the bear. "Doesn't alcohol thin the blood? You'll need a fresh bandage if you keep that up."

"Oh, fuck off. This thing's halfway healed already." Rori couldn't resist biting back, as I knew she would. "Everyone's is healing super fast." She gave a small smile that almost looked sad. "Can't help but feel like it's a final gift from our vengeful gods. Better get your ink done soon if you want the superhuman healing."

"I've hardly got any room left." Hudson chuckled as he rotated his thoroughly inked arms.

"Yeah, right. You've got this big open spot right here." Rori yanked down the front of his shirt, touching her forefinger to his sternum. "Perfect spot. Big ol' empty canvas."

"You sure it's big enough?" He smirked at her and didn't look the slightest bit uncomfortable with her standing so close, nor with her touch on his bare skin.

If anything, he seemed to be flirting right back.

"It'll do the job." Rori returned his smile and stepped back, releasing her hold on his shirt. She clearly didn't want to crowd him, didn't want to cross any boundaries he may or may not have established. "Your skin holds ink beautifully, by the way."

"Thanks." Hudson actually blushed. "Helps when they don't see much sunlight for a few years."

Rori had been in the middle of taking a sip from her drink, then promptly choked and began coughing.

"Easy." Hudson actually patted her back when she doubled over. "No need to swallow it all at once."

Rori wheezed like she couldn't figure out whether to cough or laugh. I too was dumbfounded by Hudson's flirting and innuendo. He seemed different since Rori had woken up. Happier, even.

"Well, aren't you full of surprises tonight?" Rori mused when she recovered. " Dark humor and dick jokes. Anything else I should know?"

"I just told him."

The two of them looked at me when I spoke, though my breaking the silence didn't seem to break the tension between them. If anything, it felt more like the chemistry between them expanded outward to include me.

"Told him what?" Rori asked.

"What happened when you woke up," I said. "Between you and me."

"Ah, when we kissed."

"Yeah."

Her attention returned to Hudson. "And how do you feel about that?"

He pulled in a long breath as though taking the time to ponder a big decision. "Weirdly not jealous about it."

"Well, that's a promising start," Rori observed, her eyes flicking back to me.

"He's all torn up about it, though." Hudson jerked his chin at me. "Look at him."

"Hey, I'm not—"

"He's in love with both of us." Hudson steamrolled right over my protest. "And he's conflicted because he thinks he has to choose." While I wanted to disappear into the floor, Hudson gave Rori a knowing look. "But not choosing is kind of your thing, isn't it?"

"That's...true," she said tentatively. Finally, someone else who looked as shocked as I felt. "With all consenting parties, of course. Sharing partners isn't for everyone."

"He wants us both." Hudson shrugged. "And you're a pro at the whole sharing thing. Sounds like a perfect solution to me."

"You don't need to put words in my mouth," I finally spat out. "I can decide for myself what I want."

Hudson spread his hands. "Is any of what I just said untrue?"

It wasn't, and I was only trying to protect my own ego. To no longer find myself bared to Rori fucking Wilder, the woman I tried so hard and failed to convince myself I wasn't batshit crazy for.

In all the times I'd been held, used, and humiliated by the Sisterhood, I'd never felt as vulnerable as this.

Rori approached me slowly, as cautiously as she would a wild animal. "I wouldn't make you choose, Devin. I'm open to this, as long as the two of you are."

She glanced toward Hudson, who gave an affirming nod.

"What about Torr and Santos?" My voice came out huskier than intended.

"I think they've always known this was a possibility." With a small smile, she then turned to Hudson. "What surprises me the most is you."

He nodded as if expecting that. "Your dad and I had an interesting talk just before you woke up. It put a lot in perspective, you know? Gave me a lot to think about. And even before then, I just..." He paused for a long time. "I just like you," he said with a shrug. "I admire and respect you. I don't know if my feelings go beyond that or if they ever will. But Devin," he inclined his head toward me, "means a lot to me. And it's hurting him to be without you. So why would I deny him that?"

Rori's smile grew wider. "You're a good guy, Hudson." She looked at me, a teasing glint in her eye. "Your boyfriend's a good one."

"He's—" I stopped myself, blowing out a breath. "Okay, yeah. I guess he is my boyfriend."

It felt strange, but also freeing, to not be secretive or even subtle about being with Hudson. We were supported, accepted. Neither of us were tools for some evil purpose anymore, we could just be us.

"That's right. Can't deny me anymore." He threw an arm around my shoulders and planted a big kiss on my cheek.

"When have I ever denied you anything?" I grumbled out the words but the sensation in my chest was light, bubbly and giddy, as I turned my head to find his mouth.

Rori was beaming, her warmth toward us genuine. "I'm happy for you two. As for the other part of this equation," she motioned between me and herself, "we can take it slow if you want. Being with multiple people can be strange."

Before I could respond, Torr came out of the house with a slam of the front door. He was shirtless with a large bandage taped across his chest just like Rori.

"That was fast," she remarked as he came up behind her, arms snaking around her waist as he planted a kiss on her neck.

"Your dad's the best at what he does. Hey, guys." Torr nodded at Hudson and me before bringing his chin to Rori's shoulder. "How are you, by the way?" he murmured, turning his face toward hers.

Rori snorted. "Never been better."

"Seriously, creep."

"I'm...actually okay, yeah," she assured him. "Even better than when you checked on me hours ago. I'm just ready to wipe these crazy bitches off the planet." Her smile at him was earnest, if a little wobbly. "I promise I'll work with Malik on how traumatic this was after we're done. But I have a job to do first."

"We all do," I piped up. "Every person here has a score to

settle with this cult. We're not just taking back our own lives," I squeezed around Hudson's forearm, "but the future."

"That's right." Torr held his fist out for a pound, which I gave. "But before we do that..." His arms re-wrapped around Rori, his mouth going to her ear. "Santos and I have a surprise for you upstairs."

"Oh, really?" She grinned, arching subtly to lean against him. "What kind of surprise?"

"One we're pretty sure you'll like."

"Hmm." Rori's gaze slid to me and Hudson, eyes sparking with delight. "How would you feel if these two joined us?"

"Joined? You?" I choked out in disbelief.

"You two can watch and just play with each other," Rori added quickly. "See how it feels to be part of a bigger group. If it's not your thing, you can leave. We won't be offended."

"Baby steps," Torr added with a nod, as if they had already discussed it. "I'm good with it. I'm sure Santos would be too."

My voice was lost with awe, excitement, nervousness, disbelief at what was being offered, a whole mix of emotions. So I was grateful when Hudson answered.

"Yeah, I think we'd be open to that." He kissed my neck, one hand sliding into the top of my shirt. "But you have to use your words, Dev," he chided playfully.

Finally, I found my voice. "Yes, we'll join you."

25

RORI

I paced on the landing outside my closed bedroom door. Torr and Santos were on the other side of that slab of wood. Torr said he had to, "Get Santos ready," and proceeded to shut the door in my face. That was almost twenty minutes ago.

"This better be fucking good," I grumbled impatiently. I had been excited, my fantasies playing out all kinds of delicious foreplay scenes in my head. But as time stretched on, I was beginning to feel seriously blue-balled.

Devin and Hudson waited with me, the two of them adorably wrapped up in each other. While my boots wore a hole in the floor, they kissed, embraced, and spoke softly to each other. At times, I could feel Devin's eyes on me, maybe even Hudson's too.

Once we were all in that bedroom, some touching might happen between me and one of them. But I didn't want to get between them out here. It would be their choice if they wanted me involved.

"How much longer?" I yelled through the door.

"Couple more minutes!" Torr called back.

"I bet it's food," Hudson said confidently. "He's laying Santos out on the bed and covering him in whipped cream and cherries that you can eat off him."

"I hate cherries, so he better not," I muttered.

"What? How can you hate cherries?" Devin demanded.

"'Cause they're gross!"

Finally, the door creaked ajar and a grinning Torr poked his head through. "Ready for your surprise?"

"Man, what do you think?" I was brimming with so much anticipation, I couldn't even think of a proper smartass answer to that question. I just wedged my body through the gap, forcing Torr back as I stepped inside.

I was solely focused on the bed, which turned out to be empty and neatly made. But the moment I turned, my jaw fell open. "Oh. My. God..."

Santos was sitting in a chair, wearing nothing but boxer shorts. Or rather, he was *tied* to the chair. This wasn't a quick-and-dirty tie-up job, though. The only way to describe the rope-work was *stunning*. A work of art.

An intricate pattern of ties and knots held Santos in place, from his ankles and calves being held to the chair legs, to the harness-like structure stretched over his chest and torso.

"Hey paloma," he said in a soft voice that was vulnerable, almost shy, but full of want.

That sound immediately pulled my focus from the aesthetics of his bonds to him, my Santos. "Hey, handsome. Was this your idea?"

"We both came up with it." He nodded at Torr.

"Look at you." I breathed in awe, drinking him in from head to toe. "You like being trussed up for me like this?"

"More than like." His constricted chest strained against the rope as he took a breath, the binds pressing into his skin. "I *want* this. With you."

"You're sure?" I couldn't stop taking in all the details. The contrast of the straight lines and uniform knots against the organic contours of his body was beautiful to behold. Pale threads against tan skin. His slight movements under so much restraint. Restraint that he wanted.

"God, yes." His voice became a plea, one that sent heat flooding to my core. "Your control is the only kind I've ever craved. Your pleasure is all I care about giving." His big shoulders pulled slightly at the ropes, and fuck me, why was that so hot? "So please, paloma. Use me. I'm yours for the taking."

Speechless was an understatement. I was absolutely floored by the display of devotion and trust. And not just by Santos. Unable to find anything to say, I walked a slow circle around my gift. My prize. I was only distantly aware of other movement, probably Devin and Hudson making their way into the room.

Once behind his chair, I paused to admire how Santos' arms were tied behind his back. Ropes looped around his forearms and were held together by an intricate braid of knots between the two limbs.

"You like your gift?" Torr asked, arms crossed with more than a hint of smugness.

Looking back down at my bound gladiator, I kept noticing more ties and patterns that I didn't see before. The rope went over Santos' thighs and hips and under the seat of the chair to hold him in place. Torr needed to have gotten *very* close, touched him in intimate places. I knew the two of them weren't sexually attracted to each other, but that kind of trust and comfort between each other was moving in its own right.

The thought of Torr leaning over Santos, pulling lengths of rope around his hips, securing it, and snaking the lengths up his waist, was practically foreplay in itself.

On top of all that, they had done this for *me*.

"You're not saying anything." Santos' voice hardened

slightly, losing some of that sweet, sexy begging. "Are *you* okay with this, paloma?"

"I'm just...speechless," I admitted. "I've never received such an amazing gift. Especially one wrapped so beautifully." I looked at Torr. "When did you learn how to do this?"

"When you were out for a week," he said. "I couldn't lift to cope, couldn't leave your side for a second. All I had was a length of rope, so I tied knots and made patterns."

"Amazing," I mused, returning my attention to Santos. "Can I touch you?" My hand hovered over his shoulder.

"Please," he purred.

His skin was warm under my palm. I slid a finger under the rope binding his elbows, testing its tightness. The digit slid under easily, though the rope left a clear mark on his skin.

"You're not in pain anywhere?" I asked, circling around to the front of him again. "Or going numb?"

He shook his head, tongue wetting his lips. "The only thing that hurts is that I'm not pleasing you right now."

"Oh, gorgeous man, you *are* pleasing me." I hooked a finger under the knotwork in the center of his chest and pulled slightly, until the tension snapped the rope against his skin with a soft crack. "You are just a feast for the eyes. I hardly know where to start with you."

A soft creak coming from the bed reminded me that we weren't alone. Whatever I'd be doing to Santos, I'd have an audience. Maybe even some extra participants, if I was lucky.

"You guys still good to hang out?" I said with a tilt of my head toward Devin and Hudson.

"Oh yeah."

I wasn't sure which one of them answered, but that was good enough for me. My attention was solely on the beautifully bound man in the center of the room.

"You've got to promise me one thing, Torr," I said while

walking another slow circle around Santos, gently pulling and testing at his binds as I did so.

"Yes?" Torr's voice was raspy, practically a groan already.

"Next time you wrap my present for me," I stood behind Santos and ran my palm down his chest to his firm stomach, "I want to watch you do it."

"Sure, I'd be happy to show you." Torr's eyes followed the movements of my hands as I caressed Santos. "Maybe even teach you how."

Santos dipped his head back and moaned. "Uh, yes." His body surged under the ropes.

"You would like that?" I brought my mouth directly against Santos' ear. "Feeling me tie you up before doing whatever I want with you?"

"God, yes," he breathed.

"Oh, but what to do to you now?" I kept contact with him, letting my fingers drift over his warm skin as I circled around to stand in front of him again.

"Anything you want." His shoulder muscles bunched as he watched my every movement like a hawk. "Please. All I want is to please you."

I took him in from head to toe, vaguely aware of the grin spreading on my face. *If only you could see the Butcher now, Nella.* Her fearsome gladiator, her prized possession, was exactly where *he* wanted to be. Mine.

"You see, the problem with that is," I moved one leg between his spread thighs and dropped my weight to sit on one of his knees, "All I want to do is please you too."

Santos pulled in a breath as I slid higher up his thigh, brushing my leg against his crotch.

"Make me please you," he choked out. "I'm your toy to use. Please."

"Quiet." I brought my thumb to his lips, pushing the digit

inside. "I don't want any words from you for the next ten minutes. Understand?"

"Mm-hm..." His lips wrapped around my thumb, tongue licking and teasing it as if it were the most erogenous spot on my body. When it came to Santos, any body part could become a sweet spot.

"But I do want you to make noise." My heel lifted off the ground, arching my foot and rubbing my inner thigh against his growing erection. "No words, but I want to hear exactly how much you love what I'm giving you. Understand?"

"Mmm..." Santos' quad muscles flexed, his skin biting into the ropes going across his powerful legs. He wanted to thrust, to roll his hips into my touch. But the restraints kept him in place.

I skimmed a hand down his stomach, tracing the ropework framing his hips before settling my palm on his length. He pulsed against my hand with a gasp, legs straining for more contact with me.

"Fuh—ah, hmmm..." Poor Santos was so vocal and expressive that *not* using his words served as a unique challenge to him. Good thing obeying me was a higher priority.

"We'll find something to gag you with if you can't obey simple commands." I freed his cock from the snug boxer briefs with that warning and enjoyed the sight of his head lolling back on his neck. A long, wordless moan poured out of his throat as I stroked him with a firm grip.

"Good boy." I leaned in to nip his Adam's apple and found a comfortable place to curl up and lean briefly.

The crook of his neck fit my forehead perfectly, so I rested there, kissing the hollow of his throat, enjoying the warmth of his skin and the fresh scent of him.

"I'll never get over how right you are for me," I whispered. "I'm so glad to be back and that you're still here."

He was so solid underneath me, a protective, deadly force

despite his submission in bed. The kiss he brushed over my forehead promised his strength and devotion without words.

"I love you too." With a final kiss under his jaw, I slid down his body until I was kneeling between his legs. He had allowed me a moment to melt, but I was back in my domme headspace now, gazing up at him with his cock in front of my face.

He made those moans and ragged breaths again as I pumped him from base to head. I opened my mouth and let the blunt tip brush against my tongue with every stroke. It was driving him wild, and I wanted to see if I could get a word out of him.

"Fuck," he groaned before sinking his teeth into his lip, knowing he'd messed up.

"Aw, bad boy." I released his cock with an exaggerated sigh of disappointment and looked up, finding the eyes of the other men in the room for the first time.

Torr leaned against a dresser, arms and ankles crossed in front of him. Devin and Hudson were on the bed, shirtless and spooning in a tangle of limbs. I had to jerk my attention away from them, from the shapes, lines, muscles, and tattoos that made up their bodies.

"Torr?"

"Yes?" he purred, like he thoroughly enjoyed watching my struggle.

"What can we gag Santos with for breaking the rules?" I asked.

Torr grinned evilly. "How about your panties?"

I smirked back at him as I stood, already flicking apart the button on my pants. "You were hoping for that, weren't you?"

"Not hoping. I would've made it happen. Come here."

He yanked me forward, pulling me into a rough, handsy kiss. With both hands, he palmed my ass hard, bringing them down in a slap on either side. The next thing I knew, my pants and underwear were being shoved down in rough pulls.

As soon as my bare ass was exposed, Torr slapped each side again hard enough to leave handprints. I couldn't even cry out from the sting before his mouth was on mine, hands smoothing over the bruised skin to soothe the ache. His kiss plundered my mouth, possessive and all-consuming.

The difference between my two men could not be more apparent. Torr's dominance left me dizzy, off-kilter and breathless. Santos' submission made me powerful, fired up and confident enough to rule the world. And I could not be me without them both.

With my pants and underwear off, Torr placed my panties in my hand, spun me around, and sent me back to Santos with another, lighter, slap on the ass.

"Punish your man, then torture him some more until you're dripping wet enough for me to wreck you," Torr growled.

Weak-kneed as I was, I managed to stand tall in front of Santos. "Open your mouth."

He obeyed, nearly panting as he stared up at me with huge, dark puppy eyes.

I shoved my balled-up underwear into his mouth and he moaned, accepting the slip of fabric with my taste and scent on them.

"That'll teach you to disobey orders." I returned to kneeling in front of him. "As further punishment, I'm going to deep-throat you and you're not allowed to come. How does that sound?"

His answering moan was pure sexual frustration. I watched him carefully for any signs of genuine discomfort—a shake of his head, a look in his eye, but my man was in heaven being ruled by me.

My lips slid over his blunt head, mouth stretching around

his girth as I made my way down. I opened my throat to take all of him, focusing on breathing through my nose as my lips finally met my fist wrapped around his base.

Santos moaned around my panties, and I knew he'd be begging to touch me, thrusting up to fuck my face if he were free to do so. But as long as he was my toy to play with, I'd enjoy putting him in my mouth.

And he was an absolute mouthful. Solid and burning hot, twitching when he hit the back of my throat. He wanted to come so badly, but I knew my good boy wouldn't disappoint me this time.

I was so orally fixated on him, I didn't notice Torr come up behind me until a pinch on my nipple made me squeal.

His hands were underneath my shirt, groping and grabbing with a touch that was both reverent and possessive. My shirt and bra came off, and then I ripped off the large stretch of gauze covering the fresh tattoo on my chest.

Torr's hands ran down my sides while I returned my attention to Santos' cock, showing no mercy as I resumed taking him down my throat and pumping him with my fist. His gorgeous face was in a grimace of pleasure and pain, muscles straining under the ropes. He was solid as iron on my tongue, no doubt incredibly sensitive and teetering on the verge.

"You're being so very good for me," I praised, giving him and my mouth a moment of reprieve.

He groaned around my panties, head falling back as he took ragged breaths through his nose.

Torr's hand went between my legs, a rough groan leaving his chest when he found how wet I was at Santos' submission. I spread wider for him, arching and pressing back, resting my arms and head on Santos' thighs.

"You love sucking his cock this much?" Torr purred approvingly as he dragged slick fingers to my ass, teasing my back entrance. "You like seeing him all wrapped up like a present for you?"

"Yes..." I arched deeper for him, lifting my hips.

"How would you like to ride him?" Torr's fingers pressed inside, working and stretching me while the other hand lazily stroked my pussy. "Ride both of us?"

"Yes, please," I whined.

"Come for us first." He zeroed in on my clit while stretching my ass with another finger. "Look at him while I get you ready for both of us."

I gazed up at Santos, fingers gripping the ropes at his hips to hold on through the onslaught of sensations. He met my eyes, head and shoulders angling down as much as he could, like he wanted to curl around me.

I reached up and took my panties from his mouth, discarding them somewhere on the floor. "I want to hear you when I'm riding you." A moan left my mouth, my grip tightening on his ropes as pleasure built from Torr's ministrations. "I love hearing you talk when you fuck me. It's one of my favorite things."

Santos' smile was radiant. "And I love watching you come. I love it when you hold onto me while Torr is working you. So keep looking at me, paloma. *That* is my favorite thing."

I rested my cheek on his thigh, gazing up toward his face, but my orgasm was ratcheting up so fast I gave into the impulse to shut my eyes.

Torr slapped my clit in response, the sharp, painful pleasure making me cry out. "Keep your eyes open," he growled. "He said he wants you to look at him."

The display of his dominance combined with the tender, loving look from Santos did me in. My pleasure lashed out like a lightning strike, nearly making me crumple to the floor if it wasn't for Santos's legs holding me up. Torr kept his motions up until I was begging him to stop, the aftershocks licking through me to the point of oversensitivity.

"So good," Torr praised, stroking down my back. Then he said the words that sparked a thrill in me like nothing else.

"You're going to take us both so well."

26
___

RORI

Fuck, just hearing Torr's words felt like they could spark another orgasm from me.

My gaze rolled toward the bed, once again remembering our audience. Devin and Hudson were facing each other now, kissing aggressively. Their bodies rolled and hands were hidden between each other. Hudson's back was to us, his inked skin rippling across taut muscles.

Hudson's fist gripped the hair at Devin's nape, which was making the long, dark strands come loose as the men plundered each other's mouths. With a groan, Hudson kissed the other man's jaw, making his way down Devin's neck.

And Devin looked over Hudson's shoulder to stare straight at me.

His dark eyes were hooded with lust, but no less sharp as they focused on me, his hand gripping Hudson's ass to bring the other man's leg over his waist. Devin's torso rolled and I could imagine their cocks sliding against each other, just on the other side of Hudson's hip. I wondered if they were making a sticky mess with precum, how each of them would feel in my hand.

"Like what you're seeing?" The question came from Torr,

his hand running along my shoulders and upper back. "You like watching them fuck each other?" His mouth came to my ear. "Or do you want them to fuck you?"

I shuddered at the question, fresh desire lighting up my spine and all my sensitive points.

"Keep watching them while we fuck you." Torr gripped my nape, massaging and squeezing. "Let their pleasure become yours. And who knows?" He nipped my earlobe. "Maybe one of them will let you finish him off if you're lucky."

A soft moan left my throat. Devin. It was Devin I really wanted to touch that way. That would be up to him and Hudson, but from the way he continued to watch me, I had a feeling he wanted it just as much as I did.

"Paloma." Santos' sweet, pleading voice cut into my thoughts. "Please ride me. I'm dying to feel you."

Hearing him beg was like a shot of power through my veins. Instantly, I recalled my control, my responsibility to dominate him well.

I stood from the floor, breaking eye contact with Devin to turn to my powerful gladiator, trussed up and helpless only to me. "I'll use my good little fuck toy whenever I damn well please."

Santos' eyes lit up, his cock standing even higher at attention with a cute little twitch. "Yes, paloma," he purred.

"Lucky for you," I braced my hands on his shoulders, straddling my legs over the seat of his thighs, "I could go for a nice ride right now."

"Oh God, yes," he hissed. "Ride me like you own me."

I hovered over him, just barely letting his wide head kiss my slick folds. "You don't have the right to make demands," I reminded him sternly. "Ask correctly, or I'll leave you here."

"I'm sorry," he panted, squirming under his bonds. "Will

you please ride me, paloma? I'm dying to worship your sweet cunt with my cock. Please, I would feel so honored."

How could a girl say no to that? I kissed him deeply, wrapping my arms around his shoulders as I slowly lowered down. His reverent moan into my mouth was delicious and full of longing.

"That's my good boy," I breathed when we broke apart, raising my hips only to lower down and take him fully. "You're so good to me, Santos."

"You're everything to me," he said roughly, his forehead on mine. "The world, the sun. Absolutely everything."

I knew he meant every word, and for a moment, it was just us. I held his face through another achingly perfect kiss. Giving this man everything he wanted and deserved would never make up for what he had been through. But I would spend the rest of my life trying my best.

The moment I lifted up again, I felt the heat of Torr's chest on my back. "Stay there for me," he whispered darkly.

My thighs were already burning from the effort, and I was practically on my toes.

"Lean on me," Santos urged. "I got you, paloma."

"You do," I agreed, letting my weight rest on him while Torr nudged at my back entrance. "You have me, always."

"Tell me if I need to stop." Torr nipped at my shoulder while he pressed through in short thrusts.

"I'm good, I'm good...wait."

He paused to let me adjust, teasing the sensitive nape of my neck with biting kisses, hands roughly kneading my thighs.

"You're not new to this." I could hear the smirk in his voice.

"Neither are you," I shot back over my shoulder. He and I hadn't done anal together before, but we'd both been fairly experienced before getting together, so I wasn't surprised. I was actually glad he knew enough to be considerate and slow.

"Okay, I'm good," I told him.

"You're fucking incredible is what you are," he groaned, pushing in a little deeper.

Even with Santos supporting me, my legs were tiring to the point of lowering down over his thighs and taking him deeper as well.

"Holy...fuck." By the time both men were seated inside me, I felt so full that I could scarcely breathe.

"I'm gonna start moving," Torr rasped against my nape. "Gonna start fucking this sweet, little ass. Tell me if I need to stop."

"No fucking way," I gasped, clutching Santos' shoulders for dear life. "Don't you fucking dare."

"That's what I like to hear," Torr praised. "Let me hear you beg for it."

Giving in to his demands was automatic, instinctual. "More," I whined. "You can go harder. Give me more."

Torr picked up his pace with a curse, the pressure of him filling me just as punishing as it was satisfying.

"Oh fuck me, I can feel that too," Santos hissed. He could only rock his hips in a slight cant, but coupled with Torr's brutal fucking, it was all I needed.

I was speared between them, helpless to do anything but take what they gave. The three of us were slick with sweat and panting, an expanse of skin, muscle and rope. I never wanted it to end.

The heat, sweat, and pleasure make me sinewy, all loose and languid. At some point, my head lolled and caught sight of our voyeurs.

Hudson and Devin were spooning now, the two of them facing us. Devin locked eyes with me again, the lower half of his face hidden by Hudson's shoulder. He had an arm around the other man's chest, a lean-muscled forearm cutting across an expanse of tattoos.

Hudson was panting. His blue eyes met mine briefly but quickly moved on, like someone taking in a large painting on the wall. He liked the details but also wanted to see the whole picture.

And I did the same to him. Starting at his face, then letting my gaze travel down his body. A tattooed hand clutched at Devin's arm. A pale stomach expanded and flexed with every ragged breath. My eyes followed the trail of hair below his navel further downward...and were rewarded by the sight of Devin's hand stroking up and down a long, thick cock.

Pleasure spiked through me and I cried out, my body surging with a new intensity between my two men. When I looked at the two on the bed, I saw the whole picture, not just the details. And it was nothing short of the hottest thing I'd ever seen.

The two of them lying there, Devin with one arm braced over Hudson's chest and the other hand jerking his cock. Like me, Hudson was helpless to do anything but take, feel. Watch.

Devin's eyes never wavered from mine. It almost felt like he was daring me. Like this was some kind of challenge to quit the staring contest and actually do something.

"I'm going to come," Torr growled, still stretching me to the limit. "Your ass is too fucking good."

He reached around and nimbly stroked another orgasm out of me, using me to clench around his cock so he could spill inside my ass.

Torr had barely staggered away and cleaned up when Santos called out, "Think you can untie me? I'm kinda numb in places."

"Oh shit, I'm so sorry." Mortified, I started to lift up. "We shouldn't have left you tied up this long."

"It's fine. Sit down." Santos' voice was forceful, a commanding quality that I didn't often hear from him. But one that I liked. "I want you to stay right where you are."

"Demanding," I teased, lowering to take him fully inside me again.

Torr came around with a knife and carefully cut away the bindings. I was sorry to see the beautiful rope work go but already couldn't wait to play like that again.

Worry struck me again when Santos hissed and grimaced in pain. His arm came around my waist as he started to slide from the chair.

"Santos! What's wrong?" I tried to pull away but his strength was unmatched.

"Fine," he bit out. "Just circulation coming back, it's gonna hurt for a bit." We ended up on the floor, him flat on his back and me still on top of him.

"You sure you're okay?"

"I'm perfect." He did a small roll of his hips, making me gasp. "When I'm with you like this, it's impossible to be anything short of that."

I couldn't help but admire the indentations in his skin left behind by the rope. They would fade soon but were beautiful reminders of his devotion to me.

Tracing them with my fingers, I said, "You have been very good, and still haven't come yet."

"You told me not to, paloma." He said it like it was so simple, his broad hands spanning my hips and running up to my waist. "Use me to make yourself come, and let me touch you. Please?"

"Touch me all you want," I purred, pressing my palms into his chest. "I'm just as much yours as you are mine."

His grip clamped down on my waist as he bucked into me.

My head threw back with the impact. As I crashed back down, my eyes found the two men on the bed again.

Hudson's skin was flushed, his breaths coming in fast, desperate pants as Devin jerked him with a quickening rhythm. I found myself riding Santos at the same pace of Devin's hand, my breaths finding sync with Hudson's. When he let out the first strangled groan of his orgasm, I was right there too.

Santos' fingers dug into my hips as I convulsed along his length, but my good boy remained solid as iron inside me. On my descent from the high, I folded over him and pressed a breathless kiss to his mouth. "Come with me on the next one," I whispered.

"Won't be long," he groaned through clenched teeth.

I sat upright just as Devin wrung the last jolts of pleasure from Hudson, his hand now taking a smooth, leisurely journey from the swollen head to the thick base.

"Devin." His name left my mouth like an incantation.

And like he was being summoned by me, he gave Hudson a final squeeze and a kiss before rising from the bed. His erection was heavy and taut, bobbing stiffly as he stood. My eyes traveled up Devin's body until our gazes met. I felt the need to say something, to ask for permission to touch him or ask if he was still okay with everything.

But before my scrambled, already well-fucked brain could string together a sentence, he stepped forward, bringing that jutting erection right in front of my face.

I leaned forward, lips parted, with my gaze never wavering from his. My tongue could dart out and taste him, but I paused mere inches away. He did not step back, nor did he look conflicted in the slightest. Instead, he brought his fingertips to the side of my face. With that small, tentative gesture, he urged me forward.

And I gave in to the temptation I never thought would happen.

My lips stretched around him, tongue leading the way. With a groan and a slight thrust forward, Devin's hand on my face became a more solid, sure touch. He cupped the side of my cheek, long fingers brushing back my hair like I was the most precious thing.

Santos began a slow, deep roll of his hips beneath me, holding me steady. While I crashed down to meet him, I began a tentative exploration of Devin as I took more of him in my mouth. A hand trailing up the long, lithe muscle of his thigh, fingers spreading wide when I reached the front of his hip and lower stomach. I followed the diagonal lines from his hip bones to the base of his cock, where I wrapped my fist around that stiff length.

The three of us got swept up in a rhythm of grunts, moans, ragged breaths, and slaps of slicking flesh. It was messy and pornographic. My legs ached and I was exhausted, wrung out on all the orgasms I had already, but I would not stop this for anything.

I looked up at one point to see Hudson standing behind Devin, their mouths locked in a brutal kiss as tattooed arms snaked over Devin's body. One hand slid down, caressing over Devin's stomach and hip, heading lower. That hand found its prize a moment later, cupping and massaging Devin's balls.

Desperate moans came from above me and his cock swelled in my mouth. Pleasure coiled in my clit despite my fatigue, and Santos' cock kicked inside me, urging me toward that peak. When a cool chest pressed against my sweat-slicked back, I would've grinned if my mouth wasn't full. Of course Torr had to rejoin us for the finale. It only felt right this way.

"Come for us," he commanded in my ear, fingers running

down to my pleasure center. "For all of your men. Give us one more."

My final orgasm unfolded slowly, pleasure bursting at each point of contact. Santos' wet heat spilling inside me, Devin filling my mouth as Hudson handled him, and the weight of Torr's hand at the center of it all, his voice guiding me to bliss.

27

SANTOS

Devin and I moved silently through the dark. It should have been pitch-black, but I was somehow able to find my way without issue, and he followed me with no complaint. Perhaps Tezca was lending me some of his night vision. Either way, I wasn't about to question this gift.

We had gotten out of bed way too early for this, didn't get anywhere near enough sleep after that incredible night with Rori. But I didn't feel sleep-deprived, and I'd venture a guess that Devin didn't either.

I was alert and as sharp as the edge of my machetes. All of my senses honed in on my surroundings. I was a primed and ready weapon, just waiting to be used.

I was the weapon they made me, but if today went well, it would be the last time. If everything went our way, the skills I'd learned in the fighting pit would end those who had made me a gladiator in the first place.

Rori and the others were not far behind, but Devin and I were chosen for this specifically because of our close combat skills.

The enemy would never see us coming.

We had left and hidden our bikes roughly a half mile back, where Astarte had perched on a tall boulder. Devin and I knew it was a signal to stop like we'd known our own names. From there, Tezca guided us silently through dense forests and steep hillsides.

I couldn't see him at the moment, he blended in too well for even my eyesight, but I could feel him nearby. Our compass and companion from the moment he showed us his power on the sands.

Near the edge of the treeline, Tezca stopped abruptly. Those large, yellow eyes were intense with warning as he turned his body to cross our direct path. He didn't need to speak into our minds to say, *This is as far as you go.*

I looked to Devin to discuss what to do next, but he was already moving.

Like a damn squirrel, he was climbing up the trunk of a nearby tree, barely testing the branches as he hauled himself up higher and higher. I almost laughed. Another way he was a ghost? With how fast he shimmied up that tree, he could have been weightless.

He stopped once he found a spot, and I kept an eye on the ground past the treeline while he observed from up top. All I could make out was a clearing in the distance, maybe a fence and buildings of some kind, but it was hard to tell. I could also make out small light sources, like flashlights or lanterns, moving around, though we were well out of their range now.

Devin came back to land about five minutes later and slowly moved his hands in the modified sign language Shadow and Grudge had taught us.

"There's a fence making a big square. Inside is freshly tilled earth, like planted crops. Rotating patrols all around the fence perimeter, I counted six. All armed with long-range rifles."

"What are the lights?" I asked, my hands moving just as slowly.

"Patrols have headlamps on. They look..." Devin paused as if trying to remember the sign, then he gave up and clumsily finger-spelled it. "Stupid."

I suppressed a laugh. "Roger that. What's beyond the fence?"

"Some buildings. Looks like mobile homes. Trailers and RVs. Didn't count many, but hard to see that far."

"So we're handling these perimeter guards, yeah?"

"That's what I'm thinking."

I dropped my hands and used my mouth to speak in a low whisper. "One last time as the Butcher and the Ghost, huh?"

Devin grinned and knocked his fist into mine. "For the right reasons this time."

With a soft hiss of steel, I unsheathed my machetes. A throwing knife appeared in each of Devin's hands without a sound. And with that, we were off.

We paused at the edge of the treeline to study the rotation pattern of the guards, which wasn't anything to write home about. They stood at the corner of the fence for about fifteen minutes, then the leader gave a signal and they all walked to the next corner.

Devin knocked his elbow into my arm. "Wait until they've been in one spot for a few minutes," he whispered. "Give 'em a chance to get comfy."

I nodded but felt worry needling in my gut. Something about this felt too easy. Although that was the point, wasn't it? We were here to make it easy for Rori and the others to crash through like a battering ram.

At the next rotation, Devin and I took off to find suitable positions to lie in wait before we struck. He headed for the outermost line of fencing, so I went for the back, closest to the buildings of the settlement. After we took care of the patrol, we'd go door to door and take care of the rest.

A week ago, I wouldn't have loved the idea of murdering people in their sleep, but nothing was off the table now. Their goddess had nearly taken Rori away from us. The Dark Mother did to her what she claimed she wanted to protect all women from. For bringing *that* into existence, there was no more mercy for these cultists. Only the children would be spared.

Since taking back our safe houses, we were operating under the assumption that every adult was armed anyway.

A few cars were parked between the fence and the trees, so I took cover behind one to stalk my targets. Devin was nowhere to be seen, but that was to be expected.

The guard closest to me was talking to someone further away. Their grips on their rifles were loose, and they leaned against the fence instead of standing at attention. In other words, painfully easy kills.

Their heads turned away from each other once there was a lull in conversation. My feet started moving, knowing Devin would take the opportunity to strike as well.

There was hardly any sound. No scream, not even a gurgled groan. Just the sound of a body slumping to the ground, and even that was softened, probably by Devin laying the body down gently so as to not be heard.

Still, it was enough for the woman in front of me to turn toward the sound. I was on her before she had the chance to call her friend's name, probably before she fully realized her fellow guard was no longer at her post.

One hand covered her mouth while my machete sliced cleanly through her neck like butter. She collapsed like her strings had been cut. I caught her fall, eased her to the ground, and moved on without a second thought.

The remaining patrol knew something was happening now.

Their headlamps whipped around like fireflies in the night. But Devin and I were both nimble enough to stay out of range of those lights. We were as quiet as shadows and moved just as quickly. Systematically, we disposed of the patrolling women one by one, before they had a chance to wake anybody. Devin nodded at me once he laid the final body on the ground. It was time for phase two of our assault.

With a returned nod, I pulled the small flashlight from my pocket and pointed it toward the darkness away from the settlement. I clicked the light on and off in a distinct pattern--our signal for success. The sky was lightening to a rich, dusty blue as I repeated the signal two more times. Dawn would be here soon.

A small, flickering light came alive in the darkness, clicking on and off in an answering pattern.

"They know we're good," I told Devin. "They're coming."

A flutter of wings brought our gazes skyward to the white dove flying overhead.

"Hey, paloma," I whispered. Somehow I knew it was Rori up there, watching over us and looking for the best direction to launch an attack.

A shot rang out, shattering the peaceful quiet of the pre-dawn day.

"Shit!" The white bird veered sharply off course, wings beating in panicked desperation. Another shot fired, the sound's echo crackling like lightning, and the bird dropped like a stone from the sky.

"Someone's awake. They know we're here." Devin grabbed my shoulder in a rough squeeze, bringing me back to focus. "Let's take care of that shooter."

"Rori," I choked. "If she was up there—"

"She's fine. She's back in her own body," he insisted. "The bird is just a vessel. Astarte is still here too." He shook my shoulder harder. "Don't choke on me, Santos. This is it. Let's do our job, okay?"

I nodded, rolling my wrists to swing my blades, to feel the weight of those weapons like extensions of my arms again. "Yeah, let's go."

We headed for the heart of the settlement, which was just a corridor between the two rows of structures. As Devin had said, they were mostly mobile homes plus some RVs and pop-up campers. Some spaces were made, marked with stakes and nylon rope like they were planning foundations for more permanent homes. Too bad that would never happen for these people.

Devin and I stayed out of view of windows and doors, creeping in the narrow alleys between structures. The shooter had to have been sitting on a roof or something—

The sound of something large dragging through the main corridor made me freeze, locking up every muscle in my body while I listened hard. Devin and I were back-flatted against the side of a house, the source of the sound just around a corner. He took a peek first and then made a noise that sounded distinctively like a snort.

"What?" I demanded.

He resumed his position next to me, grinning. Then he jerked his head to the side as if to say, *Take a look.*

I peeled off the wall, placing my feet carefully so as to not make a sound. What I saw around that corner was Tezca in plain view of all the homes, sitting calmly in the center of the temporary village.

His jaws were clamped around the throat of a woman, pale, limp, and unmoving. She still had the rifle strapped around her torso.

"That was our kill, damn cat," Devin muttered.

"No," I said, the understanding hitting me. "He's a vengeful god, and that woman in his jaws just killed Astarte's vessel."

Beyond the black jaguar proudly displaying his kill for all to see, there was a flurry of movement behind windows and doors. People were rousing, shouting at each other inside their homes. A window slid open and a rifle barrel poked through the crack.

"Tezca!" I shouted.

But he was already gone, tearing off like a shadow. The barrel lifted to point at me, and I darted around the corner just as a chunk of siding broke off from the house.

The roar of a dozen engines was a constant hum in the air now, a vibration that energized my blood. More shots fired, and I knew some of them had to be our people.

"Which direction are they coming from?" I asked Devin, eying that rifle now lying unused in the middle of everything.

"Sounds like it's directly east." He cocked his head from one side to the other. "Yeah, behind those houses." He indicated the row opposite from ours.

"Perfect."

The four cult leaders had now emerged and were shouting orders. "We're under attack! Eastern side, eastern side! Take your positions like we taught you!"

"Do it for your daughters!" yelled another woman, raising a rifle in the air before climbing up a ladder to the roof of an RV. Three more followed her, and other groups climbed up more rooftops. Some wore bulletproof vests and had hardened, battle-ready looks in their eyes. Others were wide-eyed with fear, still in their pajamas, holding their rifles like it was an animal about to bite them.

"Some are in the village! They got past the patrol, find them!"

With a quick nod, Devin and I separated, heading for the cover of cars, storage crates, and other items stacked behind the homes. Footsteps quickly crunched after us, loud and telling.

"We know you're hiding!" The woman fired a warning shot

that was close enough to make my ears ring. "Come out, and we may still honor you as a sacrifice." She fired another shot that shattered the window of the car next to me.

"Could you be any louder?" chastised another woman. "And don't waste ammo." The next sound she made was a gasp and then a gurgle.

"Gladys!" cried the first woman. "Oh, Dark Mother, help us!"

I took the opportunity to dart out from my cover, machetes raised and thirsty. It took me a fraction of a second to reach her, and she had no idea until I drew a red line across her throat. She'd been too distracted by Devin's knife sticking out of her friend's neck.

"Your Dark Mother is dead," I told the woman as the last of her life drained away.

"Come on." Devin slapped my shoulder before she even stopped choking on her blood. "Let's back up the others."

We ran together back into the fray. A full-scale battle was waging now, gunfire and shouts ringing in my ears. Women were lined up on the roofs of the homes and RVs, shooting into the woods. It became clear quickly that our side didn't need much help—the women were being picked off at a brisk pace.

"Damn, Hudson," Devin muttered. "Leave some for the rest of us."

"That's probably Rori and Shadow too," I mused. All of our best shooters were likely at the front line.

"Smoke them out!" one of the cultist women yelled. "Give them smoke!"

Devin and I braced together, weapons ready. "Oh shit," I said when I realized what was happening.

The cultists had matches and lighters and they were lighting strips of cloth on fire. Strips of cloth that had been stuffed into glass bottles full of clear liquid.

Devin grabbed my shoulder roughly. "Guns. The two we just killed. We gotta grab their guns and stop them from setting the whole forest on fire."

He didn't have to tell me twice. We ran back behind the buildings where the two bodies lay. In the mere seconds it took to grab their weapons, the air was filled with the unmistakable smell of burning.

We ran back to the central corridor, and a wall of fire and smoke was already building between the structures and the woods. Shit, they must have set up a perimeter around the whole place. I looked around, noticing the straw laid out in what looked like a border path that seemed to go around all of the buildings. Piles of chopped branches were laid out in several places along the straw path as if they were being gathered for firewood. But these branches were young and freshly cut, which would create lots of smoke if they caught fire.

"Shit," I said again. These cultists were craftier than anticipated.

The smoke billowed out over the village, making the landscape eerie and unsettling. Also pretty much useless for shooting. My eyes watered painfully and my throat was already feeling the effects.

But over the chaos, I heard motorcycle engines approaching and male voices shouting. Our people had been flushed out of the woods and were heading into the village to finish this up close and personal.

Devin and I stayed low and covered, shooting at dark figures on the rooftops who were now scrambling down to get out of the rising smoke. It was much harder to tell who was friend or foe now, so our shots were cautious, hesitant.

With a deep mechanical roar, two massive, black figures burst out of the smoke from the north end of the village. Shadow and Grudge emerged on their bikes like a pair of henchmen from Hell, coming to take sinners to eternal damnation with them. One look at them and cultists on the ground started running. The two veterans picked them off easily, almost like they were bored.

Once the shock and awe wore off, Devin and I ran out to meet them.

"Anyone hurt?" I asked immediately.

"So far, so good, but we're on borrowed time until smoke inhalation fucks us." Shadow's mismatched eyes roamed everywhere except for us, tracking sound and movement through the smoke. "How are you guys? Okay?"

"Fine," Devin answered curtly. "Where's Rori?"

"Not sure. Everyone scattered when the smoke came. Torr should be with her, though."

Shadow lifted his rifle suddenly, pointing it at one of the rooftops. But the figure hiding in the smoke dropped dead from someone else's shot before he could fire.

Another figure took shape in the smoke, striding toward the edge of the awning and dropping gracefully to the ground.

"You gotta be faster than that, Uncle Shadow!" Valorie's voice was muffled by a bandanna tied around the lower half of her face.

Grudge signed something to his daughter in fast, aggressive gestures. Val rolled her eyes and signed back as she spoke. "Yes, Dad. I'll stay off the roofs."

"Hey!"

Torr rode up to us then, braking his bike with a harsh jerk. "You all seen Rori?"

"I thought she was with you," Shadow growled.

Torr shook his head, worry and regret taking over his features. "We got separated in the smoke. Can't see for shit."

"Split up. Find her," Shadow ordered. "My daughter will *not* end up in their hands again, you fucking hear me?"

Our small group took off in different directions without another word. Devin and I headed toward the southern end of the village, where we'd picked off the night patrol on the fenced-in area. Parts of the fence were already broken down, like motorcycles had crashed through them.

Another shootout was happening, the Hunter squeezing off round after round with grim determination at cultists hiding behind the same cars I had.

A woman's head popped up behind the hood, and she returned two more shots before her gun clicked empty. The Hunter holstered his weapon with a triumphant grin and returned his hands to the handlebars, driving his bike forward through the tilled earth.

"Don't worry, Hunt. We got them," Devin yelled as we made our way to the cars.

But the Hunter either didn't hear or was too hopped up on vengeance and adrenaline to care. He picked up speed, heading straight for the enemies, and disappeared.

It happened so fast, I thought I was hallucinating. One second he was riding, the next, he pitched forward and disappeared like he'd been swallowed by the earth.

Fortunately, Devin caught on faster than me. "There's holes in the ground! Don't drive over that, they'll trap you!"

The time it took for us to realize what was really under the tilled earth was enough for the cultist to reload and fire at us.

A bullet whizzed by my ear, and I hit the ground, scrambling for cover. More bullets sent mini explosions of dirt and fence splinters all around me. This bitch was actually a decent shot.

"Hey, you dumb cunt! I'm over here!" More gunfire, but this time, the bullets pinged off a metallic surface.

"Fuck, Rori!" She was barely visible in the smoke, her black leather jacket and short crop of blonde hair the only features I could make out.

The beautiful, ruthless, and insane love of my life spread her arms wide in a taunt to the other shooter. "I'm the one you want, right? Come stuff your stupid goddess back in me, I dare you!"

The shooter remained silent behind her cover, but she was definitely alive and moving. Rori could see it too, and when she was this pissed, she was *not* patient enough to wait out her prey.

She stuck the gun in her holster and gripped her handlebars, jerking her wrist to accelerate the bike forward.

"No!" I screamed. "Don't drive across, you'll fall!" But the smoky air had already wreaked havoc on my throat, and my voice couldn't cross the distance between us.

Devin tried too. "Go around! Don't drive through, it's a trap!"

Rori was already several yards deep into the tilled earth patch. When she heard Devin, she actually slowed the bike and lifted her head as if looking for him.

I cupped my hands around my mouth to yell at her again, but I couldn't scream louder than the shot that rang out.

The shot that hit her in the shoulder, making her body jerk to the side with the motorcycle following.

And then the ground swallowed her whole.

Well, this was just fucking peachy.

My dominant shoulder was a throbbing, burning ball of pain. I was pinned under my bike in a damn hole in the ground, and there was dirt in my eyes, mouth, and ears. Oh yeah, and there was the fact that I'd taken a cheap shot by a cultist and had fallen into a literal trap.

"Fuck," I groaned, trying to breathe through the pain like I was going into labor. I couldn't feel my legs from the knees down, and that was also a bad sign. My back was also massively uncomfortable, like something was underneath me.

"Come on, Wilder." With my right arm useless, I had to throw everything into my left side to get the motorcycle off my legs. For a touring bike, it was pretty lightweight. That still didn't make it easy to move a four hundred pound metallic contraption with one fucking arm.

After several tries, I got just enough leverage to turn the handlebars and front wheel and pull my left leg free. With gritted teeth to brace for the pain, I wiggled my toes inside my boot. When that worked, I tried rolling my ankle. Then I flexed my foot up and down. A little sore, but it didn't feel sprained or broken.

"Alright. Now the other." I didn't know when I'd become a person that gave myself pep talks, but no one else was going to get me out of this. All my men were up on the surface, fighting for their lives. And I needed to get back up there and help as soon as possible.

Now that I had one good leg in addition to my arm, I used both to push the motorcycle off my remaining leg. I tried wiggling my toes in that boot and—

"Oh fucking Christ! Fuck me!"

The pain shooting up my leg was blinding, leaving me breathless and shocked.

"Okay," I panted when the pain reduced to a manageable level. "Not riding any time soon. Or climbing out of this hole myself, I guess."

It drove me mad that I was stuck and had to wait for help. I was the president. It was my job to lead the charge and protect my people. But my crew was capable, skilled, and not to mention vengeful. I knew they'd finish what they came here to do, then come find me when they could.

I didn't dare yell for anyone to get me out. Santos and Devin saw me fall, they knew where I was. And I didn't want to add to the noise and potentially distract someone in a life-or-death situation.

So I listened to the sounds of battle raging above me while moving as gingerly as I could. My whole right side was fucked, from ankle to shoulder. And that was damn annoying when it was my dominant side. Even with being in as much pain as I was, it was hard to shake the habit of depending on that arm, that leg.

It reminded me of one of the many lessons my dad Gunner had taught me. He made me do shooting drills over and over with my non-dominant hand until I was just as accurate with my left as I was with my right. When teaching me hand-to-hand combat, he'd even tied my right hand behind my back and had me throw punches and knife strikes for an entire month like that.

"What if you got captured and they broke your dominant hand?" he'd say whenever I complained. "What if you're tied up and you can get more leverage on your left side to wiggle free? You just going to give up because that side is weaker? No, you're not, Rori. You know why?" Then he'd pulled me into a hug after seeing how tired and frustrated I was. "Because you're *my* daughter. And no daughter of Demons is going to give up on herself."

His words repeated in my head as I leaned my weight into my left side, finding balance and steadiness in my good leg while my hand braced against the dirt wall. For the first time since falling in, I was able to get my bearings and look closer at the hole I'd found myself in.

It was big, obviously. Big enough for me and my bike to fall cleanly through, and deep enough that I wouldn't have been able to climb out even with two good legs. By my estimate, I was about eight feet deep, and the space around me couldn't have been more than six square feet.

They'd been expecting us on our bikes, it seemed. Even so, digging multiple holes of this size had to be a hell of a job. The opening had been covered by thin plywood and loose earth, disguised to look like part of a long row of tilled earth. Even I had to admit it was clever.

Loose dirt and broken pieces of plywood littered the ground where my bike and I had fallen. My bike which now had a bent frame and scratches and probably even more damage that I couldn't see.

"Don't worry, baby." I leaned my good shoulder against the

wall while I reached out with my left foot to give the front tire an affectionate stroke. "Jandro will get you right as rain when this is all over."

The bike leaned at an odd angle against dirt mounds of various sizes. I remembered the discomfort on my back, like I hadn't fallen against packed earth but something else instead.

Curious and with nothing better to distract me from the pain, I gingerly moved closer to the dirt mounds. Cradling my right arm against my chest, I used my good arm to toss aside the broken pieces of plywood and start wiping away the loose soil.

When I uncovered the face of a man, I forgot all about pain for a single instant.

I screamed and scrambled away, my right foot shooting a reminder of its condition all the way up to my skull. My breath whistled through my teeth, both because of the pain and the shock of seeing that face I couldn't look away from. He stared blankly up at the sky, eerily unmoving.

I didn't need to feel for a pulse or wipe away more dirt to see the gray of his skin. The poor man was dead. There was no other reason he'd be at the bottom of a hole, dirt carelessly thrown onto him.

It took a few more minutes of pained breathing to come to terms that I was in a hole with a dead man. Once the shock wore off, I could start to think rationally again. He wasn't stinking or decomposing yet. So he must have died recently.

Somehow, I got up the nerve to brush more dirt off of him. I wanted to see this man as he had been, as a human being who once had a life. Most likely, I wouldn't be able to tell much, but I wanted to find out what I could about who he had been.

I uncovered one of his arms and turned his hand over. God, his body wasn't even stiff yet.

The sight of his palm brought fresh tears to my eyes. The

skin was broken and raw in so many places. He'd been bleeding from his hands before he died.

That explained how these holes had been dug.

"I'm sorry." I squeezed his hand as if he could feel me doing it. "I'm so sorry we were too late for you. I hope you're at peace now." With some effort, I bent his elbow to place his hand on his chest. "If you have family, we'll find them. We'll return you to them, I promise."

I closed the man's eyelids just as a small shower of dirt and pebbles rained down, like someone was at the edge of the hole. Shielding my eyes, I looked up and squinted. The sun was rising and it was especially bright at the opening of my dark, underground prison.

I couldn't see exactly who was standing at the edge of the hole, but I did catch a leather jacket and a motorcycle helmet with the visor pulled down.

"Hey, is it over?" I called up.

The helmet nodded but otherwise stood there without saying anything. There was too much pain coursing through my body to give it much thought. All I wanted was some relief and to see that my men were unharmed.

"There's gotta be a ladder around somewhere. In one of the houses, maybe. But someone might still have to carry me. I'm kinda fucked up."

The helmeted biker again said nothing and just stood there. My reflection in the visor was tiny, a muted blonde head in a pit of darkness. Only then did I start to sense something else through the pain. My thoughts raced through the faces of my riders, especially the ones I knew the least. Who wore a helmet like that? I couldn't think of a single one.

"Who are you?" I tried to keep the pain out of my voice as I angled my bad arm and leg away from the figure. "Take your helmet off. Show yourself."

The person dropped to their haunches at the edge of the trap, then lowered their feet to dangle over the side. I backed as far away as I could while the person slid carefully down the dirt wall and landed gracefully in the hole with me.

It had to be a woman. She looked shorter than me, despite currently standing on the side panel and rear tire of my bike. She even scraped mud off her shoe against the treads of my tire. If I had use of both arms, she wouldn't have been standing up any longer. Such disrespect.

"Who the fuck are you?" I demanded again.

Two small, feminine hands went to the sides of the helmet and paused there, as if drawing out the suspense to tease me. I gritted my teeth and continued to wait, refusing to play into her game.

The helmet lifted slowly, revealing a chin, lips, nose, and finally an entire face. One that I didn't know but vaguely recognized. It hit me as she shook out shoulder length brown hair.

"You're one of them," I realized. "One of the cult leaders." She had to be the youngest one, somewhere in her mid to late thirties.

"So you do have some sense after casting out our Dark Mother." She tucked the motorcycle helmet under her arm. "And I thought you'd make this too easy on me."

I didn't dare flick my gaze up to the top of the hole, even though that was all I wanted to do. But I was injured with one of the crazy cult leaders right in front of me. I wasn't taking my eyes off this bitch for a second.

"Call for your men if you want, but they won't hear you." She put the helmet down and proceeded to shrug off the leather jacket. Everything about her movement and tone was so casual, it was eerie.

"I'm not calling for anyone," I said. "You can hide down

here, but it's just a matter of time. Your cult is gone. We've won."

"Are you so sure about that, *President?*" Her tone turned mocking as she tacked on my title. "The biker queen stuck underground with a gunshot wound and a broken ankle doesn't bode too well for your side."

I swallowed, refusing to give in to her taunting. The Sisterhood outnumbered us, but we were better skilled and experienced fighters. Santos and Devin even took out their patrol so we'd catch them unaware, although it seemed they were ready anyway. Still, I had confidence in my people, especially with my dad and uncle joining us.

"I thought I'd be impressed meeting you face-to-face," she went on after my silence. "The Dark Mother insisted you were the one, the perfect vessel to lead us into our new age but," she shook her head, her expression falling into one of disappointment, "you're just another woman weakened by men."

While she spoke, my good hand moved slowly to the gun holster under my jacket. "I would say sorry to disappoint but I honestly don't give a fuck."

In the blink of an eye, I drew and fired, but even in the small space, she managed to dodge it. She came at me with surprising speed, head and shoulders low as she tackled me around the middle. Blinding pain shot up my shoulder as she slammed me into the wall. I fought against it for clarity, for all the fighting instincts I'd been taught by my fathers until they were second nature.

I pressed the barrel of my gun against her head, but she anticipated the move and pulled it from my weakened grip. Maybe it was the desperation of the moment, maybe she didn't know guns well enough to use it, but she tossed it to the other side of the hole rather than turning it on me.

The woman clearly wasn't an experienced fighter and left so

many openings I could have exploited. She exposed her neck when she tossed the gun and had me pinned against the wall in an awkward, easily breakable position, had I been at full strength. Her only advantages were my damn injuries, and she was exploiting those in full force.

She would wait until I was trapped and maimed to fight me head-on. Cowardly bitch.

Numbness was setting in now, my vision darkening as my consciousness wobbled on a tightrope. If I passed out, she would certainly kill me. I had to gain the upper hand somehow, and fast.

I sagged against the wall, moaning and whimpering. Everything hurt like a bitch, so it wasn't entirely an act, but she fell for it anyway. Her hold let up on me just slightly, and she raised her head to look me in the face.

With what little remained of my flagging strength, I head-butted the bitch right in the nose.

The crunching sound of cartilage and her resulting cry of pain were satisfying to be sure. But what I really needed was for her to back away, to be lost in her own haze of pain for a moment.

She doubled over, clutching the front of her face, and like a dumbass, turned her back on me. It gave me just enough time to pull a switchblade from my boot, the last weapon in my arsenal. What I would give to be Devin right then, with hidden knives strapped all over my body.

Ha. I'll have to tell him that, if I see him again.

I held my knife out, staring at the woman's bent over back. Fuck, I could stab her so easily. Get her in the kidneys, her spinal cord, if only I could walk a few feet straight ahead without falling over. Throwing the knife was another option, but that wasn't what it was meant for. Plus, that wasn't my strongest skill set. I could miss, or just nick her, which would be a waste.

Another thing to learn from Devin, if I ever made it out of here.

The woman started turning back to me, and I opted to hide the knife up my sleeve. I needed her up close to use it, needed her thinking I was weaker than I actually was.

A genuine bolt of fear struck when she went for my gun that she'd tossed aside. To my dismay, she released the magazine to check the remaining ammo before slamming it back inside. She even pulled back the slide to make sure a bullet was in the chamber. This bitch knew what she was doing.

"Wait, wait." I held up my good hand, feeling the knife handle slide down toward my armpit. It wasn't too hard to sound desperate. "Let's just talk, woman to woman. I get it, okay? Men are terrible. They're entitled, stupid, and can't even wash their ass correctly."

"Too late for any of that." She trained the gun on me, eyes alight with hatred above her swelling nose bridge. "We have no use for you now. Any of you. You may have decimated our numbers but we *will* rebuild. The Dark Mother will regain consciousness through our devotion, and she will find another vessel, a better one. One that doesn't—FUCK!"

The handful of dirt I flung in her face bought me precious little time. I screamed through clenched teeth as I dragged my whole body forward, caught my knife handle in my palm, and shoved the blade into her stomach, twisting and pressing as far as it would go. She dropped the gun in her shock and I kicked it away. I saw the punch coming but didn't expect it to land so hard. My jaw lit up, as did my vision. Dots and lights sparkled like it was Christmas.

The world faded in and out, darkening and lightening up with detail like a TV screen being switched on and off. The woman was on top of me, drawing her bloody fist back again and again. I tried to hit back but couldn't tell if I landed anything. I just felt so heavy and tired.

Don't you dare. You're almost at the end, don't you dare stop fighting now. The voice came from within my own head, but those weren't my thoughts.

Astarte? I thought you died.

I'm a deity that has been self-aware since the Bronze Age. I can't die, genius. And today, neither will you.

Even then, I wanted to laugh. But my mouth wasn't working right. And it was full of something.

Turn your head. Spit out all that blood before you choke on it. There you go, little human. Now stay alive a little longer.

Easy for you to say, I thought.

Do not give in, Aurora.

You almost sound worried about me. I'm touched.

Think of your men. Your family. They will all need you for years to come.

Much like with the Dark Mother, it felt like fighting against an impossible current. A tidal wave against a grain of sand. I was being pulled under, and this time, I truly didn't have any strength left to fight it.

I'm so tired, though...I've been fighting...so much...

Aurora!

The weight on top of me had to be the woman. She'd succumbed to her injuries and somehow, I was still alive.

I shoved at her, forgetting that my right shoulder had been shot until a deep, throbbing pain pulsed all the way up my arm into my skull.

"Hey, hey, easy," a familiar voice said above my head while a soothing hand pressed down on my good shoulder. "You're safe, cuz. Come back slowly. That's just Tezca on you. He's been healing you."

"Val?" I croaked, my brain coming online slowly.

"None other. Here, have some water."

She pushed a straw between my cracked lips, which I sucked on greedily until she took it away.

I wasn't ready to open my eyes yet, but I processed my surroundings slowly, piece by piece. Reaching down, I found Tezca's head on my belly and scratched that velvety fur. His purr started up as he licked my hand, the healing rumble soothing all my aches as my injuries announced themselves.

There was another rumbling too, a vibrating sensation underneath and all around me.

"Where are we?" I rubbed my eyelids, which felt like they had been welded shut.

"In my truck bed. Torr's driving. Santos and Devin are up front with him. Right now, I'd say we're, oh, about three hours away from Four Corners."

A wave of relief immediately washed over me knowing that Torr, Santos, and Devin were okay, but the first thing out of my mouth was, "Four Corners? The fuck?"

"Yeah, you've been out for a minute." Val's hand returned to my shoulder. "It's over, Pres," she whispered. "We did it."

I wanted nothing more than to sit all the way up and demand that she tell me everything, but my injuries forced me to move slowly. And when I finally did open my eyes, I was in for another surprise. Val, Tezca, and I were not alone in the truck bed.

My eyes met those of four girls sitting against the right and left sides, all looking to be between the ages of three and eight.

"Uh, hi."

None of them replied as I slowly sat up. The younger two seemed curious. The others, suspicious.

"I went back to the safehouses for my truck after they got you out of the hole," Val explained. "Then Torr and your dad agreed we should find the kids immediately, and Tezca led us straight there. So," she nodded at the four silent girls sitting with us, "here we are."

"Was..." So many questions hit me at once, and it was a struggle choosing which to ask first. "Was there another battle?"

Val lifted one shoulder. "I wouldn't call it much of a battle. We...took care of most of them at the settlement." She spoke carefully, eyes flicking toward the children. "And the remainder were not a problem for us. The kids were kept hidden away, and once we found them, we didn't let them see what had happened."

"She won't tell us anything," declared one of the older girls, mean-mugging me as hard as she could with her arms wrapped protectively around one of the smaller children. "You kidnapped us!"

Val gave her a sympathetic look. "I know it seems that way now. But one day, you'll understand we are not the bad people in this situation."

"You have *men* with you!" the girl argued. "They're going to hurt us just like mama said!"

"No one is going to hurt you." This time Val cast her eyes toward me, a weary expression on her face.

Yeah, that look said it all. It was going to take years of patience, love, and therapy to un-indoctrinate these kids.

I wanted to ask Val more about what happened after I'd fallen in the hole, but gruesome battle details probably weren't kid-appropriate conversation.

So I opted for more basic questions instead. "How many kids?"

"Twelve in total," Val said. "Paige is riding in the other truck with the rest. None of the guys are in close proximity to them, for obvious reasons."

I nodded. "Did we lose anyone?"

Val shook her head, and I sagged with relief. "Some injuries, but you were the worst off." My cousin's expression went grave. "I had to restart your heart in front of your men and your dad. Talk about working under pressure."

I brought my hand to my chest, feeling the bruised flesh around my sternum for the first time. "You always did love to tit-punch me."

"Yeah, well, it was actually necessary this time."

A sudden thought hit me as I remembered blank, empty

eyes and a hand that had been scraped raw. I scooted closer to
Val, keeping my voice low so the children wouldn't hear. "A
man's body was in the hole. The cult forced him to dig it before
killing him, and there's probably more. We have to recover him,
and the sacrifices—"

"We will." Val took my hand and squeezed. "I promise you
we will, cuz. But we have to get you and everyone home first.
Get these kids checked out. The dead will be honored, but they
can wait a little longer."

I was quiet for a long while, letting it all sink in. "It's really
over then, isn't it?"

Val squeezed my hand harder and grinned. "Yeah. It is,
President."

* * *

TORR DIDN'T STOP DRIVING until he pulled up to the hospital
in Four Corners. The kids were ushered into the pediatric ward,
and I was immediately sent to emergency surgery to get the
bullet out of my shoulder. I kicked up as much of a fuss as I
could, telling the doctors to look over my people first, but they
were having none of it, and I was out like a light before I
knew it.

When I came to, my head felt like it had been stuffed with
cotton, but the pain was blissfully gone. It was also much easier
to open my eyes now, but that didn't prepare me for the person I
saw sitting next to my hospital bed.

"Welcome back," Hudson said softly. He started to rise. "I'll
get Torr and the others—"

"No, wait." My protest was a breathy whisper, so I tried
again. "Wait. Not yet. Give me... a few minutes before they all
rush in."

Hudson froze on his way to the door, then rushed over as I

started to sit up. "Here. The bed moves so you don't have to."

He pushed a button on the side of the bed and the head started to lift me into a sitting position, making me chuckle in embarrassment. "Oh, that's right. They can do that."

"I can raise your feet too. I can also see if it'll make you breakfast, but I don't think we're there yet."

That kept me smiling. "That's okay. I'm good, thanks."

Hudson nodded and resumed standing awkwardly next to me. "I'm glad you're feeling better."

"Me too. Drugs are awesome like that." We laughed a little together before silence returned. "Did I say anything funny while I was under?"

"Uh, well." He rubbed his jaw, trying to hide a smile. "You woke up a couple hours ago saying no one better tell your mom you were here because that'd be embarrassing. Torr broke the news that your mom already knew, and then you started talking about building a house on the moon to hide from your family."

"Wow." I laughed. "That's absurd but also makes total sense." My eyebrows lifted. "Have you met my mother yet?"

"Not yet. Someone said she was helping the pediatricians do check-ups on the kids."

"That sounds like her." I noticed his face going remote. "Hey, you okay?"

"Yeah, just..." He dragged his chair closer and dropped into it with a sigh. "They're going to run DNA tests and I know..."

He didn't have to explain it. Some, if not most of those children, will have been fathered by him.

"Hudson, look at me." It was hard to ignore my heart beating faster when those blue eyes lifted to mine. "My mother understands. Everyone who was there with us is behind you. No one is going to force responsibility or anything onto you regarding those kids."

"I still feel responsible," he admitted. "They're here now.

They're people who exist in the world. What kind of person would I be to not at least acknowledge my part in that?"

"Well, you don't have to decide right now. But anyway, I haven't asked yet. How are you? How's everyone?"

Hudson shrugged and gave a small shake of his head. "We're all fine. Just worried about you. Torr and Santos haven't slept since before we hit the settlement. I told them to go find a bed somewhere, but I think they crashed in the hallway."

I laughed at that mental image. "It's sweet of you to stay with me."

He shrugged again like it was no big deal. "Told 'em I would."

"So Devin's good? The Hunter? Paige?"

"Everyone is alive and well. We all got checked out by doctors. Some of the guys are staying at the hotel down the street, checking out the town." His gaze got heavy. "Just waiting for their president's orders."

I scoffed, looked at my right arm in a sling and my right foot elevated and in a cast. "Don't think I'm riding for a while."

"You're still our president, though."

"That 'our' sounds an awful lot like you're including yourself."

"I am." He was dead serious, his face solemn and his gaze steady. "Your dad's with your family, but as soon as he's free, I'm getting my Vengeful Gods tattoo. I'll follow you anywhere, Rori."

My throat tightened with emotion, and I blinked rapidly to keep the tears at bay. Did he have any idea how significant this moment was? He must've. The amount of trust he was placing in me was beyond my wildest dreams. It almost felt too good to be true.

"Why?" I asked. "You know you can be with Devin without following me. I would never ask you to—"

"I had a choice," he cut in. "When we cleared out the settlement and were looking for you... We swept over the field where the holes were hidden. I was the one that found you."

Hudson brought his palms together, eyes focused on his fingertips. "I looked over and saw her hitting you over and over. You were limp, just taking it. You must have been unconscious already. And I realized something." He paused as if he had to push himself to continue speaking. "I could've let her kill you, and no one would've known. Then I'd kill her myself. That would have meant two less women in the world, and the old me would have found that something to celebrate."

His eyes lifted to mine and I was stunned at the emotion in them, a stark contrast to the coldness in his words. "As soon as that thought entered my mind, I realized I couldn't let it happen. After everything you did for me, for the gladiators, I couldn't let you die. I didn't—" He swallowed and struggled again to speak. "I didn't want to live in a world without you in it."

There was a long, tense silence until I broke it. "So you saved my life."

He shook his head, refusing to look at me again. "When Val had to restart your heart, I almost lost my shit. I thought that one second of hesitation made me too late. I still can't believe that thought entered my head."

"Stop that. Come here." I held my good hand out for him to take. When he just stared at it, I added, "As your president, I order you."

That got a small smile out of him, like I'd hoped. His fingers were warm as they clasped around mine in a gentle squeeze.

"First of all, like those kids, you're undoing some indoctrination too. You've felt nothing but hate for women for years, then got thrown into dealing with *me*, of all people. It's okay if some of those old thoughts intrude, because they shaped your reality for so long."

"It's not okay, though," he argued. "Not when it comes to life and death decisions."

"I'm not done." I gave a cheeky squeeze to his hand. "Second of all, you're not perfect and nobody expects you to be. No one is policing your thoughts, and it's your actions that matter anyway. You acted quickly enough to save my life. And third of all." I released his hand and held my arm out in a *ta-da* motion. "I'm alive and on some damn good painkillers. So don't beat yourself up when it all worked out in the end."

Hudson laughed, and it sounded like actual joy bubbled out of his chest for the first time in a while. "You make it hard to argue, President."

He looked happy, genuinely so. It looked good on him, and I couldn't stop smiling. "I'm glad you're here, Hudson."

"Me too, Rori."

The next thing I knew, he was smoothing my hair back and placing a kiss on my forehead. Only then did I think about how shitty I must have looked, considering how many punches to the face I had received.

Hudson lingered with his lips on my forehead for a moment, long enough for me to wonder if he'd consider becoming more than just one of the men who followed me.

Would he ever join the ones who stood beside me?

Before I could venture any kind of questions in that direction, he straightened and backed away. "I'll let the guys know you're awake."

Then he turned and left the room.

Two weeks after arriving in Four Corners, Rori and Devin waited with me in the doctor's office. Rori paced around the room, seemingly unable to sit still despite the walking boot on her foot. When she did sit down on the doctor's little rolling stool, her left knee bounced up and down.

"Will you stop?" Devin grumbled at her. "You're making *me* nervous."

"Sorry." She drummed her fingers on her knee, looking toward the door. Her right arm was no longer in a cast, though she still held it tucked close to her body. "I don't know why I'm so worked up."

"It's okay." I knocked my shoulder into Devin's, who was sitting beside me on the exam table. "Watching her fidget keeps my mind off of whatever the news is gonna be."

"See?" Rori held her hand out toward me. "I'm helping."

A knock came to the door then, and it opened from the outside a few moments later.

"Hi, everyone," came the friendly greeting from the doctor,

an attractive woman in her late forties with olive skin and long, brown hair. "How are we doing?"

"Hi, Mom," Rori answered. "They seem good, but I'm on pins and needles over here."

Dr. Wilder chuckled as she planted a kiss on her daughter's forehead, then playfully smacked her shoulder with the paper folder in her hand. "Move it, mija. You're in my seat."

With an exaggerated sigh and groan, Rori stood from the rolling stool and crossed the room to stand by Devin and me.

As her mother took her place on the stool and wheeled closer to us, I could see the resemblance more clearly. She and Rori had the same cheekbones, nose, and lips.

"So," the doctor placed the folder on her lap, "are we ready to know? Do you have any questions for me first?"

I felt Rori and Devin's eyes on me as I shook my head. "Just give it to me straight, Dr. Wilder."

"Of course. And please call me Mari."

There was a warmth about Rori's mother that I felt the moment she came in. She had a calming, comforting presence, to the point where I felt no anxiety when she opened the folder's cover. No wonder Shadow's uneasy soul had been so drawn to her.

"Of the twelve children rescued from the Sisterhood," Mari's eyes scanned the document in her lap, her finger trailing over the DNA results, "four of them are biologically yours, Hudson."

"Four," I breathed, letting the information sink in. "That's... actually less than I expected."

Mari nodded. "The oldest is five. The youngest is six months."

Devin cleared his throat. "The other kids that aren't his. Are any of them, uh..."

"None are yours or Santos'," Mari said with a gentle smile.

280

"They all have different fathers, actually. I imagine most of the mothers came to the cult while pregnant or after their children were already born."

"Where are the kids now?" Rori asked.

"And are they safe?" A protective urge rose up in me that I didn't expect.

"They're in foster homes and are completely safe," Mari assured us. "The foster families are vetted and interviewed extensively. We also have a team of nurses who go out and do check-ups on the children weekly. Along with any medical issues, they're trained to look for and report any signs of abuse or neglect. I promise you, the children are as well taken care of as they can be."

The doctor focused her gaze on me. "As for the ones sired by you, you have choices, Hudson. You can meet them, if you'd like, and decide if you want a relationship with them. The families they're with have been told a very basic overview of your situation, and they're open to visits from you, if you'd like. If you're not ready for that at this time, that's okay too."

The room fell silent, waiting for an answer from me.

"What happens if I...I don't?" I clasped my fingers together, searching for words that were oddly difficult to spit out. "If I don't...claim them as my own?"

"After some time to adjust, they will be eligible for adoption," Mari answered. "The territory is giving you priority and a grace period to decide, since you are the biological father. But if you don't seek parental rights after twelve months, they will seek to place those children in adoptive families."

Devin wrapped a hand around my upper arm and placed his chin on my shoulder. "No one will blame you if you're not ready to be a parent in a year. You never wanted this. You never agreed to have kids. And they'll still be happy and cared for."

Mari nodded sagely. "The territory and adoption agency are

sympathetic as to what happened in that cult, but they must act in the best interest of the children. These kids need stability and a very gentle introduction to normal society so they can thrive."

"I want to meet them." The declaration was out of my mouth before I could give it much thought, but it felt right as soon as I said it. "Well, maybe one of them to start."

Mari smiled warmly again. "How about two? The two older ones are with one family and the two younger ones are with another."

I swallowed and nodded, nerves lighting up my stomach. But if anything, that was just further proof I was doing the right thing. "Okay, sure. Two of them. Maybe the older two first? I don't know, I've never spent much time around kids."

Mari closed her folder and beamed at me. "Just be yourself, Hudson. You'll do great."

* * *

Rori and I pulled up to a small house three days later. She wasn't in riding shape yet, so we borrowed her brother's car to make this visit together. It didn't hit me until right then that this was what couples did. Partners in love met children for the first time, not friends or...whatever we were.

Really, it should have been Devin with me. But the kids were still distrustful of men, if not absolutely terrified of them. Mari and the social worker I talked to recommended that I have a woman with me when I met my children for the first time.

My children. I was still getting used to that idea.

But I wasn't bothered by the idea that Rori and I looked like a couple. There was actually no one better to do this, and I was glad she was here. My feelings were complicated, but for now, I was just grateful for her support.

"Cute little place," Rori remarked when I cut the engine.

The house did look cozy and well-maintained. Flower bushes of some kind lined the walkway. The exterior was painted a soft blue with an off-white trim and had painted shutters framing the windows. It looked every bit like a warm, happy home where kids were loved and content.

A stab of inadequacy hit me. How was I the number one candidate with rights to these children? I had nothing. No home or way to make a living. Even the clothes on my back were borrowed. Just because we shared blood didn't mean I could be a father.

"You good?" Rori asked gently. "We can try another day, if you want."

It was a fair question. Was I actually ready for this?

I was here now. Uncomfortable and completely out of my element, yes. But if I left now, would I really come back? Or would I just avoid this discomfort, this massive potential responsibility being held out to me? I was getting stronger in trusting myself but wasn't all the way there yet.

"Yeah, I'm good," I told Rori as casually as I could manage.

I gestured for her to go ahead of me, an idea we'd discussed with June and Lisa, the foster parents, over the phone. The children would be more at ease seeing another woman first.

Rori gave my arm a squeeze as she walked past me, heading up the charming mosaic-tiled walkway to the front door where she knocked gently.

A Black woman almost as tall as Rori and with long, multicolored braided hair opened the door, smiling warmly as she stepped aside to let us in. "Hello, come in! I'm Lisa. June's watching the girls out back."

"Thank you for letting us come over," Rori answered. "I'm Rori, this is Hudson."

"Well, I can see the resemblance," Lisa said as she shook my hand. "Maia, the older one, looks just like you."

"Thanks." I laughed nervously. "That's promising, I hope."

I was antsy to meet these kids, I realized. I wanted to learn about them, their likes and dislikes, their dreams and fears.

"Please make yourselves comfortable." Lisa gestured toward a cozy living room with deep set couches. "I was just making some tea, would you all like some?"

"That would be lovely, thank you." Rori took a seat and smiled graciously. It was a trip seeing her this way, all warm and polite. I almost couldn't believe this same woman was the foul-mouthed biker president with a thirst for revenge.

But that thirst had been sated now, I reminded myself. The nightmare was really over.

Once settled on the couch with tea, I could see through a bay window to a large backyard. A Caucasian woman with dark hair up in a messy bun sat on the other side of the window. We could hear her talking to the two girls, though they weren't in view.

"Sounds like they're settling in well," Rori remarked.

"Every day is a little bit better," Lisa said with a nod. "The younger one, Elodie, probably won't remember the cult. But Maia is old enough to remember, and she struggles to under-stand some things. She asks about her mom a lot. We try to tell her that her mom wasn't a bad person, but she had brought Maia into a dangerous situation. So she had to come with us to be safe."

"Do they have the same mother?" I asked.

"No, different mothers," Lisa said. "Those two are like peas in a pod, though. Very emotionally close, like true sisters." Lisa placed her mug down on the coffee table and brought her hands to her lap. "Are you ready to meet them?"

"Yes," I said. "I would like to."

"Are we still okay doing it as we discussed?" Lisa's gaze shifted from me to Rori.

"Yes," I said again. "Whatever it takes to make them feel more comfortable."

"Alright then."

She stood from the couch and headed for the backyard, with Rori and me following. After opening the sliding door, she and Rori stepped outside while I stayed behind.

I could see and hear the kids from where I stood, but they wouldn't see me until I was signaled to come out. The children had been taught by the Sisterhood not to have any interaction with outsiders and that men were especially unsafe. So our plan was to introduce them to Rori first, and then, based on their reactions, see if they were open to meeting me.

"Hey hun, Rori's here," Lisa said to her wife. "Girls, this is our friend, Rori. Can you say hello and introduce yourselves?"

"Hiii!" Elodie, the almost-four year old, waved and smiled brightly at Rori. "We're playing sandbox."

The younger of the two had russet brown hair curling around her face, much like mine had at that age. Her expression was open, happy, and curious about her foster mothers' new friend. Maia, on the other hand, remained silent and withdrawn, watching Rori suspiciously. She *did* look like me, down to the blue eyes and furrowed brows.

Lisa and June didn't push Maia for an introduction, and Rori seemed to take note of her frostiness, crossing her legs to sit on the grass just outside of the girls' sandbox. "I like all your shovels and tools in there." Rori gestured to the brightly colored plastic buckets, rakes, and other sandcastle building supplies. "Can you show me what you're making?"

Elodie babbled happily about her sandcastle process, showing Rori everything she used and what it made. Maia, however, silently continued her own project in the far corner of the sandbox.

"This is so cool." Rori was engaged and attentive to Elodie

the whole time. "You've got a whole workshop. My dad has a workshop too, only his stuff is for building motorcycles."

"Dad?" Maia asked in shock, speaking up for the first time. "You have a dad?"

"I do, four of them actually." Rori smiled at her. "And I love them just as much as I love my mom."

Damn, that was slick. Way to shift the conversation in an age-appropriate way.

"My mom said all dads were bad, and that's why we didn't have any," Maia argued.

"Some dads are bad, that's true. But so are some moms. Moms and dads are just people, so there are good and bad ones out there."

"I had an amazing dad." Lisa had sat on the bench next to June and clasped the other woman's hand. "He supported us through everything. I miss him every day."

"I'm sorry you lost him," Rori said gently.

As the conversation progressed, Maia gradually moved closer to Rori. "What's it like having a dad?"

"Well, it's different for everyone. But for me, it was great. Sometimes a little overbearing because I had four of them, but they taught me so much. How to defend myself and ride motor-cycles. How to treat other people and care for the ones I love. When I was really little, it was like having four superheroes. Big, strong guys who would protect me from anything."

"They protected you?" Maia's attention was rapt on Rori, like she was learning the secrets of the universe.

Rori nodded. "A good dad will always protect you. Some-times even when you don't want protection," she added with a laugh.

"I wish I had a good dad," Elodie sighed wistfully as she smacked a plastic shovel on her sand tower.

Rori looked at the two foster mothers first and then at me, mouthing with a smile, "Ready?"

I nodded, my heart pounding in my chest.

"If you two would like to meet him, I know someone who'd be a great dad." Rori grinned at the two girls. "He'd love a chance to be yours."

"A dad? For us?" Maia looked suspicious but also intrigued.

"Not just any old dad, but an excellent one. He's a great protector, he's big and strong, and he won't let anyone hurt you." Rori's smile softened and her cheeks darkened with a flush. "He's also smart and funny, and he's honest. He's a good listener, and he gives great hugs. I know for a fact you girls will be safe with him."

I was so floored by everything she'd said, I almost missed the head nod she did as my cue to come out. Even as I walked over, my thoughts were in a daze. She knew I could hear everything, but she wouldn't lie to those kids, right? Rori Wilder would never speak so highly of anyone unless she believed it was the truth.

"Girls, this is my friend, Hudson." She tugged at my pant leg a bit, and I took the invitation to sit on the ground next to her, eye level with the two children.

With my daughters.

"Are you a dad?" Maia gave me a hard stare, already starting the interrogation.

"Well, I've never been one before," I answered. "But if you give me a chance, I'd like to try."

"What's that?" Elodie pointed at a tattoo on my wrist, a compass rose. Her little finger rested just above the point for North.

"These are tattoos." I extended my arm so she could see more of them. "They're drawings that will never wash off."

"What?!" Maia was so bewildered that she came right next to her sister for a closer look. "How do they never come off?"

"Oh, I can't wait to hear this." Rori stretched her legs long in front of her and planted her palms behind her. She relaxed and listened with a smile as my children and I got to know each other.

EPILOGUE

RORI

One year later

"I can't believe he finally did it." Devin lay diagonally on our bed, bare feet crossed at the ankles, hands laced behind his head. "He's been hemming and hawing at it for months. I was about to decapitate him myself out of frustration."

"Oh, come on. You know you can't push him if he's not ready." I inserted the silver hoop earrings into my lobes, then stepped back from the mirror, angling my body from side to side to check my reflection.

"If I didn't push, you wouldn't be dressing up for a date with him right now," Devin retorted. "It would have been five years from now." He turned on his side, propping up onto his elbow. "You look incredible, by the way."

"You think so?" I swayed my hips, making the long skirt swish along with the movement. My leather jacket was slim-fitting and cropped, more for fashion than actual riding. It added a little edge to my feminine dress and earrings.

Lucia picked out the dress and jacket for me. Even my fashion-loving little sister knew I couldn't go full girly-girl for a date. And I was pretty sure Hudson was going to pick me up on a motorcycle.

"I know it for a fact." Devin came up to sitting on the edge of the bed, meeting my gaze in the mirror. "You don't even have to try for him, you know. He's already crazy about you."

I turned away from the mirror to face him, bringing a hand to my hip. "He needs this sense of normalcy though, and honestly, I like it." I brought a hand to the back of my neck as my face heated. "I've never been asked on a date before."

"No?" Devin's eyebrows shot up. "Torr, Santos, and I will have to fix that."

"It's different with you guys," I laughed. "I mean, I'm not saying no to that, but Hudson needs this, you know? He's worked so hard over the last year."

"He has," Devin said quietly with a nod. "I'm really proud of him."

I gave him a stern look. "I hope you tell him that."

"I do." Devin smirked deviously. "Usually while he's sucking my cock, but—"

"Oh, fuck you." I grabbed the nearest thing that wouldn't cause permanent damage, a makeup bag, and threw it at him.

Devin caught it easily and brought his arm up to throw it back. He cackled when I brought my arms up, shielding my face.

"No! You are not allowed to ruin my face, hair, or outfit!"

"Well shit, I think that's the first time I've seen you cower from anything."

"I am *not* cowering!"

A knock came to the door before we could continue fighting. Which was a good thing, because arguments with Devin usually led to intense, passionate sex. Which was always incredible but

290

probably not the most appropriate thing to do right before a date.

Devin turned out to be that perfect medium between Torr and Santos that I didn't know existed. He liked to push my buttons and get me to react, but he didn't want submission. Sex between us was a battle, a rough, tumbling, push and pull until we were both sated and exhausted. That was just the dynamic between us. Instead of butting heads, we bit each other's lips, shoved, grabbed, groped, and tested each other's limits.

Most of our verbal arguments weren't serious now, and we actually did get along the majority of the time. But neither of us wanted to have fight-sex all the time, so it worked out perfectly that we had other partners.

If tonight went well, however, his other partner could become mine too.

"I'll get the door." Devin stood and smacked a kiss on my lips before I could react.

"You jerk, now I have to re-apply it," I groaned, turning back to the mirror.

"Worth it." Devin chuckled as he left the bedroom.

While I carefully tried to fix the lip color Lucia had put on me, I tried to ignore the fluttering in my belly. Why was I nervous? I *knew* Hudson, had gradually gotten to know him better over the last year. When he wasn't working or spending time with his daughters, he was with me and my guys. We both fucked Devin, for Christ's sake.

He had been especially busy as of late, though. I hadn't seen him for a few weeks, so when he asked me—and only me—to dinner the other day, to say I was pleasantly surprised was an understatement.

It felt like this might be a turning point for us, a new chapter in our relationship. And I couldn't lie, I felt nervous, like a long-time crush had finally noticed me.

Hudson and Devin's voices were a soft, comforting murmur as I finally left the bedroom, trying not to let my nerves show as I walked down the hall. I kept my chin lifted, my steps assured and confident, trying to channel the strength of my domme persona.

Hudson looked, well, really fucking hot. He'd gotten a haircut and his face was clean-shaven. The blue shirt he wore under his leather jacket brought out his eyes. His boots were polished and his dark jeans were slim-fitting, hugging his muscular thighs in all the right places.

The smile that lit up his face when he saw me did nothing to assuage my belly flutters. "Hey, Rori."

"Hey," I returned more breathily than I intended. "Long time no see."

"Yeah, hope I can make up for that tonight." His eyes continued to drink me in, and I never wanted him to stop looking at me. "You look amazing."

"So do you." My heart jumped into my throat as I said that, but I never was a girl to hold back what I felt.

"Yeah, both of you are hot as hell." Devin grinned smugly before fixing Hudson with an icy glare. "I want her home by midnight—"

"Oh, fuck off." I shoved at his shoulder.

"But if that means you come home *with* her," he continued, ignoring me. "I certainly won't mind."

Hudson laughed, a blush creeping up his neck. Over the past year, he'd been a branch extending off our group relationship. Sometimes he and Devin would spend time alone, other times he'd hang out with us as a group. But he'd always maintained a little bit of distance. Devin was the only one he had a sexual relationship with. So far.

"We'll see where the night takes us," Hudson said coyly before accepting a kiss from Devin.

"Have fun." Devin kissed me on the neck this time. "I'm meeting up with Santos and Torr at Bryce's. Join us after your dinner." He smirked. "If you don't suddenly get *busy*, that is."

"Alright, we're out of here." I wrapped my hand around Hudson's bicep with a dramatic sigh. "He's been doing this all day."

"You poor thing." He laughed.

We headed out the door with our arms linked together. "How does an MC president feel about riding on the back of my bike?" Hudson asked, his tone playful.

"I have no problem with letting a gentleman lead every once in a while." My arm wrapped a little tighter around his. "Honestly, it's nice to not be in the driver's seat all the time."

"Should I keep dinner a surprise, then? Or would you like to know, and possibly veto, my choice?" We came to his bike and I released his arm to let him climb on.

"I'd like to know." Once he was seated, I swung my leg over and allowed my body to press snugly into his back. "Not to veto your choice, just because I don't like being kept in suspense."

"It's Nina's." Hudson spoke to me over his shoulder, our faces close. "The new place downtown. Lisa and June are friends with the owners, and they said the food is incredible."

"Sounds great." I wrapped an embrace around his stomach and propped my chin on his shoulder, wondering if he'd take the chance to kiss me right then.

He didn't, but that was okay. We had all night.

HUDSON and I were seated by a friendly hostess and then ordered drinks and appetizers from a very attentive server. The moment we were finally alone at our table, Hudson blurted out, "So, I want you to be the first to know something."

"Okay. I'm listening." He looked nervous but also on the verge of bursting with happiness.

He broke out into the widest grin I'd ever seen on his face. "It's happening. I'm officially adopting Elodie and Maia."

"Oh my God, Hudson!" I immediately slapped a hand over my mouth, realizing my shriek had attracted some curious stares from other customers. "Hudson, that's fantastic," I said more quietly. "Congratulations!"

"Thank you." He rubbed his palms together, shifting in his seat. "I'm kind of terrified but also really excited to be a dad full-time."

"You are so ready for it," I told him. "You've worked so hard over this past year. Not just on yourself but getting to know them, learning about what they need. You'll do great, Hudson. I'm so happy for you."

Our conversation paused while the server returned with our drinks and appetizers.

"What a thing to celebrate." I held my drink out to him. "Cheers to that."

After we toasted and drank, I asked, "How's it going with the younger two? Is bringing them home with you on the horizon?"

Hudson sighed, a frown making his brows pinch. "It doesn't look like it right now. We've tried some bonding activities, and they're just not very responsive to me. I get it, they're really young, and I'm still basically a stranger to them. They're really attached to their foster parents. Who are great, don't get me wrong. But it's clear they're not choosing me, and that sucks a little."

"I'm sorry." Without thinking, I reached across the table and put my hand over his. "They are still babies. I'm sure they'll understand more when they're older. You'll be able to keep seeing them, right?"

"Yeah. It seems like their foster parents are hoping to adopt them, and they said they want me to continue having a relationship with them. So, I'm sure we can work something out."

"That's good to hear."

He nodded, stroking his thumb over my fingers. "I want to start bringing Maia and Elodie to see them too. They're all sisters, so they should get to know each other."

"I think that's a great idea."

There was another pause in the conversation as our main dishes were brought out.

"How's Torr's mom?" Hudson placed his napkin in his lap. "Any improvement since the last update?"

I gave him an uneasy smile and his frown deepened. "Not much has changed," I admitted. "She has her good days and bad. She is remembering Torr more often though. The doctors say he just needs to keep seeing her, stay consistent so he'll stick in her memory. It's hard on him, but he keeps showing up for her. That's just the man he is."

"Shit, I'm sorry."

"It's not all bad. When she's lucid, she's so spunky and hilarious. We're just taking it one day at a time."

We turned to lighter topics as we ate, talking about work and what else we'd been up to since we last saw each other. Since moving to Four Corners, Hudson had found his calling in tech communications. Thanks to him and a small team, the town had reliable internet for the first time since my parents were in their twenties. It wasn't very fast yet, but it was a booming industry that was constantly advancing.

As for me? I was still running Vengeful Gods MC with primarily the same crew of ex-gladiators. We aided Four Corners and other neighboring territories with the transportation of goods, usually as escorts to deter any theft or violence.

"If your girls are ready for it," I said when I was nearly

finished with my food. "Maybe they can come to one of the parties at my parents' house. There's lots of kids around the same age."

"Um." Hudson cleared his throat and wiped his mouth with a napkin. "That's kind of something I wanted to talk to you about too."

I had been relaxed most of the evening, but now that fluttering in my stomach returned. "Okay."

"I..." Hudson pulled in a deep breath and tried again. "I want you in the girls' lives. You, and the guys too."

Neither of us said anything for a moment. "In what way?" I asked.

"I'm not asking you to become their mother," Hudson said quickly. But I...they..." He swallowed and tried again. "The girls love you, Rori. They idolize you. Maia wants to be exactly like you."

"I love them too," I admitted. "They're such sweet, smart people. And they've been through so much at such a young age. I'd go to war for them, and I'm a hundred percent serious."

"They're amazing," Hudson agreed. "I still can't believe they're mine sometimes. And I'm, um, rambling and stalling, but what I'm trying to say is..." He paused and took a deep breath. "I just want *you*, Rori. I want us."

"Us," I repeated, trying to calm the fireworks lighting up my chest. "You mean like *us* us?"

Hudson grinned, sheepish and adorable. "I want to share you with the three other men who love you, who I also love, are my best friends, and the people I want my daughters around. I want you with them, and I also want you alone. Like we are now." He reached across the table for my hand and I placed it in his. "What do you say, Aurora Wilder?"

"I think," I said coyly, "that we can do much better things alone than just sitting and talking."

He didn't miss a beat. "Then I'm getting the damn check."

We paid our bill and headed out of the restaurant in a hurry, going straight to his motorcycle parked out front. Hudson spun to face me the moment we stood next to his bike. His hands went to my waist and mine went around his neck as we came together in a deep, all-consuming kiss.

That kiss was a release of a year's worth of pent-up attraction, of growth and setbacks for both of us. A year of orbiting each other, of processing our individual traumas both privately and with others, before we were finally ready to collide into each other.

And what a collision it was.

Breaking apart for a breath was barely a separation at all, we remained wrapped up in each other, our mouths hovering mere inches away as the heat of our breaths mingled in the space between.

"I want us too, Hudson," I whispered. "I just need to know that you're sure. Us sharing Devin is one thing, but—"

He cut me off with another kiss, a lighter, more playful one that I could feel his smile through. "I want it all. Everything, as long as I have you. You saved me, Rori. And I don't just mean the night you got me out of that house."

"The night you shot me, you mean."

He chuckled, because that's what it was to us now. A memory so distant that it became a joke. It almost felt like that night happened between two other people, not us. "If that's how you want to remember it, fine."

I pressed my smile to his, winding my arms around him tighter. "It's a good thing you saved me too, then."

His hands slid around my ribs, molding to my sides. "I'd say that makes us even."

"Mm, well, I never shot you, so I dunno about *that*."

Hudson laughed and dropped his forehead to my neck,

which allowed me to say into his ear. "You come with some pretty cute kids though, so I'll let that even the score."

He took a shuddering breath, wrapping me into an embrace that crushed me against his chest. "Thank you for...waiting," he whispered. "For letting me get my shit together, learn how to become a father, and put that whole ordeal in the rearview mirror. Thank you for allowing me to become a man worthy of you."

I blinked away the sudden tears that rose, not expecting him to go from joking to all swoony and romantic.

"I would've waited forever," I admitted. "Not for my chance or anything, but for you. More than anything, I wanted you to heal. I would've waited forever to see you whole and happy again. And if you found happiness with someone else..."

"But I didn't," he said when I trailed off. "I found it right here."

"So did I."

I smiled up at him, and we came together in another kiss.

One that would be followed by many more that night, and for the rest of our lives.

Thank you so much for reading Deathless! Not ready to stop going on wild motorcycle adventures? Ride with Mari and her four biker husbands in the Steel Demons MC! This series is complete and available in Kindle Unlimited!

Start the Steel Demons MC series:
https://books2read.com/SDMC1

If you're craving a standalone story with three chaotic bisexual men, Valorie's parents have a book too!

Read all about Kyrie and the Sons of Odin in Their Property:

https://books2read.com/theirpropertysonsofodin

WANT BIKERS AND SHIFTERS?

Check out my new M/F paranormal romance series, Howling Death MC, on my pen name Sophie Ash! All books can be read as standalones.

Book 1: **Traitor Wolf**
Book 2: **Enemy Wolf**
Book 3: Cursed Wolf
(coming Spring 2024!)

* * *

To keep up with all my releases, join my Facebook group, The Ash Coven:
https://www.facebook.com/groups/ashcoven

ALSO BY CRYSTAL ASH

Harem of Freaks: The Complete Series

Say Your Prayers

Steel Demons MC

Lawless

Powerless

Fearless

Painless

Helpless

Heartless

Senseless

Ruthless

Merciless

Endless

Shifted Mates Trilogy

Unholy Trinity: The Complete Series

For a complete list of books by Crystal Ash, visit her Amazon page.

ABOUT THE AUTHOR

Crystal Ash is a USA Today Bestselling Author from California. She loves writing steamy, heart-wrenching romance with tortured heroes, especially if they're in a reverse harem. Crystal's other loves include animals, mythology, and well-crafted alcohol, most of which can also be found in her stories.

When she's not writing, she's probably drinking craft beer with her husband or trying to coax her feral cat into accepting affection.

crystalashbooks.com

f facebook.com/Crystal.Ash.Romance

instagram.com/crystalashbooks

a amazon.com/author/crystalash

BB bookbub.com/profile/crystal-ash